OLIVIA FANE has endured one divorce, married two husbands, been awarded three MAs in Classics, Social Work and Theology, written five novels and given birth to five sons. Fane's combination of intellectual ideas and clear, involving prose won her a Betty Trask Award for *Landing on Clouds*. She lives in Sussex.

POSSIBLY A LOVE STORY

Arcadia Books Ltd
139 Highlever Road
London W10 6PH

www.arcadiabooks.co.uk

First published in Great Britain 2017
Copyright © Olivia Fane 2017

ISBN 978-1-910050-96-5

A catalogue record for this book is available from the British Library.

Typeset in Garamond by MacGuru Ltd

Printed and bound by T J International, Padstow PL28 8RW

ARCADIA BOOKS DISTRIBUTORS ARE AS FOLLOWS:

in the UK and elsewhere in Europe:
BookSource
50 Cambuslang Road
Cambuslang
Glasgow G32 8NB

in the USA and Canada:
Dufour Editions
PO Box 7
Chester Springs
PA 19425

in Australia/New Zealand:
NewSouth Books
University of New South Wales
Sydney NSW 2052

POSSIBLY A LOVE STORY

OLIVIA FANE

A

For my cousin Sarah

1

Most people envied Laura Glass. You would be a fool not to.

In fact, there were some in Lavender Street, South Clapham, who would time their journeys to work specifically to coincide with the lovely Laura in her Lycra, delivering a tightly packed red plastic bag into her dustbin at 7.45 on the dot, before setting out on a five-mile jog round the common, rain or shine.

She was already forty-one when this story begins, but a quick glance – or two, because it was nigh impossible not to give her a second glance – might have placed her nearer thirty. She was tall and slim and moved with a certain grace, which her numerous friends often commented on, and which she attributed to an old headmistress of hers, who had put 'deportment' above geography on the educational agenda. 'Facts are for exams, poise is for life,' she would bark at the fourteen-year-old girls pacing up and down the dining room with wooden spoons tucked into the back of their bras. 'We are turning into a nation of jellyfish!'

Laura never went to university, and often regretted it. But what she didn't regret was the reason: her husband, Hugo. For this was the most enviable thing about Laura: she was still, after twenty years of marriage, unquestioningly devoted to the man she'd met on the first day of her first job, a temporary secretarial position with Wilder and Co., Advertising Agency.

Laura had been barely eighteen, Hugo had seemed a lofty twenty-two. A fortnight later, the handsome dark gallant had proposed to her, and persuaded her to join him in his light, airy, third-floor flat in The Chase, Clapham. He had style, Hugo. He had one hundred

red roses delivered to the table where he popped the question, or rather made the demand, 'Marry me, Laura!' The attractions of a cold, Hugo-less, Scottish university rapidly waned, and Laura never looked back.

Their courtship had been a happy, undemanding one. They often wondered what it actually meant to 'work' at a relationship, because theirs had fallen into place so easily. They took delight in remembering the anniversaries that others forgot: the first time they met, the first time they kissed, the first time they made love ('the night of the burgeoning blossom' as they called it), and their first evening together as a couple in Clapham. In fact, the month of January was more or less their own. The final winter's flourish was Valentine's Day, when the two young lovers would open a bottle of champagne for breakfast, and feed each other croissants.

They married on May Day, when Laura was twenty-one and a half years old. They went to town designing a wedding that no one would forget, and no one did. Laura's parents (who were delighted by Laura's 'catch' and didn't mind in the least that their daughter had forsaken a degree in History of Art), lived in a large Georgian rectory bang in the middle of Hardy country, in the village of Piddlestock, and hosted an event so spectacular that it was a 'feature' in the local press.

Not content with renting a marquee in dull, cream canvas, Laura and Hugo had requisitioned a circus tent in orange, yellow and red, above which flew their very own flag, designed by Hugo himself. Their names were intertwined in a clever way, and above them a male and a female hand were clasped. It all looked rather impressive until at the last moment Hugo decided to add arms, so that they looked like they were arm-wrestling; but no one noticed that on the day. Only in the years to come did friends joke about the framed flag hanging in their loo. Hugo could see the funny side of it and laughed with them, but Laura was finally driven to hide it away in the attic.

The circus performers who actually owned the tent wanted to be included too. So the good-hearted Laura stitched up some jesters' outfits, sewing bells on to felt slippers and stuffing three-pronged pointed hats with her old tights. The troupe of jesters juggled amongst the guests, delighting all; and when they sat down to the wedding lunch, two trapeze artists balanced precariously on a tight-rope dangling above them, and the best man mentioned them in his speech. 'What an appropriate metaphor for marriage!' he said. Laura had wanted to whisper to Hugo that she felt such comments wholly inappropriate at *their* wedding, but didn't. She laughed, alongside everyone else.

But the moment everyone remembers took place at half past four in the afternoon. For Laura and Hugo had wanted their very own maypole and had even commissioned a choreographer to create a dance for them, the purpose of which was to tie the happy couple together in ribbons, and indeed to the maypole itself. They had even tried – money no object – to persuade Andrew Lloyd-Webber to set music to Robert Herrick's famous Maypole poem, but in the end had employed a red-headed folk singer called Valeria to do her best with those immortal words:

I sing of brooks, of blossoms, birds and bowers:
Of April, May, of June, and July flowers.
I sing of May-poles, Hock-carts, wassails, wakes,
Of bridegrooms, brides, and of their bridal-cakes.

Valeria sang her heart out, beautifully and mournfully, as she struck the time with a wooden stick with bells on the top. Even the weather was cinematic: a pregnant dark grey bursting with light, the rain finally breaking on a hill beyond, while over the wedding party hung a vivid blue.

Most of the guests were suitably mesmerised by the event, and, happy to say, Laura and Hugo were so under the spell of their own devising – seven fourteen-year-old girls tying them in silk ribbons of every colour of the rainbow – that they found the experience both moving and erotic. Only the bridesmaids giggled, whispering to one another that they looked just like Peter Pan and Wendy, tied to the mast of Captain Hook's ship.

The young Hugo had made Laura his PA the moment he had had the power to do so, less than a year after she joined him in his office. Wilder and Co. recognised and rewarded the couple's talents handsomely: commission after commission came their way, and Hugo Glass was a name to be reckoned with in the world of advertising. Most of his campaigns led to a four-fold increase in profits for the companies who sought him out. Some lucky clients found their profits rise sky-high. He renamed a fledgling chewing-gum company Chew Blue, and all over London vast blue billboards sprung up along railway sidings, the colour of heaven, with instructions to 'CHEW BLUE' in Copperplate Gothic, small and discreet in the bottom right-hand corner.

Nor was it only the blue gum-spotted streets of British towns that testified to Hugo's success. For ten years now the greatest phenomenon in the British high street had been the second-hand clothes store, Second Helpings, where buyers like gods decreed whether someone's cast-offs made the mark and could thereby become part of their stock. Hugo's contribution was his idea to *flatter* the seller into selling his or her clothes at a knockdown price. *'Have you got what other people want?'* was the slogan on which an empire was built.

Hugo made money, lots of it. When Laura and Hugo had children, they left their sunny flat for a six-bedroomed house, five storeys high. Five years later, the house next door came on the market and they suddenly realised the trouble with their house was that it was much too *thin*. They just hadn't noticed it before. Their open-plan kitchen/sitting room where the family came together to eat and watch telly was just so *mean*. The drawing room and the dining room where they entertained friends were just so *rectangular*. They also thought that in this day and age it wasn't good enough for everyone to be sharing just two bathrooms. How did other people manage? Or perhaps others didn't have as many friends come to stay as they did. So they bought the house next door as well, and all their rooms became large and generous: a yellow drawing room on the left, always immaculate, a family sitting room on the right, and at the back of the house a vast, square kitchen with fitted units in reclaimed pine, an Aga, and an old farmhouse table imported from Provence and big enough to seat fourteen.

The two front doors – to the left and right of their triple-sized hall – didn't bother them at all. In fact, the whole family – for they had two delightful children, Leo and Jemima, aged fourteen and sixteen respectively – wondered how other people narrowed their horizons to one, when having two was such unadulterated *fun*. Laura, who loved colour, was forever painting them: black and white, orange and yellow, blue and green. The children would instruct visitors to enter one door, and leave through the other, quite randomly. Or once, when they thought it would be fun to have one entrance for girls and another for boys, Laura clapped her hands in glee and promptly painted the doors pink and blue. And over the years they thought of countless reasons to use one door ahead of the other – dark or fair, rich or poor, adult or child.

At the time this story begins, it so happened that the doors were painted red and grey, and they had been for some months now. The Glass family had thought it would be a great wheeze to use the red door when you were happy and the grey door when you were sad. Needless to say, they rarely used the grey – a spoilt exercise book at school, a filling in a tooth, a tiff with a best friend. Well, they had to use the grey door sometimes or there'd be no point, would there? For all four of them – Laura, Hugo, Jemima and Leo – had all been extraordinarily blessed in this life, and had barely a gloomy memory to look back on.

But on Monday the ninth of January 1995, things were going to change in ways none of them could have imagined.

❖

At seven in the morning Laura was in a particularly buoyant mood. She was lying in bed, her head against the pillows, sipping the tea that Hugo had brought up to her before setting out for work. He had also opened the curtains for her, because that was also part of the routine of their marriage, despite it still being dark outside and the streetlight throwing its harsh sodium rays on to her white quilt. He had also kissed her cheek. In fact, it was the kiss that woke her. She smiled at the memory of it. Life was good.

There were other reasons to be happy. The previous evening, she had driven her children back to their boarding school in Hampshire. Both she and Hugo had taken to Bedales from the very first. They needed no persuasion that the encouragement of self-expression was more important than rule-following: and here was a school with no hierarchy, no uniforms, and teachers were called by their Christian names. No wonder Jemima and Leo had barely said goodbye to her, in the flurry of coats and scarves and bear-hugs. That was as it should be, thought Laura, generously. Driving back to London, listening to a CD of gentle jazz, she had felt relief that a new era of calm was to descend on to the Glass household.

Laura gazed towards the window willing the morning light to come so that she could get on with the day. When it promised to be a fine one she almost skipped out of bed to find her running gear, and after a brief foray in the bathroom to wash and do her teeth, she smoothed on to herself her second skin, enjoying the contours of her body as she did so. Today the colour of her Lycra was yellow.

At half-past seven Laura was in her kitchen tidying up. Hugo never put his cereal bowl in the dishwasher, and Laura never complained. She was momentarily anguished by the five remaining Shreddies in the cereal packet: to chuck or not to chuck? Hugo always did this. It so annoyed her. But Laura knew better than to mention it. That was the sort of conversation that made him bridle. In the end she opened up a new packet of Shreddies, and scrupulously added the five to the top of it. Then she vigorously squashed up the empty packet, and added it to the rubbish.

At a quarter to eight Laura went outside with a tightly wrapped red parcel and pushed it deeply down into the wheelie bin on top of another ten such bags. (Colour Now! was another of Hugo's successful ventures – rubbish bags in the four primary colours, et al.) That done, she stretched her limbs, kicking each leg behind her in turn and catching hold of her foot. She looked up, and smiled broadly at a couple of covert admirers: George, a geeky-looking thirty-something from two doors down, was taking lights off his bike and putting them into his rucksack. She gave him a little wave and said, 'Hi there! Lovely morning!' And she delighted in the knowledge that George, setting off for a job in IT, would still have a smile plastered on to his face half a mile into his journey.

'How easy it is to make people happy,' she thought to herself.

Laura had thick, shoulder-length blonde hair, which she put into a high ponytail when she went running. As she set out for the common that morning, she was conscious of the swing of it, to the left, to the right, and enjoyed its weight and rhythm. She enjoyed the crunch of her step on the thick frost, which glistened in the early morning sun. Laura loved London, and the common in particular. Here were people of every colour, age and station in life going about their business, criss-crossing along the paths, like a wonderful dance.

Laura was acutely aware of her good luck in life, and grateful for it. Unlike friends who felt they deserved their wealth because they had 'worked bloody hard' for it, she thought of their own good fortune as a prize, which might have fallen into anyone's lap, but which just happened to have fallen into theirs. And she was abundant in compassion for others for whom life hadn't turned out quite so well, which was, more or less, everyone. She didn't bear a grudge against a single living soul.

As she crossed the main road and broke into a jog, Laura was feeling particularly benevolent. Everything about her looked bright and new. She even espied twins tucked up in their double pushchair, and stopped running to greet them. And all those who fell in Laura's shadow were rewarded with a radiant smile, for there was yet another reason why Laura was happy that morning.

At the weekend she'd gone shopping in the Oxford Street sales with her daughter Jemima, kitting her out with winter clothes for school. Her favourite shop in the world was Browns in South Molton Street, where a single angora jumper might set you back a few hundred pounds, and while Jemima was immersed in about twenty items in the open-plan changing rooms at Topshop, Laura had run off there to take a quick browse. The sale wasn't beginning till the Monday, however. She sighed as she stroked a ravishing faux fur coat for £2,800. A shop assistant had winked at her conspiratorially.

'That'll be half price next week, if you're interested,' she'd said.

Now Monday dawned! And in amongst the beauty of the morning, the delicious weight of her swinging hair, the litheness of her svelte body, the life-affirming charm of all the passers-by, was the vision of the fur coat, which, God willing, would soon be hers.

Such was her mood that she even considered running to the shop, but you can't go shopping at Browns in Lycra. So she went home, took a shower, wrapped herself in a towel and dried her hair. In fact, she spent longer choosing what to wear for her shopping trip than she would have done if she'd been lunching with friends.

In the end, she chose a bottle-green dress in fine wool, which gripped her body snugly down to her calves, and some high Jimmy Choo boots. The truth was, you never knew whom you might bump into in that neck of the woods.

After applying a little make-up – some green eye shadow to set off her hazel eyes, and an orangey-red lipstick – she flung on an old, black coat (part of the fun of shopping lay in that sense of *transformation*) and walked back up to the common to wait for a bus.

Laura always used public transport. She wasn't one of those rich women who put up an invisible barrier between them and us – going everywhere by taxi, having their shopping delivered ahead of jostling with Joe Public. In fact she'd been heard to say that she actually enjoyed jostling with Joe Public. It made her feel alive, she said, like she was just one small part of this great and beautiful world. She also liked being looked at, which made her feel one big part of a less than beautiful world. Though, of course, she didn't tell anybody that.

Laura thanked the bus driver as she boarded, gave him the correct change, and found herself a place to sit in the front of the upper deck of the bus. The early morning sun had all but disappeared, not that she noticed. She sat still, tall and elegant, lost in her own thoughts. She hadn't mentioned the coat to Hugo. Sometimes he was angry with her for spending too much on clothes, and had even threatened to have her name removed from their joint account. 'You only live once!' was her habitual defence. Hugo might then retort: 'I don't care how many times you live! What's the point of another effing ....? Haven't you got enough?'

But after these rows, or 'rowettes' as Laura used to call them, they always seemed to have the most incredible sex. And as the bus trundled up Battersea Bridge Road, she imagined herself naked under the aforesaid faux fur coat, and thought, happily, that'll shut him up.

As the bus approached Bond Street, she carefully made her way down the stairs and got ready to leap off. She wanted to thank the driver for her journey – Laura was always thanking everyone for everything – but the driver didn't look round. She felt oddly disappointed, like a possible relationship had been cut short.

She walked the hundred yards or so to her destination like a model, self-consciously. High heels make you do that, she thought. You couldn't help but hold yourself high, or you'd look quite ridiculous, like a leaning tower. Ah well, almost there. The boots were beginning to rub against her heels. My punishment for my petty extravagances, she thought to herself, uncomplainingly. But worth it. You only live once.

A small crowd of women had accumulated outside the shop. It was still a quarter of an hour before the shop opened. She saw first to her delight, but then to her dismay, that her fur coat was part of the window display. It was even more beautiful than she had remembered it: tight fitting in the arms and bodice, but then flowing romantically from the empire line, in the softest, finest fur like a baby rabbit's, speckled fawn on white. It was no longer a question of her walking into the shop and politely asking a shop assistant if she might try it on. Oh, why hadn't she just bought it at the full price on the Saturday? She surveyed the figures of her competitors, and counted six more or less the same shape as she was. It was going to be the most unseemly scramble. Quite honestly, she couldn't bear it.

With seven minutes to go, and nowhere near the first wave of women, who were thrusting at the shop door as gracefully as they could, she decided the suspense was too much for her. She would nonchalantly walk down the street to take her mind off things. She relaxed momentarily in front of a shoe shop. She spotted some pink four-inch stilettos, just *glorious*, in the window.

Then she spotted something else.

Five minutes later all thought of the coat had gone. She was sitting in a taxi, kicking off her boots, sobbing her heart out, her sweet, tender girl's heart, that had never known grief.

She saw the golden plait first, in a doorway, and was curious to see the owner of such a fine head of hair. She was slim, young, petite and wore flowery jeans with flat pumps. The girl was kissing someone. Not bad for 10 a.m. on a Monday morning, she thought, generously. Laura loved watching couples together, to see how they did things, to see how they kept the passion alive.

Then she saw that the girl's lover was Hugo.

Not fun.

When Laura was a girl of fourteen, her mother had said to her, 'Darling, remember this: men aren't to be trusted. They're on a different planet to us women. They fall in love at the drop of a hat, and at the drop of another they're out of love again. Your best bet in marriage is affection. Go for a good, solid, Labrador type of man, like your father. Someone who knows who his mistress is, wags a lot, and stays loyal to her all his life!'

Though Laura was a good girl and biddable, on the subject of romance, Laura didn't listen to a word her mother said. She was waiting for the *one*, and the *one and only* was Hugo. They say girls who love their fathers marry them, and Laura adored hers, who was kind and generous to a tee. But who at eighteen looks for such mundane qualities in a man? Hugo had none of her father's qualities, and affection, when it was given, was given perfunctorily, in the way that one might remember to water the cabbages.

Laura's mother was acute in such matters and even from their very first weekend together (croquet, Pimm's on the terrace, that sort of thing), she had taken her daughter aside to tell her that Hugo hadn't been kind to Maisie, their black Labrador.

Laura, it's true, was momentarily alarmed. But it turned out that no, Hugo hadn't hit dear Maisie or anything as wicked as that, which really would have made Laura think twice. It was just that Hugo hadn't submitted to Maisie's charms, hadn't taken her proffered paw and shaken it affectionately as most people did.

'Hugo just hasn't grown up with dogs!' said Laura, defensively.

'Nonetheless, affection is important in a marriage.'

'Of course he's affectionate!' insisted Laura. 'And anyway, was Heathcliff affectionate? Was Cathy crying out night after night for a man to watch telly with on the sofa?'

And Laura's Heathcliff was beautiful, dark, brilliant, sexy and endlessly creative. No, he didn't own dog-eared slippers and bring cups of cocoa to bed. Lovers don't do that kind of thing. Lovers bring flute glasses and crack open the bubbly.

Laura paid more attention, however, to her mother's wise words on the subject of friendship. 'Your girlfriends will be with you for life,' she had told her, 'and the closest will be the ones you make at school. You'll see each other through thick and thin: marriage and children, middle age, old age. Your children will leave home. Your husband, well, he'll be in the garden shed most likely, if he's not on the golf course. But your girlfriends will always be just a phone call away, and will always be there for you!'

Laura was a kindly soul and a trustworthy friend. In fact, she'd kept in contact with five of the original eight girls in her first school dormitory, and kept a birthday book, always remembering to send a card. But her three best friends had joined her at St Benedict's, Bridport, in the sixth form. All three, the sexy redhead Arabella (with the Pre-Raphaelite hair), the drug-fuelled Rachel (skinny and Jewish), and the anarchist Ann (pale and freckled, with lips, determined and thin), had got expelled from their London day schools for unwholesome activities of various kinds and had been sent by their parents to an all-girls school deep in the country for some fresh air and a new beginning.

For, if truth be told, Laura had always found herself attracted to people who coloured over the lines, as it were. And though her friends (twenty-three years on) had all been tamed by their various adventures, these were the three to whom she had always turned for advice.

Arabella was at work when Laura phoned her.

'I can't talk now,' she said. 'I'm going into a meeting. Ring in an hour.'

'Please, Arabella! Hugo has a mistress. A child mistress, as far as I could make out. She looks about seventeen.'

'They all do,' said Arabella, nonchalantly. 'Listen, I'm really sorry, let's talk later.'

'But what am I to do?' sobbed Laura.

'Leave him, of course. He's no better than Charlie was. Sex crazy. They all are. If he's behaving like this in broad daylight, do you think it's the first time he's been unfaithful to you? He even used to flirt with me when you weren't watching. He's a bad 'un, sorry to say. Leave him. I'll be your lawyer. I'll get you a fortune.'

'But I don't want a fortune!'

'I can't talk now! Listen, let's have lunch – can you hang on till two? What about meeting at Whistler's? Reserve a table. Leave a message with my secretary. Must dash! Love you!'

The phone call was such a failure that the poor Laura began pacing the length of her long house, pulling at her hair. How could Arabella talk of a twenty-year old marriage so lightly, as though it could just be disposed of at its first hitch? Was she envious of her? Was that her problem? And what about poor Jemima and Leo, how would they feel if they got divorced?

Divorce! Divorce! The very word was so harsh, so unforgiving. Laura went into her bathroom to retch. Her mouth tasted acrid. She looked into the mirror, which was almost the length of the wall and surrounded by the same light bulbs used in actors' dressing rooms. Up to that moment, she fancied she'd been lucky to escape the clutches of age. But now she was merciless with herself. Her skin looked dry and flaky, and blotchy from crying; her hair was thinning, she was quite sure of it. She noticed to her horror the beginnings of a double chin, despite doing chin exercises since she was a teenager. And though the muscles on her arms were toned, soft flesh hung away from them, not only *away*, but *down* too, *earthwards*. As an object, she counted herself spent, ugly even. No wonder Hugo had looked elsewhere.

Again she began to pace. It wasn't even midday. What was she to do with herself until two? And could she really face being in a public space with Arabella rabbiting on about *divorce*? Was she not to be offered *hope* first?

Then she stopped dead in her hall of the two doors, the red and the grey. She had left through the red door twice that morning, without thinking, and had come back through the red door, without thinking. Did Hugo think she was stupid as well as old? He never remarked on her little schemes. He seemed to go through the doors quite as he pleased, even going through the pink door when she had them designated male and female. Had Hugo just been teasing her, humouring her all through their marriage? Did he, when push came to shove, think her absurd?

Poor Laura found herself kicking at the red door. She would have painted it black there and then if she'd had the paint. She hated it. Only she hated herself more, and began to weep even more profusely.

At last she was calm enough to go back to her phone book in the kitchen. Arabella had failed her, even if she had been busy. Well, Rachel would have time for her. Rachel would know what to do.

Rachel was trying to warm up her studio when the phone rang. She was beginning work on a couple of new commissions: the restoration of an eighteenth-century portrait of a servant, probably Dutch, and a twentieth-century landscape by Mark Gertler. She was pleased to be distracted by her old friend. Her husband Jerry was in Senegal, painting the villagers and colourful markets for which he was so justly renowned, and her daughter Clara had returned to student life in Manchester over the weekend. She had time in abundance.

'Hello, Rachel!' Laura said. 'How are things?' She tried hard to make her voice sound normal and cheery, but gave up immediately when Rachel asked her what was wrong.

'The most terrible thing has happened,' blubbed Laura, 'and I don't know what to do! I just don't know what to do! Hugo is having an affair!'

'You poor girl!' said Rachel sympathetically.

'What shall I do? What shall I do? Do you think we should divorce? Oh, I just don't want a divorce!'

'Of course you shouldn't get divorced!'

'That's what Arabella says I should do.'

'That's because she's a divorce lawyer, of course. She'd like everyone to be divorced, not least because of what happened to her. But Hugo's not Charlie, you know. I never liked him, even before the accident. There's one thing I promise you, Laura. Hugo's devoted to you, I've noticed that often. You've got a wonderful marriage.'

'How can he be devoted to me if he does something like this?'

'I imagine most men have affairs.' Rachel paused to wonder if that was fair. 'I must say, I can't imagine Patrick having an affair. But he's so terribly …'

'Dull, he is, isn't he, Rach!' laughed Laura even through her tears. 'But how can you be so cool, how can you think it's just all right to …'

'Listen, Laura. I've been with Jerry five years now. But God knows what he gets up to in Africa. I'm quite sure he seduces all those black women he paints. Well, he's hinted as much. And what am I supposed to do about it? He's the best thing that's ever happened to me. If I were weaker, I'd go for a nice dull man like Patrick. But Ann needed a steady sort just to be there and adore her, what with her family background. We're stronger than she is, and we went for gold. That means we have to share them a little.'

Laura hadn't a clue that Ann had had a troubled family history, and on any other day would have wanted to discuss it *ad infinitum*. But right now she had to get her head straight about something else.

'Don't you mind that Jerry's unfaithful to you?'

'Why should I mind? He loves me! He's totally dependent on me, even if he doesn't realise it. As is Hugo dependent on you. Of course he flirts, he needs the adoration of every woman he meets. But there's only one woman he really worships, and that's you. I've watched him lusting for you at dinner parties. It's you he wants.'

'But you haven't been living in London for five years, Rachel. He might have been lusting for me when you knew him. I don't know if he still does.'

'Are you still having sex?'

'Well, yes, of course.'

'Often?'

'About twice a week,' said Laura, shyly. 'That's normal, isn't it? I mean, it doesn't take terribly long, not like … The truth is, I don't even know how long sex is supposed to take.'

'Have you ever slept with anyone *but* Hugo?'

'You know I haven't, Rachel! I would never be unfaithful to him!'

'Why not?'

'Of course I wouldn't! I don't go in for that kind of thing!'

'I've been unfaithful to Jerry.'

'But I thought you loved him!'

'I do, and always will. An occasional affair doesn't do any harm to a relationship. That's my experience, for what it's worth. Providing it's discreet, no one even needs to know about it. Hugo tried to keep his own peccadillo discreet but failed.'

There was renewed sobbing down the phone. Rachel patiently let it subside.

'Listen, Laura. Hugo loves you. That I know. You have a marriage made in heaven. I doubt there are many marriages that don't have occasional lapses, fidelity-wise. Forget you ever saw him this morning. Dress in your sexiest clothes for when he comes back. Make him a delicious supper. Don't let this come between you, for God's sake. What about Jemima and Leo? They'd be devastated if you ever separated or did something stupid like that. Shit happens. This is shit. But move on as fast as you possibly can, and hopefully you *will* have moved on by this evening. Why don't you enjoy yourself down at the sales this afternoon? You know how much you love that kind of thing. Treat yourself!'

'Oh Rachel! You make it all sound so easy. I don't think you can imagine what this feels like. I feel so stupid, so betrayed. I don't think he respects me. That's the root of it. You say he loves me, but I'm just not feeling that love. I used to feel it. We used to have something really magic, Hugo and I. It's just not there any more. It's just not there!'

'Look, if you want a break for a while, why don't you come down here? If I think of all the times you've been there for me. I shall make you cup after cup of hot chocolate.'

Laura managed to laugh amidst her tears. 'I think I'll stay here,' she said. 'I think that's the brave thing to do. Not that I'm feeling at all brave.'

'If you want to run away, you know where to come.'

'Thank you, Rachel, thank you! I knew I could depend on you. I do very much feel like running away. But I'll try and brave it out.'

The two friends said goodbye, but Laura found she could brave it out for all of five minutes.

Her mistake was to begin rummaging through the pockets of Hugo's jackets, looking for evidence against him. She found it soon enough. A hotel bill, six months old. The Marigold Hotel, Chester. She remembered him telling her about some new contract in Chester, fuck him. And suddenly here were two fucking dinners, fucking champagne, two fucking breakfasts, what a fucking fool she was.

Laura never swore, never. Patient to a tee, her children would have told you she had never even lost her temper. When the children were young, she had au pairs. That helped. She could slip away to the aerobics class and sweat out any residual irritation with her offspring. Now where oh where were all these words coming from?

'Fucking au pairs!' she said next. 'Right under my fucking nose!'

She clambered up another two flights of stairs to the attic rooms, where Brigitte, Axelle, Hedda and pretty Amelie had slept over the years. She stripped the bed. What was she expecting to find, a used condom? Three years after Amelie had left them, and countless kids had had sleepovers in that very room? She flung open the wardrobe. Empty, just a few hangers. But she had more luck with the chest of drawers. Hidden under the drawer lining was a letter written in German, dated, but unsigned. Unfinished, perhaps. The sixth of June, 1980. That was Brigitte's era, when Jemima was still a baby. What was she writing? That the father of the house had come knocking at her door? That she didn't know whether to tell his wife?

'I loathe you, Hugo, you idiot, you fuckhead!'

Then the phone rang.

She ran down to her bedroom and picked it up.

'Who is it?' she said, coldly.

'It's Ann. God, Laura, is something wrong?'

'You bet the fuck it is!'

'Do you want me to come round?'

'Nope. I don't actually.'

'You sound awful.'

'You can come if you don't bring your ... daughters.'

'But you know I have the girls in the afternoons! Becky and Sal finish school at midday and ...'

'That's fine. Don't come.'

'For God's sake, Laura! This isn't you speaking. It's some troll.'

'Well, perhaps I am a troll. Perhaps that's the real me!'

'It's not the real you! I know you, and you're the kindest person …'

'I'm a fraud! May you be the first to know it!'

'If you're a fraud, so am I!'

'Well, we all know you're a fraud. What happened to you, Ann? You used to be so free. You used to say just what you thought about everything. We could always rely on you to show a little spirit. Perhaps you should never have had children. Twins, what a nightmare!'

There was a sudden silence on the other end of the phone. Then Laura broke down into floods of tears. 'I hate myself, I'm so sorry. You see I am a troll! A vicious, vicious troll!'

'I'm coming right round. I want to get to the bottom of this.'

'No, no, I'm going out to lunch!'

'You're not fit to go out to lunch! What's happened, Laura? What's going on?'

'Hugo's having an affair. And he's always been having them. I don't know how many. It's like I don't exist.'

'But Hugo thinks the world of you! Everyone knows that!'

'I don't know what to do. I don't know if I'm coming or going. Arabella says I should divorce him. But I love him! I don't want a divorce! I don't want to be a bitter old divorcee who hates men! Then Rachel says I should just ignore it. But I'm not in any fit state to ignore it. Part of me wants to kill him. Yes, if he comes back tonight and acts as if nothing has happened I'm going to kill him. What am I saying, Ann? I'm going crazy. That's no good, is it? If he sees me like this, he'll just walk out anyway and spend the night with Miss Golden Plait.'

'Do you know her, then?'

'Of course I don't know her. I didn't know she even existed until three hours ago. I'm such a fool! I'm such a fool!' And poor Laura began to weep her heart out all over again.

'Look, cancel your lunch. I'm coming right over!'

'What? You'll have me traumatise your girls?'

'I'll find a babysitter. Wait for me.'

The wait was a long one. Laura cancelled her lunch with Arabella, telling her she wasn't ready for divorce quite yet. Oddly, that gave her a sense of perspective on the situation. She no longer felt she was falling off a cliff. She poured herself a glass of wine and nibbled at some pitta bread and taramasalata. She even began to consider Rachel's advice. If she were strong enough, that was how she would *like* to behave, certainly. Could she really be that cool?

Half an hour later, the phone went again.

'No luck, I'm afraid. The childminder's filled her quota for the afternoon and the girls' numerous babysitters are still at school.'

'That's okay,' sighed Laura, surprised at how disappointed she felt. She wanted company.

'But listen to me, Laura. Don't think I've lost my wildness just because I'm a mother. I am the old Ann, you know. I have an instinct about how to punish wrongdoers. I always have had. Laura, listen to me. You have to take revenge. I've been hatching a plan. How does this sound to you?'

It's not often 'revenge' is given the credit of being the 'middle way'. But this was how, quite honestly, it seemed to Laura. She was to take matters into her own hands and leave him – just temporarily, of course, but write a note suggesting it was forever. Then, suggested Ann, get him where it hurts – in the wallet! Wasn't Hugo always on at her for spending too much? And didn't she have a joint account? Go on a spending bonanza!

'He'd kill me!'

'You'd kill him, more like!'

'But where would I go?'

'This is the best bit! Haven't you always wanted to go to the Caribbean? To bathe in those glorious limpid blue seas, empty golden beaches, palm trees, drinking tequilas at sunset …'

'Can you imagine how lonely I'd feel, with all those happy honeymooners?'

'Not everyone's going to be on honeymoon. There'll be business-men recharging their batteries, singletons looking for romance.'

'Romance is the last thing I need at this moment, I can tell you that for starters. I never want to see a man again.'

'What I'm saying is, the world is yours for the taking, so take it, do whatever you like. Go on a world cruise! You always told me you wanted to see the pyramids.'

'Even going to see the pyramids seems a bit daunting on my own.'

'Come on, Laura, show some spirit! Do something that you would never normally do. Take the plunge. Carpe diem! Seize the day! As you've been so frank with me today, I'll be frank with you. Ever since your children went away to boarding school, you've been drifting through your life at half-mast. I'm sure to the world you must seem to have everything – good looks, money, even Hugo. But human beings need more than that, something more substantial.'

'I do charity work. I'm on the local board of the NSPCC, I'm always arranging Macmillan coffee mornings, do you remember ...'

'I'm not talking about the charitable works of the great and the good. I'm talking about a deeper exploration of life.'

'Are you suggesting I go to evening classes?'

'Look, let's talk about today. Something shocking happened. Something life-altering. You, Laura, are going to change from this day on. You're going to be reborn. You're a sweet woman, but you've been sleepwalking, and now you're thoroughly awake. How exciting is that?'

'I don't want to be reborn. I want my old life back.'

'But your old life was a lazy one, an easy one. The unexamined life is not worth living. That's Socrates for you. Take his advice.'

'God, do you really think I need to go somewhere? Rachel said I can go and stay with her in Bruton.'

'No, Laura, wrong! Not Bruton! Think exotic.'

'I could go to Peru!'

'Hooray!'

'The Maldives!'

'Yes!'

'Australia!'

'That's more like it!'

'What do I write in the note, Ann?'

'Something short and to the point. How about, "You bastard!"?'

'Shouldn't I tell him where I am? What if he's worried about me?'

'You have no concept of revenge at all, do you? You *want* him to worry! In fact, you don't happen to have lurking in your address book the name of a bloke you fancy who might want to come with you?'

'What's got into you, Ann?'

'This is me talking here, this is Ann the Anarchist, silly!'

'How do I buy a flight? Do I go to a travel agent?'

'Oh Laura, you really have no idea, do you? Just go to the airport, see what flights are leaving when, and take your pick. And your passport. Don't forget to take your passport.'

'Is it really as easy as that?'

'Yep.'

'And you think I should go shopping first, do you?'

'Laura, honestly, do whatever you feel like doing! Now is the time to start living authentically.'

'What do you mean, "authentically"?'

'I mean, from your heart outwards. Don't try and please people all the time. Live for the moment.'

'Okay, if you think that's what I should do,' gulped Laura.

'And if Hugo rings tonight I'll tell him I haven't heard from you, okay?'

'I trust you, Ann,' said Laura, tentatively.

'The person you should trust is yourself. Now, I'm going to feed these girls, who have been miraculously patient, and send you on your way. All you need is Hugo's bank card, your passport and some *joie de vivre*. Good luck to you!'

When she hung up, Laura's mood was still and thoughtful. She was sitting at the kitchen table, wondering what to do next. The pad of paper on which she wrote her weekly shopping lists was within an arm's reach, so mechanically she reached out for it.

'YOU BASTARD!' she wrote, obediently.

Then she wondered about her children, who might or might not be coming home that weekend. She could never divorce Hugo for their sake, she realised. They'd be devastated. Laura didn't approve of divorce, ever, where children's lives were at stake. She considered it a selfish, defeatist act, beyond the pale. Except, she supposed, if there was physical violence.

So she added: 'If the children come home, tell them I'm on a skiing holiday with friends.'

Momentarily her heart went out to her dear children, her sweet boy, her darling daughter. They must never become the innocent victims of this terrible thing. They must never learn that anything is amiss at all. Underneath her first two messages to Hugo she wrote a third: 'And tell Jemima she forgot her PE shirt and it's on the ironing board.'

Then she went up to her bedroom and gathered a few things together. Well, one thing was for sure, she'd be going to a hot country. She rummaged through her drawers and was in no mood to choose a wardrobe at all. A couple of T-shirts, a Janet Reger apricot negligee, a silver lamé bikini she hadn't worn in years, a pair of shorts and a couple of mini-skirts, two halter neck dresses in different colours. Perhaps a couple of mohair shawls for the evenings. She'd buy anything else she wanted out there. Shoes! Her Jimmy Choo boots lay discarded in the hall. She wasn't going to be putting on those mini torture chambers again, that was for sure. Some sensible, one-inch-heeled pink soirée silk court shoes. Those were the shoes to begin the rest of her life in.

Laura walked through the grey door, for the first time ever. Then she turned round to spit on it.

She caught a taxi this time. She realised that standing at a bus stop required a certain energy she just didn't have any more. When the taxi driver asked her where she wanted to go to, she felt like crying. She wanted to say, 'Back home, where I belong!' She felt like a pigeon with a broken wing, not a kestrel eyeing its quarry. She wasn't good at this revenge malarkey.

Knowing that home was denied her, her instinct was to head for the airport and get the hell out of London, where she could only envision unhappiness for God knows how many weeks, months or years. But quite suddenly, in spite of herself, a vision of that coat popped into her head.

'South Molton Street,' she said. 'Do you know the shop Browns? It's the Bond Street end.'

'Right you are,' said the taxi driver.

Oh God, what was she thinking of? She was going back to the scene of the crime, going back to the porch where she had seen *them!*

She bent double, like she was going to be sick. But the sight of her pink silk shoes encouraged her again. Wasn't Dorothy given some shoes in the *Wizard of Oz,* which protected her from evil? Couldn't she fly with them, too?

She was quite sure that such a splendid thing as that coat would have been bought up by now, many times over, but what if it was still there, in the shop window? Wouldn't that be some solace, at least?

When she got out of the taxi and paid her fare she barely registered the surprised look on the driver's face, who was, in fact, wondering if she was stoned.

'Here,' she said, 'keep the change.'

The coat was not there. Well, that wasn't particularly surprising. Masochistically, Laura walked towards the offending porch, and did a bitter little twirl right in the place they had stood. This energised her somewhat, and for want of something better to do, she went into Browns to see if there was something else that might take her fancy.

She tried to imagine herself in Barbados. What might she need for Barbados?

'Have you got your summer stock yet, by any chance?' Laura asked a shop assistant.

'It's in the stockroom, still in boxes. Come back in a couple of weeks.'

Even the phrase *a couple of weeks* renewed poor Laura's pain. She felt dizzy at the prospect of time just carrying on without her. Or rather, with her. Things were going to happen, and she didn't know what they were going to be. The thought of that was enough to make her stomach churn.

'Are you looking for anything in particular?' asked the shop assistant, politely.

'Well, not really. I noticed a rather lovely coat last week which some lucky person will be wearing right now … actually, you could tell me who bought it, if you know … faux fur, tight bodice, full skirt, a lovely thing that was in your window.'

'You mean this? No one has been able to fit into it!' The shop assistant brought Laura the coat from the rack by the changing rooms. 'It was probably made for a size eight model six foot tall. The other sizes left the shop the same week they came in. It's been like Cinderella and the glass slipper all day.'

Laura stroked the coat affectionately.

'Could it possibly be my luck is going to change today?'

'Give it a go!' The assistant surveyed Laura's figure with a practised eye and said, 'If the coat is going to fit anyone, it's you. It might just have your name on it!'

They don't just call shopping 'therapy' for nothing. The coat fitted like a glove. Laura saw her reflection in the changing room, and was too delighted by what she saw to keep it to herself. So she went out into the main shop and got all the admiring glances a woman could wish for.

'Well it fits!' she said. 'As long as I don't even wear a cardigan under it.'

The assistants gathered together to clap her.

'It couldn't be going to a better home,' they said. 'You look wonderful in it!'

Laura smiled graciously, caught sight of a couple of jade necklaces and lay them on the counter.

'I'll have these, too,' she enthused. 'I'm going to spoil myself today.'

She did. She had to buy a new suitcase for her haul. Even those pink stilettos she'd seen earlier were still there, waiting for her. She felt like dancing down the street. She gave her old wool coat to a charity shop, spent a fortune on make-up and scent, and then put her hair up in the public loo. She was naughtily aware of the pleasure she derived from being stared at. Earlier, she wouldn't have dreamt of taking the tube to the airport. In the mood she was in, the victorious snow queen, she couldn't think of anything she'd rather do.

She took her place between a Rastafarian plugged into his Sony Walkman and an elderly gent. Overwhelmed by the day's events she was too highly charged just to sit still, so she tried to engage them in conversation. She asked the gentleman, now engrossed in his copy of the *Evening Standard*, whether he was going anywhere special.

He mumbled, 'No, not really,' and went back to his paper.

Thwarted, she began making eyes at the Rasta, smiling broadly at him until he was obliged to take his earphones out and ask her politely, 'Is there anything you want, lady?'

'Well actually,' she said, embarrassed, 'I was wondering whether you thought Jamaica was a good place to go on holiday?'

'You going to Jamaica?'

'Well, yes, quite possibly. Would you recommend it?'

The Rastafarian grimaced. 'I've not been there myself. But I guess it's a good place.' He looked at her quizzically, as if to say, 'Any other questions?'

Laura blushed, smiled again, and closed her eyes, holding fast to her suitcase.

She knew this journey well, down the Piccadilly line to Heathrow Airport. She was aware of the train braking as it was coming into a station, the noise of the doors opening and closing, like a machine might sound, if it breathed. She heard the passengers coming on, and getting off. She felt them staring at her, but she didn't mind. She and her suitcase were embarking on an adventure. It was half past four in the afternoon. Still she had no idea where she would finally lay her head that night. She tried to see this in a positive light. She tried to remain curious and upbeat, but then found herself holding on to the seat to prevent herself from jumping up and aborting her mission completely.

The journey seemed to last forever. Sometimes she tried to imagine she was in a hot bath. In fact, when she was *really* in a hot bath she liked to turn the lights off and close her eyes. It relaxed her. She also remembered the breathing exercises from her yoga class. She breathed deep into her diaphragm, held it there a moment, and then exhaled. She felt the train emptying out.

She thought of Hugo getting back to an empty house. How hard would he try to find out where she had gone? Would he feel anxious? Would he feel remorse? Let him feel all those things, and more. And the fridge was empty, she thought with satisfaction. I never did the Monday shop for you today, you bastard. Perhaps I never will again.

One station after another, onward, onward, to where?

Perhaps she'd spend the night on a plane. Perhaps she'd end up in Australia, or New Zealand. Perhaps she'd end up in Florida. One of her old school friends lived in Florida. Perhaps she'd pay her a visit.

When she opened her eyes again she saw that she was being stared at. Not by a crowd of perplexed fellow travellers, but by a young lad of about twenty years old. She straightened her back and pouted her lips, ever so slightly. Laura had been too absorbed in her own husband to notice there might be life beyond him. The boy continued to stare, shamelessly. He was wearing a black leather jacket and jeans. He had a small, green enamel stud in one ear and hair that might naturally have been tight, blond curls, but which he was keeping at bay by cutting it short. But what bewitched Laura most of all was the singular beauty of his face.

Laura knew what 'sexy' meant, or thought she did. When she'd go shopping with her friends they'd spot a good bum and pretend to be terribly turned on. Or at least, how could anyone be turned on by a bum of all things?

They were passing stations far too fast. Osterley Park, Boston Manor, Northfields.

At Hounslow West the boy got off.

Laura followed him.

2

When Laura emerged from the entrance of Hounslow West tube station, she immediately looked out for the boy, who was walking away from her at some speed. Her case was heavy with the spoils of the day, and she regretted an earlier decision to change from her low silk pink pumps into her new stilettos. She wanted to call him, but didn't know his name. She let out a half-hearted 'You there!' and a couple of Indian lads looked at her. She suddenly felt absurd and humiliated, stuck out here on a dual carriageway in the middle of nowhere looking like an ageing film star draped in fur. She had never wished to blend into the world, preferably disappear within it, quite so much.

But then she noticed that the boy was still only fifty yards away from her, waiting to cross the road, and she suddenly felt her luck was in. Never had she felt more grateful for a rush hour. She ran towards him – never mind the suitcase and the heels, she actually ran.

The boy turned round.

'Are you following me?' he said.

Laura smiled apologetically.

'Yes,' she said, weakly, catching her breath. 'Kind of.'

'What d'you want?' the boy asked, in a matter-of-fact tone.

The first word she thought of was 'you' but she just shrugged.

'Nice coat,' said the boy. He kept his distance.

How could he not see how she needed him?

For a short while the pair of them were silent. The traffic roared within inches of them. Laura tried to put into words some kind of feasible excuse for her behaviour. In the end she managed: 'Is this where you live?'

Laura looked around her. Everything was dark and cold and loud. The lights glowing on the other side of the dual carriageway were from small Indian supermarkets, their wares displayed in stalls on the street. Not a Costa Coffee to be seen. Not even a house, as far as she could make out. Where were all the houses? How could anyone live in this din? She could never have imagined a place as bleak as this. When the boy said nothing, Laura was more courageous still.

'Can I come home with you?' she said.

The boy paused. Then he said, 'No.' But he stopped looking for his moment to cross the road and looked at her, and the way he did so gave Laura hope.

'It's so cold here,' Laura said.

'Yes,' said the boy.

'I'm on my way to Heathrow Airport. The truth is, I'm not sure where I'll be flying to yet. A warm place, but where, God only knows. Do you want to come with me?'

She looked pleadingly at the boy.

'All expenses paid, and all that. I'm just kind of running away from this dreary winter. It's been dragging on and on and on, and I want a break from it!' Laura forced a light, ordinary tone.

'I haven't got a passport,' said the boy.

'But we have to go somewhere! We can't just stand here all night!'

He came up to her and looked into her eyes so intently she imagined he saw every last vestige of her soul.

'You are so fucking beautiful,' he said.

That was when the boy kissed her.

So tenderly, so full of longing. Laura had never been held like that, squeezed in an embrace of such overpowering strength. She couldn't even remember her first kiss with Hugo, though they celebrated it every year. And now was not the time to be remembering it (though she couldn't help comparing). Now was the time to be born anew.

At Heathrow Airport Laura was showing her new friend Jed the list of departures. Jed had agreed to follow her to the end of the fucking earth, but in fact, without a passport, they couldn't go far.

'Choose from up there!' enthused Laura. 'Edinburgh, Cardiff, Douglas – that's in the Isle of Man – Newcastle, Inverness, Leeds.'

'Douglas,' Jed said. 'I've got an uncle called Douglas.'

'Good choice! I went to the Isle of Man when I was a girl. It's a lovely place. Fairies live there. And there's a great kipper factory.'

Laura bought the tickets, first class naturally. Jed proffered his provisional driving licence as ID, and no one queried it.

During the flight they found little to say to each other. Jed sat by the window and spent the journey looking out.

'The stars,' he said. That was all.

Laura took off her coat and carefully folded it, putting it in the luggage compartment above them. She sat down again and admired the new dress she was wearing in white linen, just a simple well-cut Christian Dior dress with short sleeves. She'd been expecting to be flying somewhere hot, after all. She wanted Jed to turn towards her and notice it. Hugo never noticed her clothes, or if he did he would raise an eyebrow, which asked the question, 'How much did that set me back?'

The trolley came round with sandwiches and drinks.

'Jed, do you want a drink?' asked Laura.

'No thanks,' said Jed, looking briefly towards her.

Laura said she hadn't eaten all day and was starving. Jed didn't respond. She bought herself a cheese sandwich and a glass of wine. She was about to press Jed again but it was obvious this was his first time in a plane and she didn't wish to disturb his reverie. In fact, she enjoyed it. Everyone was so spoilt nowadays, they didn't look out of windows any more. It was good to be with someone who appreciated the smaller things in life.

Halfway through the small plastic bottle of Merlot, Laura began to feel bolder. With Jed looking away from her, she could enjoy his physical presence all the more. His jeans were dirty, worn and too loose, but the outline of his thighs excited her. His hands were dirty, too, despite her suggesting at the airport that he might like to wash them. But she was pleased he hadn't. Somehow he was more intriguing for resisting her.

It occurred to Laura that she had never felt more virginal. She felt she was twenty-one years old setting off on her honeymoon. Oh no, she was more excited than that! For when she married Hugo, she'd already lived with him, she knew exactly what was in store. They'd already been on several holidays together. Their honeymoon in Marrakesh was, when she came to think of it, just another holiday. But Jed was like an unopened present. For a few days – for all she knew, the rest of her life – she would slowly unpack him, get to know him. Another human being, just for her. Another human being to have sex with. She closed her eyes and relived the kiss at Hounslow West.

Laura looked at her watch. Half past seven. Hugo would be home by now, ringing her friends to find out where she'd gone. Well, no one would be suspecting the Isle of Man! She smiled to herself, but felt sick to the stomach. What was she doing flying, as the captain had just informed them, over Manchester?

They took a taxi to Douglas from the airport and suddenly Laura blurted out: 'Have we forgotten to say hello to the fairies?'

Jed looked at her as if she was mad; but the taxi driver looked behind him in mild amusement, and said, in all seriousness: 'They live under the next bridge.'

'I knew it,' said Laura, with pride. 'I'm pleased the fairies are still there. Jed, you have to say hello to them and they bring you good luck.'

Jed did not say hello, and Laura was too shy to greet the fairies alone, so they drove over the bridge in silence.

Laura was suddenly so deflated she couldn't speak or think.

On they went, Jed seemingly transfixed by the dark outside the window, Laura almost in tears.

But then Jed realised and said, 'Don't worry, Laura. You'll get your good luck.'

Laura took his hand and kissed it. 'Thank you,' she said.

They were staying right on the seafront. An icy blast of sea air and spray hit them as they got out of the car.

'God, I needed that,' laughed Laura, as her fur coat ballooned in the wind. 'When was the last time you saw a sea like that? It's wonderful, isn't it?'

The tide heaved against the stony shore in a vast majestic rhythm, but the night was a dingy black and there was little more they could see.

'Yeah, Laura,' said Jed, and he clambered up on to the sea wall while Laura paid the taxi driver and got her suitcase out of the boot. She waited for Jed to have his fill of it, anxious not to interrupt his communion with nature, before calling out, 'It's freezing! I'm going into the hotel. Are you coming?'

The Hilton, Douglas, isn't quite like the Hilton, London. It's a large Victorian building bang on the seafront with an ugly, modern extension used as a casino. Yet Laura was delighted with it. It was warm for one thing, and she went up to the reception to sign them in.

The hall had the air of a conservatory: palm trees were growing up to a glass ceiling, and there was a fish pond right in the middle of it, surrounded by a stone wall. Jed went straight up to the pond and leant over to try and catch a large goldfish in his hands, while Laura booked the best room in the hotel.

The receptionist asked for their names. She was a woman of about sixty who looked like a school matron. Laura blushed. She had never committed adultery before.

'Laura and Jed Glass,' she said.

Jed looked up at her. She shrugged apologetically.

'Twin or double?'

'I'm sorry?'

'Do you want twin beds, or one large bed?'

'You mean … is Jed my …' Laura realised to her horror that she was being accused of being Jed's mother.

But then she managed, 'King-size, please. And I was wondering whether we might have some supper brought up to our room. Something light.'

The receptionist looked at her watch and explained that last orders were at 10 and it was already five past. But looking at Laura's forlorn face she said, 'I might manage to get you a couple of ham rolls.'

'That would be so very kind. And a bottle of champagne, please.'

Jed released the fish and came over to the reception desk.

'Beer for me,' he said.

'Beer for him,' laughed Laura nervously. 'Do you sell peanuts?'

'There's a mini-bar in the room and you'll find peanuts in there,' said the receptionist.

'A mini-bar! I love mini-bars! Do you know, my husband Hugo won't let me have a tiny gin and tonic from a mini-bar, he's that mean!'

'Well, fuck him,' said Jed.

'Oh fuck him!' said Laura with delight.

'Your key,' said the receptionist, now visibly embarrassed.

'I'll take that,' said Jed.

Laura carried the suitcase.

The bedroom was not as unconditionally glamorous as Laura had hoped it might be. The walls were painted green, and the bed was large and soft, with a dip in the middle. The wardrobe and dressing table were ugly modern things, which dominated the room. They were, in fact, art deco from the 1930s but Laura didn't recognise the style and thought they were tatty. Jed didn't even bother to look about him.

'I can't believe this is their best room,' said Laura.

He walked up to Laura and kissed her, unbuttoning her coat as he did so.

Laura saw Jed's hands approaching her beautiful white linen dress.

'Oh Jed, wait a while. Wouldn't you like a shower?'

'Where's the zip?' asked Jed, genuinely puzzled.

'You can't just throw my coat on the floor!' said Laura.

'We're not here to watch fucking TV. Come here, Laura.'

She did as she was told.

'Take that dress off.'

'The sandwiches will be here in a minute!' Laura put her coat on the chair and sat down on the bed. 'Don't be so fast,' she said.

'Hey, what are we here for, Laura?' said Jed. He sat down beside her and lay his hand on her thigh.

The sandwiches came. Laura drank champagne, and Jed drank beer. They sat next to each other on the end of the bed and rested their glasses on the same table as the TV. In the event, Jed ate both ham rolls.

After five minutes when Laura didn't have a clue what she was doing in that hideous room with a man who was stuffing bread into his mouth like he hadn't eaten for a week, she asked, 'How long have you lived in Hounslow West?'

'Fuck Hounslow West,' said Jed.

'Do you work?'

'It depends what you call work,' said Jed.

'Do you enjoy what you do?'

'Yep.'

'Are you going to tell me about it?'

'Ah! I see now. There are buttons going up the side. Fucking nifty.'

Jed wiped his hands on his jeans and promptly began to undo them.

Laura stood up and exclaimed: 'This dress is white, Jed, and your hands are filthy!'

Jed stood up to confront her. He poured her another glass of champagne and said, 'Here, drink this.'

She did.

'Now, are you feeling better?'

'Please, please, just wash them,' begged Laura. She looked up at him sheepishly, worried she might just have spoiled the spontaneity of the moment.

'You can fucking take it off yourself, then,' said Jed.

Then Jed took three pillows and lay them down the centre of the bed, like a bier.

'Take that dress off and lie on here,' he said.

'What about you? Are you going to take your clothes off?' asked Laura. 'How ridiculous I sound!' she thought. Oh, why couldn't they just be naked together and be done with it?

Jed ignored the question and went into the bathroom. Laura could hear him having a shower and was grateful to him. For want of anything better to do, she did exactly as she was told. She even hung her dress in the wardrobe and folded her underwear on the chair. Ridiculous really, she thought to herself. It crossed her mind that he would kill her and throw her body into the sea, and no one would ever know where she had gone. She helped herself to another glass of champagne and then lay, stark naked, on the three pillows running down the centre of the bed.

A memory of her former self, that happy wife, that happy mum, floated into her head. She felt giddy. When she briefly tried to make sense of things she felt frightened. She felt like a sacrificial virgin on the altar. She thought of Hugo having sex with Miss Golden Plait. She didn't even feel angry with Hugo, just perplexed. She thought of Jed with other women. Then she thought of plain sex.

'Why do we do this? Why do we submit?' Her head was so light now, letting itself sink into the pillow. Her stomach knotted, but in a good way, now. 'It's such an extreme thing to do, to hand yourself over like that. Like this.'

When Jed came back into the room he was wearing jeans.

'That's cheating,' said Laura.

Jed just stared at her. 'You're fucking beautiful,' he said.

Laura got up briefly to prop herself on her elbow. She noticed a small tattoo of a funny little aeroplane at the top of one arm, as if a child had drawn it. His chest was more boy than man, quite hairless.

'Come on, Jed, why did you put your jeans back on?'

'Lie down,' commanded Jed. 'And shut up.'

Jed knelt on the floor next to her and felt her lower belly, suddenly so gentle, even reverential. Then he leant over and kissed it, while his hand put two fingers inside her. Laura willed them to stay there, but he walked over to the other side of the bed and stared at her so hard, at every part of her naked body, it might have counted as penetration in its own right. She had never felt so vulnerable, so yearning to be touched again.

Then Jed leant over to lick her, slowly, down the centre of her body, and once more she felt his fingers inside her, more roughly this time. When she flinched he slapped her thigh.

'Don't move,' he said.

Again Jed paused to look at her. Now Jed began to lick her ears and stroke her breasts. Then, quite roughly, he opened her legs.

Hugo had been Laura's only lover. She was waiting for Jed to get on top of her, waiting for him to make love to her. There were just some things that the innocent Laura had never known, even imagined in her wildest fantasy. For Jed was a true master with his tongue, a true lover.

Jed was not content to give her one orgasm, but four.

And that first night, they didn't even have sex. Sex proper began at 4 a.m. the next morning. The lovers didn't pause until noon.

'Shit,' said Laura, 'we've missed breakfast!'

Jed got out of bed to go to the bathroom. He didn't kiss her before he left her, and Laura's mind switched involuntarily back to Hugo. She thought of the cup of tea he always brought her before he set off for work at seven, his kiss on her cheek or forehead, sometimes even a 'Love you!' Was it all just an act, a habit? Was it all done in the spirit of flossing his teeth, dull but necessary to maintain the status quo? She looked at the phone on her bedside table. She considered a quick phone call to Rachel or her parents. That's where he'd imagine she'd gone, somewhere out of London. She wanted to know if he'd been in touch. But then Jed came in wearing one of the hotel bathrobes. He was smiling broadly.

'It's fucking amazing here,' he said, appreciatively. 'Look at this!' He went to the curtains and opened them with a great theatrical sweep.

Laura's heart swelled with gratitude for Jed's gratitude, and she happily wrapped herself in a sheet and joined him at the window. The sky was pearly grey, lit up by an invisible sun, and the January-black sea heaved against the stony beach of Douglas harbour. Both pairs of eyes sought out the horizon, separating all that had been with all that was possible, and for a moment or two they were lost to it.

Then Jed began opening the window. It was a sash window that looked like it hadn't been opened in years, but Jed was forcing it upwards.

'Jed, what are you doing?'

'What do you think I'm fucking doing?'

'You'll break it!'

'There's a balcony out there!'

'That's not a real balcony, we're not supposed to stand on that!'

'A balcony is a fucking balcony,' said Jed.

At last the window creaked into action and Jed crawled out on to a space one foot deep with a stone balustrade. He stood in his white robe with his arms outstretched to the sky and said, 'Come on, Laura!'

'I'll just get dressed,' said Laura anxiously. 'I can't go out there dressed in a sheet!'

'What's your problem?' said Jed, slightly irritated. He put out his hand to her and tried to pull her under the window to join him, but the sheet kept slipping. Jed laughed at her attempts to cover a naked breast.

'Please, Jed!'

But Laura would not be humiliated. She let go of Jed's hand and made a supreme effort to wrap the sheet around her as tightly as she could. Then she clambered under the window before standing proud and tall at Jed's side. It was so cold she could scarcely breathe, and even though a road lay between them and the sea itself, their faces were soon wet with spray.

If Jed had been Hugo, Laura would have been furious. A part of her looked in dismay at the streaks of dirt on the white sheet, and was wondering whether, if all the dirt was on one side of it, she could make the bed up so no one would notice this childish behaviour of theirs. But a part of Laura felt oddly liberated. To feel so cold in such a beautiful place by such a beautiful man and stand with her chin held high was exhilarating.

And this latter mood was what carried her through the rest of the day. Laura wanted no truck with the past. She scarcely thought of Hugo, and never the children.

They had lunch in The Bohemian Café in a side street. Laura chose it because she liked the name and the colour it was painted: a warm terracotta red. It was small and dark inside: even at lunchtime there were candles on the tables. On the walls were large, framed negatives of seashells. There was also a less satisfactory poster of a woman with blanked-out eyes whose hair was splayed out above her. At first glance it looked like a traditional, if rather eccentric portrait. But if you looked again it was just possible the woman was dead. When Jed pointed this out, Laura laughed. 'It's a bohemian café,' she said, 'anything goes.' Jed didn't know what a 'bohemian' was.

'It's when you are wild and free and clever,' explained Laura. 'It's when you do exactly what you want. You don't believe in all those tedious social conventions. You're generally terribly poor, and you try and make your living doing something artistic. In fact, Jed, I think you're a bohemian at heart. You look like you would paint awfully well. You have the perfect mouth for chewing thoughtfully on the end of a paintbrush. Do you paint, Jed?'

'I don't do any art stuff,' said Jed.

'But you must try! Perhaps there's an art shop in Douglas. I shall kit you out.'

'But I'm good with my hands. I'm good at making things. I can weave with hazel.'

'You mean you make baskets?' Laura did well to conceal her disappointment.

'Yeah, I've made baskets, and I made ...'

'Have you ever thought of being a sculptor, Jed? If you're good with your hands ...'

'No,' said Jed.

They were in no mood to choose from a menu and ordered the lunch of the day, without much noticing what they ate. Jed ate ravenously: Laura put the rest of her mediocre Lancashire hotpot on to his plate. They were the only customers, but Laura neither noticed or cared. As far as she was concerned, they were the only two people in the world.

'I know what I'd like to do after lunch,' said Laura.

'Go on,' said Jed.

'I'd like to look in an estate agents'. I know that sounds really odd, because I really don't know you at all.'

'I don't follow.'

'The truth is, I love imagining other lives. Well, Hugo's a bastard, and I might divorce him. He's also rich. We could buy a lovely cottage together on the divorce proceedings. Now, I'm nowhere near divorce, it's total pie in the sky. But I'm someone who likes to dream. Is that ridiculous or what?'

'Yep,' said Jed, enigmatically.

'You mean you'll come?'

'No, it's ridiculous.'

'But it's not, Jed! Now, how can I persuade you? We could just start our lives again. My life has been spoilt, irredeemably spoilt. The only man I have ever loved has been Hugo ... God I can't even bear the sound of his name. If we lived here ... It's just so beautiful, isn't it?'

'You don't stop loving someone just because they treat you badly,' said Jed.

'Oh God! You are not only the sexiest person I have ever set eyes on – you are also the wisest. But even if deep down I do love Hugo, I tell you, I don't feel any love now. In fact, if I'm to be totally honest, I don't even feel I love my children.'

'You can never say that,' said Jed.

'Of course I love them, they're my life. Or they have been my life. I have a beautiful older daughter, Jemima. We used to be so close, Jed. She used to confide everything in me, but not any more. They're at boarding school. I'm no longer part of their lives. They've outgrown me.'

'Kids never outgrow their parents.'

'You know what, Jed, we had a row over Christmas. It was a row about nothing. Ah yes, the heating. They like it on full blast twenty-four hours a day, intolerable. I said to them, "If you're cold, put a jumper on. What are jumpers for?" You know what, Jed, it's not the argument I remember. It's the way they looked at me. With such contempt!'

'Why did you send them away?'

'You make me sound so awful, Jed. I never sent them away. I'd have been quite happy if they'd gone to a good day school in London. It was *they* who wanted to go. I can't tell you what their school is like. You would have thrived there. They've even got their own recording studio on the premises just in case you feel like cutting a CD. Or you can make bread, shear a sheep. Do you think I'm a bad mother, then?'

'I wouldn't send my kids away,' said Jed, 'and I wouldn't leave them either.'

'Then you're a better person than me,' said Laura.

The two ordered pudding from an elderly man with such a stoop that it was all Laura could do not to offer to help him carry the plates back into the kitchen.

'I suppose this place closes down in winter,' whispered Laura. 'It's lucky to get any staff at all.'

'Perhaps he's a bohemian,' said Jed. 'And that's the picture of his dead wife on the wall. Probably he killed her.'

'Bohemians don't murder people!' said Laura.

'Who would you murder if you could, Laura? Would you murder Hugo?'

Laura laughed uncomfortably. It popped into her head that he might mean it. 'No, I don't think I'd murder him. I'd stop at torture. I'd like to see him writhe in pain.' (Though even as she spoke she realised even that wasn't true.)

'If you want me to do anything for you,' said Jed, helpfully.

Laura looked at him but simply couldn't tell if he was joking. There was something about his deadpan delivery that unnerved her.

'Perhaps I just want him to miss me.'

Jed said nothing more; an awkward silence ensued which Laura broke only after the waiter had given them each a plate of treacle tart and cream. 'Mm, that looks delicious,' she enthused, but found she had no appetite for it. 'Now, Jed,' she said, in a tone more like an aunt than a lover, 'have you thought what you're going to do with your life?'

'Nothing much,' said Jed. He was tucking into the tart with abandon. 'I don't have ambitions.'

'But that's ridiculous!' exclaimed Laura. 'Everyone has ambitions.'

Laura surveyed the waiter hovering at the kitchen door. A thin, grey wiry fringe hung over his forehead; his eyes sagged with exhaustion, like he'd spent a lifetime trying to keep them open, his jowls were like those of a basset hound in a cartoon. She thought, 'Did this man have ambitions once?'

'What's all this crap about ambition? Why do we all have to be ambitious?'

'Because you'll end up like our waiter,' thought Laura. But she let Jed continue.

'Ambition is ...' Jed struggled to find the right word. 'Noisy. Ambition shouts, "Look at me! I'm fucking great, aren't I?"'

'What do you mean? You can be an ambitious stamp collector. Everyone has ambitions one way or another, or you might as well not exist.'

'What about you, Laura? What have you done with your life, then?'

For a moment Laura couldn't think what to say. 'I've had a family.'

'Well, then, that makes the whole world ambitious, doesn't it? You just have to want kids. You're no more ambitious than I am, Laura. That's why I like you.'

Laura felt herself wanting to say, 'Look at me, can't you see? I'm at the top of the tree!' Instead of which, she tried again. 'Jed, what is it that you want from life? Perhaps "ambition" is the wrong word.'

'I just want people to fucking go away,' said Jed, with feeling. 'Does that count?'

'Oh my God, Jed! Is someone making your life difficult?'

Jed shrugged.

'Are you in some sort of trouble?'

Jed didn't answer her.

'You never said what you do. Is it someone at work?'

'I don't want to talk about this,' said Jed.

'Oh sweet Jed!' exclaimed Laura, taking hold of his hands, one of which still wielded a spoon. 'I will go to the end of the earth to help you! You know that!'

Jed took his hand away and carried on eating.

After lunch they had a quick walk up and down the high street and Laura found an estate agents'. There were such heavenly little cottages for sale! How happy they would be together! Hadn't Jed said that he wished people would leave him alone? Well, no one would find him in the Isle of Man. But Laura didn't notice Jed slip away from her. She felt such a fool, walking at some speed in both directions to find him. In the event, he had crossed the road and was sitting on the beach. Her instinct was to be angry with him, but she found herself apologising.

Laura found the cleanest stones she could (thinking of her coat) and sat down gingerly beside him.

'An old habit,' she said, 'which I suppose I ought to be rid of.'

'Yep,' said Jed.

'Haven't you ever wanted your own home? Do your parents own their house?'

'My mum lives in a council house,' Jed said.

'She must know about the right to buy and all that.'

'Shh,' said Jed.

There was a screeching of gulls that reminded Laura of her childhood holidays at Lyme Regis. She was about to mention it but Jed seemed so far away, so lost in his own thoughts, that she knew she must be quiet. Then Jed took her hand and the warm comfort of his suffused her and reminded her what happiness was.

'My dear Jed, what a precious young man he is!' thought Laura. 'He's just so deep! What a terrible life he must have led! Thank God I have the chance to make things better for him!'

Laura tried to work out what it was that Jed was looking at so fixedly. When she followed the direction of his gaze, all she could see was mist and spray. But then she saw something more interesting.

'Do you think someone actually lives in that little castle over there, on that tiny island?' asked Laura, after what she considered to be a respectful silence of twenty minutes or so.

'No,' said Jed.

'Would you like to live in it?'

'No,' he said. He withdrew his hand, and it immediately felt as though the light inside her had gone out again.

'I must be quiet,' she reminded herself, as she surveyed her lover. She felt as though she had caught some wild bird, an injured bird she could help, but which at any moment might fly off again and die unloved in the wilderness.

When it began to rain Jed didn't even seem to notice. But at last they agreed they would go back to the hotel. Laura noticed to her slight embarrassment that they had been given new bed linen, but she didn't mention it to Jed. The rain outside was gathering force. Jed opened the window. Laura snuggled back into bed in her clothes. Jed joined her there and they kissed.

'Don't you just love the feeling of being warm and safe when it's pouring with rain outside?'

'Yep,' said Jed, and he put his arm around her.

Laura felt they were like two souls stranded together against adversity, against a world that didn't understand them. But no sooner had she thought that, she decided upon its very opposite: that here she was in bed with a total stranger that she couldn't make head nor tail of, and her real life was somewhere else. The thought briefly made her nauseous, but then Jed kissed her again and all was well.

'I don't understand men,' she said. 'It's weird how men and women are so different. What does it *feel* like to be a *man*, Jed? When you're having a shower and you look down at your body, what do you *think* about, Jed?'

'Sometimes I think about women,' said Jed.

'Any particular woman?' Laura, who had never felt jealous in her life till about twenty-four hours ago, was surprised to feel it now.

'Not really,' said Jed. 'So what do you think about when you're in the shower?'

Laura closed her eyes and imagined herself under her power shower in Lavender Street, surrounded by hand-made Italian tiles in warm hues.

'Things I'll be doing in the day, what I'll cook for supper, and ...' said Laura, pausing anxiously, 'shopping. That sounds terribly shallow, doesn't it? But from today I am going to be honest about everything. Do men think about shopping, ever?'

'Sometimes.'

'I mean, that's a really nice leather jacket you have. You must have put some thought into that?'

'I was given it.'

'You mean a girlfriend gave it to you?'

'No, my mum did.'

Laura was surprised by her feelings of relief.

'Come on, then, tell me. What is it that you've ever wanted? Has there been something you've saved up for, something big and expensive?'

'I had a motorbike once. A Harley Davison. But it got nicked.'

'Didn't the insurance company get you another?'

Jed threw her a look that said, 'Insurance? What planet are you on?'

Laura wanted to say, 'But isn't it illegal not to have insurance?' Instead she said, 'Poor Jed! What about that earring? Did you choose that?'

'No, my girlfriend did.'

Laura's face fell a mile.

'It's not like that,' Jed said. 'We were mates at school. We've been off and on ever since really.'

'When were you last "on", Jed? Are you "on" now?'

'We have sex sometimes, that's all,' said Jed. He sounded almost bored to mention it.

'How can you talk like that?'

'How am I talking?'

'As though sex didn't matter.'

'Does it matter much?'

'But, Jed, don't you think there's something more to sex than sex?'

Jed pretended to think, and then said, 'Nope.'

'I'm sure there's something deep in that, but I can't for the life of me think what it is.'

'Sex is sex. Find all the depth you like in that. And come here.'

The hours passed. Laura was beginning to have the experience that her body was no longer her own. Every little crevice of her body she had handed, wholesale, to her beautiful lover. They raided the mini-bar, they snacked on peanuts. They even watched *The Simpsons* together. At seven in the evening, Laura had a bath and was wondering what to wear for dinner. They had decided to eat in the hotel restaurant. As she'd packed for a five star hotel in the Caribbean, she was deciding between a blue halter neck dress or an orange one, both floor-length, both held up by a jewelled strap. And truth be told, she also had her eye on the casino.

In the end she went for the blue, because it went well with her new pink stilettos. Jed wanted to undress her again as soon as she had dressed, but she told him to wait in a friendly, firm voice that you might use with a puppy in training.

They found themselves in a large Victorian dining room with sombre wallpaper and heavy antique furniture. Jed baulked at its formality, but Laura was happy. There were four young waiters, standing like footmen round the room, waiting for customers. So far, they were the only ones there. A waiter came up and took them over to a table. He gave both of them menus and, after a detectable pause, handed the wine list to Jed. It was evident that Jed had never seen such a thing, which amused Laura and made her love him all the more.

Jed held the wine list and sighed. Laura was waiting for him to ask her advice, but he didn't.

'A bottle of Chablisse,' he said. '1991 vintage, please.'

'That was almost very good,' said Laura, affectionately. 'But you don't pronounce the *s*.'

'No, Laura, I do pronounce the *s*.'

The waiter went away to fetch the bottle.

'Yes, Jed, you do, but you ought not to!'

Jed regarded the older woman coldly. 'Chablisse,' he said, provocatively. Laura felt his look like a dart and almost crumbled. But Jed noticed and picked up her hand and kissed it.

'What does it fucking matter what I call it?' said Jed, quietly, tenderly.

'You're right, Jed,' said Laura. 'It doesn't matter at all.' She felt she might burst into tears any moment, such was the odd mood she was in. She picked up the large leather-bound menu and hid herself behind it, passing Jed his and telling him to pick whatever he fancied.

Choosing from a menu is such a comfortingly banal thing to do when you've left your husband and you've known your lover for a little over twenty-four hours. Laura hadn't had a prawn cocktail in years, perhaps not since she'd stayed at the hotel in Lyme Regis. Jed also remembered a time when he'd had prawn cocktail as a kid, and he followed suit. Then when Jed said he wanted fish and chips, they both chose the fish course with *pommes frites* as a side dish. Things were back on course: when the waiter returned with a chilled Chablis (which Jed declared 'tasty') and took down their order, Laura's spirit returned.

'Now, Jed,' she said. 'Have you ever tried your hand at gambling?'

Jed made a face as if to say, 'Why would anyone want to do that?'

'Oh Jed, don't be a spoilsport! It's fun!'

'What do you have to do?' Jed sounded bored already.

'I can't believe you don't know! You must have seen the Bond films. We could pretend we were in a Bond movie. You could do the gambling and I could stand behind you looking aloof and sexy. Then you could win loads of money and take me to bed. How does that sound?'

'I haven't got the cash.'

'But I have lots,' said Laura. 'My husband is as rich as Croesus. I have two grand in notes upstairs. As far as I'm concerned, it's yours!'

'I suppose it would wind him up,' said Jed.

'Oh it would *so* wind him up! It will do him good to have a little less of it. It's in twenty-pound notes. I'll give you five hundred straightaway.'

'I wouldn't know what to do with it.'

'Oh *please,* Jed! Just once! We must do everything once in our lives!'

'For you, Laura.'

'Oh thank you Jed! If it's rubbish, I promise you we'll go right back upstairs.'

It was a difficult dinner to get through, not half as intimate as their lunch had been. Laura thought the fish was too dry but didn't say anything because Jed seemed to be enjoying his and she didn't want to spoil it for him. Sometimes they looked at each other like passionate lovers, sometimes they ate head down like total strangers, as they veered between absolute engagement with the other and a lonely retreat back into themselves. It was hard to tell what Jed was thinking, but he sat still and focused. Laura, meanwhile, was fidgeting anxiously, her mind flitting from one subject to another. Eventually she said, 'It's unbelievable. I thought I'd be in the Caribbean tonight. I thought I'd be sitting at a bar on a warm and sultry beach.'

'Were you just going to run away by yourself?'

'Was that an absurd idea?'

'Is that what you were really going to do, lie all alone among the palm trees?'

'I like palm trees. I saw you looking admiringly at the ones in the hall.'

'Not admiringly. More a feeling of wanting to set them free.'

Laura laughed uneasily. There was something about Jed that she just couldn't get.

The Hilton casino at Douglas bore a pitiable resemblance to any other casino in the world. At least the ones in movies. If Laura hadn't been so keen to play her role, they might have walked away at a first glimpse of the place. It was just one large ugly room, with a bar in the middle, lit up by what looked like ultraviolet wands standing from floor to ceiling. The bar stools were old, upholstered in plastic faux leather, and through an occasional rip dirty yellow sponge emerged like a disease.

The gambling tables were covered in dust cloths, waiting for someone to take an interest in them. Perhaps some nights no one turned up at all. Tonight there were four would-be punters, excluding themselves, sitting at the bar. All men. All middle-aged. All looking like they had been bored for at least a decade, and they weren't doing anything to confront that boredom, either, like address a word to anyone else.

They visibly perked up when they saw Laura, but when they saw who she was with looked more tragic than ever. Laura gave them a friendly little wave. Jed didn't like that little wave. He wanted to cut and run.

'Now, Jed, what will you have to drink?' Laura had perched herself on a stool and caught a pleasing glance of herself in the mirrored shelves behind the barman, decorated with random bottles of spirits. Jed asked for a pint and she ordered a spritzer.

'I recognise you from the restaurant,' she said to the barman, 'you're certainly multi-tasking tonight.'

The barman smiled politely, but appeared not to know what she was talking about. He put their drinks on the counter. Laura happily rummaged through the wad of notes in her pretty turquoise clutch bag and handed him a tenner without bothering to ask the price.

'Do we buy the chips from you?'

'Yes,' said the barman, fetching her change. She was going to ask him when it was all going to start but then he went off to serve someone else. Jed sipped at his beer sulkily.

'Cheer up,' said Laura. 'I promise you gambling is incredibly good fun. I can't believe you've never done it. Surely you've put a bet on a horse?'

'Nope.'

'So you're a kind of gambling virgin.'

One of the punters snickered. Jed winced.

Then another of the waiters came in, this time dressed as a croupier in full evening dress. He looked just the part, Greek and handsome. He went up to the roulette table and removed the dust cloth with an extravagant flourish. Laura wanted to clap her hands for delight (but resisted). The evening was looking up.

Already the other punters were buying their chips. Laura was desperately trying to hand Jed a wad of notes under the lip of the bar, but Jed pretended he didn't know what she was on about. Laura was thinking, 'Come on, Jed, be a man! Buy the chips! Show the others that you're not only more handsome than they are, but you're richer too!'

But Jed didn't play ball.

'You buy them,' he said.

'Okay. But these chips are for you, you know. If you win, you keep the money. I mean it.'

Laura asked the barman for twenty red chips at £20 a piece. Jed walked over to the window, and drew back the curtain to look out. But she had had her fill of admiring glances from the other four gentlemen. She reassessed them. They didn't seem quite so decrepit as when she had first looked. One in particular half-smiled at her: mid-fifties, rugged, a man with a history, thought Laura. She liked his suit: fine weave of cloth, probably bespoke, and his slim, silk tie. She half-smiled back.

'Jed,' called Laura. She suddenly felt slightly embarrassed by his jeans. She wondered if there was a dress code. Jed didn't even bother to turn round.

'Come on, Jed. Roulette is much more fun than you think. Please, have a go, for me! You promised at dinner.'

Jed followed her to the table, looking sour.

Things kept on getting better. Another six punters came in at the last minute, including a couple of women who'd also dressed up. They were younger than her, but not so classy, and one of them should certainly not have chosen to wear something above the knee with those legs. While they went off to buy chips at the bar, Laura, Jed and the original four were taking their places round the roulette table. It was huge, with thick, fluted mahogany legs, and the roulette wheel was surprisingly splendid. What's more, the harsh wall lights were turned well down, and a large, rectangular light with a gentle, evocative glow hung over it. Suddenly the stage was set closer to Laura's dreams.

'Look at that,' said Laura admiringly. 'It's a proper roulette wheel. Ebony and ivory. It must be a hundred years old. It's a rather beautiful object, don't you think, Jed?'

Laura didn't notice that everyone else was quiet. It was as if she had admired the manufacture of a Buddha in a temple, while the faithful were praying.

The croupier was taking metal balls out of a velvet purse hidden under the rim of the wheel.

'Betz pleeze!' he said, in a thick accent.

'Go on then, Jed! Place your bet!'

When he didn't budge, she feverishly began to explain how to do so. Black or white, odds or evens, those fours, those twos, or just any number he chose, but then the odds would only be one in thirty-six.

'Thirty-seven,' said the man in the bespoke suit and the slim tie. 'You've forgotten the zero. There's a one in thirty-seven chance you'll win.'

Wasn't there just the slightest lilt of a Scottish accent? He was beginning to play the part Laura had so willed upon Jed to a tee.

'There's quite a gale out there,' said Jed.

Laura put the chips into Jed's hand and tried to attract his attention. 'Here you are!' she said. 'A hundred quid's worth. Put them anywhere you like! And remember, you keep the winnings.'

Jed put all five red chips on the number twenty.

Laura looked at him as if to say, 'What the hell?'

'I've just had my twentieth birthday,' he explained. 'Lucky twenty.'

Was he mocking her? Laura let it pass. And the hundred quid.

The real James Bond, meanwhile, had won with his more considered approach to the game. He looked up at Laura, just briefly, to check she'd noticed. Naturally, she had. Perhaps he had assessed the situation between Laura and the boy, and realised he had an outside chance with her. The ball spun again and again. Jed continued to make ridiculous, random bets, sometimes not even watching the metal ball spinning in its groove, till all the chips were gone. In a Bond movie, she would have traded allegiances. Every time the croupier pushed his winnings towards him with his little rake, he would meet her eye, as if to say, 'Young beauty isn't everything, you know. You should have been here with me. I could have given you a better time!'

They left the casino after half an hour. They was no point buying any more chips, thought Laura. What a complete spoilsport. She gave the victor an admiring farewell glance, and left with Jed, taking him by the hand.

Back in the bedroom, Jed was angry with her. His kisses turned to little bites, his gentle caresses were rough and desirous. He broke the halter string of Laura's dress and tiny diamonds scattered over the floor.

'Now look what you've done!' said Laura. She knelt on the floor and began to pick them up. 'You could have at least tried! You could have at least pretended to have enjoyed yourself for my sake!'

'We were wasting time, Laura,' said Jed. 'What were we doing in that place?'

He began kicking the little diamonds all around the floor. Then he saw that Laura's dress was starting to fall down, and he decided to help it on its way. He knelt down beside her and whispered in her ear: 'You know that all I want to do is fuck you.'

He then pushed her on to the floor and took off her dress, like it was her skin. But he didn't touch her. He just looked at her a while, naked. Laura could tell he was still angry with her. But the old petty Laura, the Laura who had already thought that she could pick up the diamonds when Jed was in the shower in the morning, disappeared under his gaze.

'Get on the bed,' he said to her. 'Put a pillow on your face. I don't want to see it.'

Laura did as she was told. She wondered if Jed was going to suffocate her. Adrenalin pumped through her.

Laura felt herself being raised on her haunches. Jed slid her knickers down her legs and stuffed pillows under her bottom. She found it a relief not to have a face on show, not to have the responsibility of making an expression. In her facial sanctuary, the pillow cool and soft against her, she closed her eyes tight and waited.

Jed's fluctuating moods played out on Laura's slender body. She felt his fingers going up inside her, two, three, four, and she cried out. He bit the inside of her thigh, and when she kicked out in self-defence, he slapped her hard on her hip.

But Laura surrendered utterly, obediently holding the pillow to her face with her pretty hands, and Jed was pleased with her. He kissed her feet, her shins, her knees, her thighs. But as Laura waited for his tongue to caress her, he was angry all over again. He bit her, he slapped her, he took her from behind.

Laura submitted to whatever he did to her, hour upon hour. Laura was a good girl. Dead in the night he took the pillow from her face and kissed her tenderly.

On the following day, Jed stole a motorbike.

What drove him to it? A hard call. Jed had consented to being dragged up and down Douglas High Street looking for a new pair of jeans. Laura also bought him underwear, socks, two jumpers and three shirts. Jed feigned gratitude. But his heart was with the weather. The sun was out. It was a beautiful, breezy day. He hated shops.

And the second reason was that the owner of the bike had left the key in the luggage box. They were just off to enjoy a walk in the country after a sandwich in the hotel, walking through the white-washed prosperous suburbs of Douglas, when Jed noticed it.

He tried to put it this way to poor Laura, who was horrified. 'If a bloke leaves the fucking key in the luggage box, he's asking for it.'

'But he's just gone inside for a moment. Didn't you see him, in the orange leather?'

'Of course I fucking saw him. Get on this bike and hurry up!'

'But it's stealing!'

'It's not, Laura, it's borrowing, I couldn't get it off the island if I wanted to. We'll give it back, later.'

'If you promise to give it back, then.'

'Of course I'll give it back! That's all I'm doing, borrowing! Get on the fucking bike!'

Laura did as she was told, and away they went. It was a Kawasaki four cylinder with a green and blue body, newly washed and waxed that morning.

'This'll go,' said Jed.

Laura had never been on a motorbike before. She was worried that they didn't have helmets on, and she didn't like the way the bike swayed from side to side when they turned a corner, and the way the skirt of her fur coat was flying behind them. After about a mile Jed turned up a lane and stopped the bike behind a clump of trees.

'You've not been on a bike before, have you?'

'I'm worried my coat's going to get stuck in the wheels,' explained Laura apologetically. 'And isn't it the law to wear helmets?'

Jed looked at her as if she was mad.

'Or perhaps it isn't on the Isle of Man? Don't they have different laws from ours?'

'Hey, live, Laura! Live for a day!'

Jed had a knack for making things seem all right. Hadn't she noticed all the bike shops in Douglas? Didn't she realise they were in a biker's paradise? Hadn't she even heard of the TT races, perhaps the most important motorbike convention in the world?

'The roads on this fucking island are a fucking race track!' he said.

'Serendipity!' exclaimed Laura. 'I bet the roads in the Caribbean are crap.'

'You bet they're crap!'

'But I wish I had a leather jacket like yours!'

'Give me your wallet and I'll drive back into Douglas and get you one. I'll make you my queen,' said Jed.

Jed put out his hand and Laura gave him her wallet with the rest of her cash and Hugo's bank cards.

She thought, 'What have I done?' in the twenty or so minutes when he was gone. 'How will I pay the hotel bill?' Jed had even set off in the wrong direction. Yet weaving in and out of her anxiety was the joyful prospect of being Jed's queen. Surely Jed was just avoiding the bike's owner, she reasoned. And then again, 'Am I really going to be spending the afternoon on a stolen motorbike?' and she thought of the man in the orange leather who was looking forward to a day out, but who would now be ranting and raving in his house waiting for the police to call round. But her momentary anxiety was swiftly supplanted by the pleasure of seeing her lover again, who jumped off the bike, kissed her, and then presented her with a large package from the luggage box.

'Oh Jed, what a treat!' said Laura. There was an emblazoned Biker's World in gold scrawled across the bag. Inside there was a leather turquoise jacket and some trousers to match. He'd also bought gloves for both of them. 'Oh Jed,' she said, 'it's beautiful! You have immaculate taste!'

Laura changed behind a bush. So strange to be changing behind a bush when Jed had already visited every place of her naked body many times, but it was force of habit. The leather clung to her in such a way that even putting it on aroused her. When Jed saw her he snogged her and put his hand between her legs, squeezing her.

'You are so fucking sexy,' he said. 'It breaks my heart to wait till later.'

Jed set about cramming and crushing Laura's coat to get it into the luggage box. She stood by and resisted the urge to say 'Take care!' Nor did she spoil the day by asking for her wallet back.

Then they got back on the bike and Jed said, 'Get closer, get really tight. Our bodies have to be as one. Come so close to me that not a hair could fit between us. So when I lean over towards the right, you lean over towards the right. When I lean to the left, you lean to the left. It's that simple. It's about trust, Laura. Do you trust me?'

'Oh yes, Jed! With all my heart!' exclaimed Laura.

And they were off.

Laura felt the power of the machine rush through her, even as Jed accelerated away. She had never known anything in her whole life that could compare to this, and she gave herself to it. She felt herself getting drunk on the cold, clean air and the broad blue sky. A huge smile was fixed on her face, stiff with cold. She had never realised before that a motorbike could feel like an extension of yourself, unlike a car, which held you captive. They turned the corners like they were dancing. Jed's movements were smooth and sure. How was it possible to feel so wild and free, and yet know that you were utterly safe at the same time?

The lanes were all theirs for the day. They scarcely passed another car, only whitewashed cottages and thatched roofs, pretty gables and crenelated walls: a landscape, indeed, for a fairy kingdom. They drove through valleys and moors, vast empty spaces, mile upon mile, with only the sea beyond them. Jed reached eighty, ninety, one hundred miles an hour, and Laura hung on to to him, in a kind of catatonic bliss.

When they reached a beach, North of Ramsey, they stopped. Jed locked up the bike and took Laura down a path to the sea. To left and right there were fuchsias, still in bloom. Laura felt light-headed. She no longer cared whether she had a past or a future. When they reached the shore they found a beach where every tiny stone looked like a precious gem.

'It's so beautiful here,' said Laura, with feeling.

'I'll tell you what's beautiful. You are, Laura. You're the most beautiful woman I've ever met.'

Hugo hadn't told her that for years. She flung her arms around Jed's neck and kissed him, joyfully.

Jed unzipped her jacket and cupped her breast with his hand. Then the two began to make love all over again, and even a temperature of five degrees centigrade did nothing to cool their ardour.

Jed and Laura were to stay on the island eight more days. They hid the bike in some bushes a mile outside Douglas and spent their days zooming up and down the lanes as happy as children, and just before they flew home Jed was as good as his word and returned the bike without a blemish and with a full tank of petrol. (That was Laura's idea, to make up for any inconvenience.)

It was Hugo who interrupted their romance. Not that he ever found out where his wife had gone to, but because she found herself thinking about him more and more. She also remembered her children. Quite irrationally, she began wondering whether they had come home for the weekend, whether Hugo had followed her instructions to give Jemima her gym shirt, whether he'd told them she'd gone skiing with friends, or what it was that he'd told them if he'd made up some other story. Or perhaps he'd even gone so far as to tell the children what had actually happened: their mother had just disappeared into thin air, and he was frantic with worry.

Poor Hugo! She imagined him ringing up Ann and saying, 'Where's she gone? Life without Laura is intolerable, Ann! I can't eat! I can't think! I can't work! You have to tell me where she is!'

But even Ann didn't know where she was. No one knew.

Why is it that the most perfect bliss ever has to be dented? Why is it that outside forces always seem to get in the way? Why was it that she and Jed couldn't buy a little house on the seafront and shut out the world forever? The world that said, come back, Laura. Your great big house in Clapham needs you. Hugo hasn't even done the washing-up.

3

Jed travelled all the way back with Laura to Lavender Street, Clapham. He told her he wanted to see where she lived. He said he'd never seen a house with two front doors before. Before he left her he said he wanted to see the house for himself so he could picture her sometimes, running up and down five storeys of stairs.

It was three in the afternoon, ten days precisely since she had left through the grey door. They were standing by the dustbins. Laura overcame an instinct to take a quick look and see if Hugo had been putting out the rubbish. Then, to her horror, she saw his parked car a few yards away. He was never home on a weekday afternoon! Was he trying to trace her? Was he too upset to go to work? Were the children at home with him?

Jed handed her her case.

'Thanks, Laura. Thanks for everything,' he said to her.

'I'd invite you in but I think …'

'You think His Majesty might be at home.'

'You read me like a book, Jed.' She kissed him. Not like the kisses of old but an affectionate peck of farewell. 'You've given me the best week of my life. I mean that,' she said. Then she turned her back on him and began to drag her suitcase up to the red door, smiling to herself.

The smile was short-lived. Glancing through the yellow chiffon curtain of the drawing room, she noticed a thick golden plait hanging down one end of the sofa, and some little pump shoes thrown off in a hurry. They still had their clothes on, but they wouldn't for long. Hugo was wearing jeans and a T-shirt, and was snogging Miss Golden Plait for all he was worth. Neither saw her. She felt like throwing up but didn't know where. She fumbled for her keys, but then she had an idea. Oh my God, did she have an idea. She left her case at the front door and ran for Jed.

Jed was a fast walker; Laura had to run to catch up with him. She knew he'd be heading for the tube station across the common. She threw off her high heels, opened the buttons of her tight coat, and ran across the common in green silk tights.

'Jed, Jed!' she cried, waving her shoes at him. 'You've got to come back!'

Jed looked round. He was smoking a cigarette but when he saw Laura approaching he threw it on the ground and stamped on it.

'I never knew you smoked,' Laura said.

'I don't, really.'

'Oh Jed, you look really sad! You miss me already, don't you?'

Jed said that he did.

Laura began to cry. It was all so confusing. 'I need you so much,' she wailed. 'You have to come back. You have to make that shit of a husband of mine see sense.'

Laura explained her plan as they walked back across the common. Hugo had been skiving work to shag his little bint and it made her sick, she told him.

'This might end in divorce, Jed, it really might. How dare he treat me like this? You're a man, Jed. Are unfaithful men always unfaithful? I mean, do you think he's been like this all our married life and I've just not known about it?'

Jed put an arm about her shoulder, and Laura anxiously looked round to check if anyone had seen. 'Not here, Jed, but soon!'

They were walking back towards Lavender Street. Laura was still in her stockings, dangling her shoes at her side, explaining to Jed what she wanted him to do.

'We're going to creep quietly into the house. The drawing-room door is ajar. Sneak into the room with me and then start kissing me.

Kiss me like the first time we met in Hounslow West. Kiss me with all the passion you can muster.'

'Gotcha,' said Jed.

As they approached the house, Laura noticed to her alarm that the golden plait was now hanging down a totally naked back.

'You can undress me too, if you like,' she whispered. 'Just carry on till he notices, the bastard.'

'He won't turn violent on me, will he?'

'Of course not! He's not a maniac.'

'What if I turn violent on him?'

'Do whatever you like. Shh! We're going in.'

Jed gave a really good performance. It was a full two minutes till Hugo looked up. By then her coat was on the floor (that poor crushed coat), her shirt was at her waist and Jed had one hand on her breast. And when Hugo got up from the sofa and shouted, 'You whore!' they didn't even stop kissing.

'Fuck off, Hugo!' Laura said, coolly, resuming her embrace.

Miss Golden Plait quickly put her shirt back on and tried to wriggle by them, but they were blocking the door and she was forced to say, 'Excuse me, Mrs Glass.'

'Amy, is that you?'

Amy shrugged nervously

Amy was a hairdresser at Toni & Guy, Oxford St. She'd cut the children's hair for years. Occasionally Hugo had taken them there on a Saturday morning, before buying them an ice cream at Baskin Robbins.

'How dare you?' said Laura coldly.

'I didn't mean ...' Her puce face crumbled under Laura's unforgiving eye.

'Just who do you think you are?'

'For God's sake, Laura, she's just a kid.'

'Just a kid! Just a kid! Does that make things better or worse? What does that make you, Hugo?'

'I'm twenty-two,' said Amy. 'Let me pass.'

Laura was standing in the doorway, menacingly.

'Don't be such a bully. Let her go,' said Hugo.

'I'm off, too,' said Jed.

Laura turned towards her lover. She looked pleadingly at him. It was a look that said, 'Don't betray me now, we still love each other, don't we?'

Jed and Amy left together. It was better that way. Hugo and Laura had a lot to talk about.

'Do you care nothing for me?' Laura asked, her hands wrapped around the hot teapot, which was, at that moment, the only reliable comfort object she could find.

They were sitting together in the kitchen, at their large pine table from Provence.

Neither could help thinking that the other looked good. It's true what they say about the post-coital glow, and they both had it.

But this was an argument they were having, not a love-in.

'Where did you think I had gone to, Hugo?'

'What, with six grand in cash? Do you think I thought you'd thrown yourself off Beachy Head or something? I thought you were on a skiing holiday with friends,' Hugo said sarcastically.

'What did you tell the kids?'

'I couldn't be bothered to make up another lie. They didn't come at the weekend. You know how these Bedalians like to party.'

Laura glanced behind her and saw Jemima's PE shirt still on the ironing board, just where she'd left it.

'That's one good thing,' sighed Laura.

Hugo couldn't keep his eyes off his wife. Still so absurdly beautiful.

'You're more fanciable than ever,' he said, suddenly. He leant over the table and kissed her. 'We're all square now, aren't we? One all. You got your revenge. I don't need to know where you've been bonking him. That's none of my business. And we've got a few anniversaries coming up, remember. I owe you some roses.'

'Is that all you're going to say?' asked Laura. She liked his little speech, and wanted more of it.

'What do you want me to say? I'm sorry. I'm sorry you felt you had to do what you did. And Laura, you are so, so sexy.'

Laura wanted to say something to the effect that flattery wouldn't get him anywhere, but flattery always did, and they both knew it.

Hugo stood up and came over to his wife, taking both her hands in his. 'You're the one that I love, Laura. I've never loved anyone but you. What I had with Amy was just sex. Sex is meaningless for a man. Sex is instant gratification, nothing more. It's what we're biologically programmed to do. But you, Laura, are the mother of my children! Not some floozy. You're the best. Come on upstairs. Let me love you how I want to.'

Laura began crying with relief and happiness. The truth was, much as she adored Jed, she realised that a life with him would be an impossibility. What would she have said to her parents, for a start? Or rather, what would they have said to her? Laura had been brought up to believe that sexual fidelity in marriage was the first commandment. How appalled they'd be if they ever found out what she and Hugo had been up to. Introducing Jed to her dear, honourable father, watching the sides of his mouth dip in the way they did when he was disappointed about something but was putting on a brave face, quite honestly it didn't bear thinking of.

During those last few nights at the Hilton she had found herself missing her children, her kitchen, her home comforts. She missed her long phone chats to her friends, snuggling up in the corner of the sofa with a cup of tea. Jed had been this fantastic adventure, but the Isle of Man seemed as remote to her now as Clapham had when she'd been making love in a large container of kippers, only a couple of days ago. 'Oh Jed, you dear young man! But we're just too different, you and I!'

So Hugo and Laura made up and made love in the marital bed,

and Hugo said afterwards, 'Bloody hell, Laura, what's that bloke done to you?' Laura smiled a secret smile. She never told him.

Two weeks later, life had slotted back into the old routine. At first, even the routine was a delight to Laura. She was happy to be woken with a kiss and a cup of tea at seven in the morning. She was pleased to be reunited with her favourite muesli, pouring it into her favourite green pottery bowl, which she had bought some years ago at a craft fair. Even moseying around the kitchen contented her, and wiping the pine counter tops with a brand new striped dishcloth from Hugo's Colour Now! range. Then, out on the common for her morning run, all seemed well with the world.

Laura was one of those 'ladies who lunches' and she had some catching up to do. They fed off healthy salads, quiche Lorraine, and gossip, whereby one or other of them would relay the latest scandal in their circle of friends. They talked of lovers, separations, jealousy, depression. Friends who had lost jobs, others who had started new companies. They talked of fashion and skiing in the winter, and fashion and tennis in the summer.

Laura had always loved these lunches. Compared to everyone else, it seemed to her, her life was going rather well. You can never be too rich nor too slim, as the saying goes, and she scored well on both counts. Even her children had never caused her a particular problem. So the most uncomfortable feeling Laura had ever experienced was pity, or 'empathy' as she called it.

But since her little adventure, these lunches had become a bore. She had felt, somehow, that the spotlight was now on *her*. For the first time in her life she was the outsider, the one on trial. 'Are you one of us, or not?' they seemed to say to her. The other ladies would look at her, patiently, as though they were waiting for her to confess something. Had the gossip already begun about her? Had Ann let something slip? But no one, no one knew where she'd been. She hadn't even told Hugo. The Isle of Man was her secret. The Man was her secret, too.

Another thing Laura realised. These women bored her. They were all very nice and all that, she couldn't say a word against them. But when you've been on a motorbike without a helmet on at one hundred miles an hour, holding on to a body like Jed's, it's a bit difficult to get excited about Miranda and Lucinda, Clarissa and Jo. Was this really what her life was made of? When push came to shove, she found she no longer cared about their holiday plans or marital spats or diets.

The children came back at weekends. But teenagers, alas, aren't like small children who bring you Mothers' Day cards from nursery school and treat you like you're the centre of the universe. They have their own lives to lead. In fact, they hadn't even realised she'd gone missing.

There was a time when nuzzling up with the family on their vast Conran Shop sofa, gorging themselves on fish and chips from Clapham High Street and watching *Back to the Future* for the nth time, was Laura's definition of paradise. Those days were gone, now.

Laura considered getting a job, but the only skill she could offer the world was a typing speed of eighty words a minute. Her shorthand was long-forgotten. Perhaps now was the time to study for a university degree? Now, that was something she hankered for, a student life. How she would love those late-night conversations round the bar! She was conscious of feeling hollowed out, like there was no real centre of gravity in her. If she had read a little more, perhaps dabbled a little more in politics or gone to a few evening classes, would she be feeling as empty as she was?

Laura and Hugo were having sex night after night. Laura was thinking of Jed and wondered whether Hugo was thinking of Amy. Nothing was *wrong*, exactly. Yet Laura found herself watching Hugo. She might watch him open a bottle of Chablis to eat with their fish, with a critical fascination. The way he said Chablis with a French accent irritated her to the core. How tense the muscles of his face were when he pulled at the cork! The way he sat down, pulling his jeans up at his knees when he did so. Why did he do that? Were his jeans too tight for him? The way he read the newspaper: AIDS was intent on ravaging populations, oil spills were killing hundreds of thousands of seabirds, but Hugo only ever made a dash for the sports pages, living on his own private island of sports scores and advertising contracts.

On the return trip back to Heathrow Jed and Laura had exchanged addresses and phone numbers. At the time, Laura had no intention of contacting Jed ever again. It was much too dangerous. She had put the piece of paper in the inner silk pocket of her fur coat, *right next to my heart,* she had told Jed. Now the very danger involved increased the temptation to meet up with him again.

It was the twenty-eight of January, the night of the hundred roses, as they called it, the anniversary of the night when Hugo asked Laura to marry him. Usually Hugo brought back as many roses as he could physically carry from the florist's immediately outside his office; this particular evening he brought a single rose in a glass case. 'To the one I love' read the inscription on its gold-painted wooden plinth.

Laura received the rose graciously. For as long as she'd known Hugo, she had trusted him on all matters of taste. If Hugo thought that a single rose presented well was the equivalent of a hundred thrust into her arms, then Hugo was somehow right, it went without question. So she blamed herself for her dead heart. She blamed herself for thinking of Jed, day and night.

'Thank you, Hugo! That's so beautiful!' enthused Laura. She was about to say, 'And you are the one that I love!' but the words jammed in her throat.

Laura had been aware all day of a certain lethargy in her movements. She had set out on her run, for example, five minutes late. She had forgotten to bring out the rubbish with her, and couldn't be bothered to pop back in to fetch it. She hadn't smiled at her neighbours, because the truth was, she hadn't even noticed them. She normally ran two circuits of the common, but after one and a half had found herself resting on a bench in the playground, watching a young Pakistani mum coping with her four young children. The mum looked tired and careworn. On a normal day Laura might have befriended her, and even pushed a child on a swing, or fed a baby a bottle of milk. Laura was good with strangers and always kind. But Laura had no energy even to proffer a smile. Rather she sat, bent double, getting her breath back.

Laura was equally non-committal to a romantic supper *à deux*. In former years she might have spent a morning smelling scented candles, unable to choose whether to envelop her house in a warm apricot or exotic vanilla. She might have travelled across London to buy monkfish from Smithfield market, or fresh pistachio nuts from Soho. She would pore over her cookery books for at least a week, such was her love for Hugo, and her childish delight in pleasing him. By three in the afternoon she was wondering whether to get a shepherd's pie out of the freezer. Or perhaps it was time for a major row: had she not let him off rather easily for his infidelity to her? He was the one who started this! How happy their Christmas had been down in Dorset with her parents! And on Boxing Day, when her dad had taken Hugo on a day's shooting in the rain, she and her mum and the kids had spent the day cosy and happy by a roaring fire, doing one of her grandmother's old wooden jigsaw puzzles. How sweet, how uncomplicated life used to be!

And what a wonderful New Year's Eve they had all had in Trafalgar Square. A whole gang of them had gone. Ann and Patrick and the twins, and a couple of other families they used to know well when Leo and Jemima were at prep school. The champagne, the fireworks, the celebration of life! But life had to be founded on something solid and Hugo had taken that away from her.

In the end Laura found some rather good fish stew left over from a dinner party, right at the bottom of her freezer, just when she was beginning to despair. She served it up with frozen peas and a tomato salad. Hugo was all compliments. She couldn't decide whether she'd be angrier with him if he'd noticed her rather hasty supper, or flattered her on her cooking. Preparation time: seven and a half minutes.

It was while lying in bed that night that the gulf between them yawned open. They were like parallel rods. Laura was as surprised as Hugo when she heard herself say: 'Did you sleep with Birgitte?'

'Who the fuck is Birgitte?' asked Hugo, staring at the ceiling.

'Our German au pair who wore thigh boots. Our first au pair. Jemima must have been about three months old. Bad skin.'

'Great body, though.'

'You did shag her then.'

'Who do you take me for, Laura?'

'Arabella says this wasn't your first affair.'

'Arabella can say what she bloody likes,' said Hugo, scornfully.

'You might as well tell me the truth. Because right now, I feel so cold towards you that whatever you confessed to would just brush off me. You could tell me anything, it would barely make me stir. You can tell me Amy's your first love affair. Or you could tell me you were shagging some Moroccan maid on honeymoon when you told me you were having an early-morning dip. You could tell me, "All men have lovers, it's in their nature," and in my present mood, Hugo, it just wouldn't bother me. I'm in the mood for the truth. You may as well seize the opportunity.'

There was a silence.

Laura felt her stomach lurch.

Hugo didn't need to say what he said, Laura already knew it.

A minute went by. Laura's heart was now beating fast and furious.

'All men have lovers, it's in their nature,' said Hugo. He put out his hand to Laura's and held it.

But Laura wasn't quite as cool about things as she thought she might be. She snatched her hand away from his and slapped him for all she was worth, shouting at him that he was a shit and a bastard and how could she have devoted her life to such a man as him. Then she leapt out of bed and ran from room to room looking for refuge and finding none. For some moments she lay between Jemima's cold sheets, clutching at her old teddy; finding no solace, she ran up to the attic as the furthest place from Hugo, only to find Birgitte's letter on the chest of drawers. It was midnight: she couldn't even phone a friend. She even considered going jogging, but some woman had recently been stabbed to death on the common. It was while Laura was speed-walking the circuit of her ground floor, round the kitchen, through the hall, a figure-of eight between the drawing room and the sitting room, that Hugo roused himself and went downstairs to plead with her.

'Laura,' he said to her, 'I've never felt so close to you, never loved you so much, as I do now. You are the only woman in the world that matters to me, you know that. We have spent our whole adult lives together …'

'Shut up,' said Laura. He was standing in his boxer shorts shivering. 'Perhaps I should leave you for good, now.'

'That's great, Laura. Go and move in with your boyfriend, then. As for me I'm going to go back to bed.'

Laura spent the rest of the night watching black and white romantic movies in the sitting room. It was Celia Johnson in *Brief Encounter* who sent her on her way, and by the time Dooley Wilson began singing 'A kiss is just a kiss' in *Casablanca* she was truly smitten. And the object of her love became Jed.

Number 82, Basildene Road, Hounslow West was a small house rendered in pebbledash, dating from the 1950s. It was in a row of other similar houses: but whereas they might have newly painted front doors or a couple of roses planted in the front garden, Jed's house looked tired and unloved. It had a large front window but the curtains were closed. The timber was rotting on the two smaller upstairs windows, and the paint had peeled away. All the glass, noticed Laura, was filthy.

Laura was wearing make-up and some fine Italian high-heeled

boots she'd dug out from the back of her wardrobe. She was wearing her faux fur coat with Jed's address still stashed away in an inside pocket, and was bitterly regretting it. She wasn't in the mood for the eyes that followed her: Indian, Sikh, white, almost exclusively male.

They looked harmless enough, but it crossed her mind that she might be mugged. And then she thought, so what if I am. It would be Hugo's money, Hugo's rings they'd be snatching. And if they held her against the pavement, grazing her cheeks, what of it? Adrenalin was rushing through her, but the cause of it, Laura considered, was not fear, but desire.

Laura rang the bell, and waited. She could hear the soundtrack of *Postman Pat* chiming innocently from the front room. A couple of minutes later she rang again. A woman opened the door. A beautiful woman, mid-thirties, perhaps, wearing Jed's black leather jacket. She was as tall as Laura, dazzling blue eyes, almost as slim.

'Yeah?' she said, in a tone that said. 'Who the hell are you?'

The two women looked hard at each other for some seconds. Then Laura looked down and thought she didn't like those Italian boots any more. She thought she might give them to Oxfam. In fact, perhaps she should volunteer in some hot country far from Hounslow West, where little black children in brightly coloured dresses would love her and she would find some meaning in her life.

'I'm looking for Jed,' she said.

'Go on up,' said the woman, 'you wake him. He won't moan at you.'

Laura looked at her watch and began, 'I would hate to …'

'It's fucking midday. Up there, on the right,' said the woman.

'I don't want to be interfering …'

'Go and wake him fucking up!'

Laura had never been into such a small house. She worked out that the whole surface area of the ground floor was about a quarter of the size of her kitchen. She glimpsed into the sitting room and saw the backs of two blond heads staring at the TV, and two pairs of small feet, still wearing slippers. The walls were nicotine-stained:

no pictures, no bookshelves, no knick-knacks, barely any furniture beyond the knackered sofa the kids were sitting on. No air, either, that was fit to breathe: over-warm and reeking of cigarette smoke.

She walked up the stairs, as instructed. Even the banister was grimy, and she took her hand away from it as brusquely as if it had burnt her. There was a bathroom straight ahead, painted pink with a lino floor, and her instinct was to wash her hands. But the woman was watching her, and for the life of her she couldn't remember whether to go to the right or left. She was quite sure that the woman was setting her up. A lover who wanted to get him in trouble, and Laura was falling into her trap.

The right-hand door was shut, the left ajar. She peeped in. The only piece of furniture was a double bed with no headboard. Layers of clothes were strewn around it: no cupboard, even, to put them in. Jed wasn't there, he must have gone out without his girlfriend realising. The smell of stale sex wounded her to the quick.

'On the right!' the woman reiterated, watching her.

But the bedroom on the right was the kids' room. Four single beds were squashed together, with another sea of dirty clothes at their foot. The stench of the house pervaded even here, heedless of the Tom and Jerry, Pluto the dog, and My Little Pony motifs on the duvet covers. Then suddenly Laura noticed movement under Action Man.

Jed's head appeared above it.

'Fuck,' he said. But it was an affectionate 'fuck' and Laura felt encouraged. She took off her coat and boots, happily discarding them on the floor as was the habit in that house, and walked across the first two beds to lie beside him on a happy pony.

Leaning on her elbow and smiling benevolently, she said, 'I've missed you, Jed.'

Jed undid a couple of buttons on her shirt and slipped his hand into Laura's bra (a red lacy bra she had never worn since the day Hugo embarrassed her by giving it to her). Laura closed her eyes momentarily to relish the bliss of those hands once more, cupping her breast, gentle and eager, but continued to talk.

'Oh Jed, if you only knew the dullness of my life you'd take pity on me! I am living half a life with half a husband. My marriage is dead. I know he's thinking of that girl. He's living in another world. I can't go on living this lie. It's you I want, Jed. The ten days I spent with you were the best in my life.'

Jed put his hand deep into her crotch and squeezed hard. But Laura was more intent on delivering her message than succumbing. After throwing back her head a little and emitting an involuntary sigh, she continued, 'I've been wondering so hard what to do. I want you as part of my life, Jed. I think of you day and night. If I were a man I'd buy you a little flat somewhere and come and visit you and bring you little trinkets, and big trinkets …'

Jed leant over now and pulled her hair and bit her ear so hard Laura wondered whether he had drawn blood. She would have preferred tender kisses and affirmations of love, but she could see he was in no mood for that. Within moments Jed emerged naked from under his Action Man duvet and was undoing the button of her jeans.

'No, no, no, Jed, what about your girlfriend? Come home with me, so we can be private! Or we can go to a hotel! We can spend the day in one of those grand hotels at Heathrow Airport, loads of them have swimming pools …'

'I don't have a fucking girlfriend,' said Jed.

'But the woman downstairs …' whispered Laura.

'She's my fucking mum.' Angrily Jed put his hand down into Laura's red lacy knickers, but Laura was too appalled to notice.

'That's never your mum!'

'What's your problem?'

'She's just so young! I feel so …' *Old*, thought Laura, but said, instead, 'silly.'

Suddenly Jed pushed her away and got back into his bed.

A boy of about three years old was standing in the doorway, watching them. In one hand he held an old yellow blanket, the corner of which he was stroking urgently with his thumb. His other thumb was in his mouth.

Laura deftly buttoned her shirt and sat up. 'Hello,' she said, in a friendly way. 'What's your name?'

The child said nothing but just stared at her. Nor did Jed say a word.

'I suppose I'd better be going,' said Laura. She waited for Jed to dissuade her, but he didn't.

She crawled to the end of her bed and walked over the wad of clothes till she reached her trusty coat and boots.

'It was great to find you, Jed. I'll see you soon, I hope. You know where I live. Drop by, won't you? I'm always alone in the day. Weekdays.'

'Will do,' said Jed. He didn't even look at her, but turned his attention to his little brother.

This was not enough for Laura, whose strength deserted her on the tube journey back to central London. She felt the eyes of her fellow travellers on her, knew her mascara had run and her lipstick had smudged, but her instinct was to hide her face, not to take out her compact mirror and correct it. She wrapped her long legs tensely around each other, divorcing herself from the looks of pity and wonder around her, and with some effort, held on to her tears till she was back in the safety and monotony of her bed and home, where she gave vent to sorrow upon sorrow.

No, there was not a shred of comfort to be found. The prospect of a dinner party that evening appalled her. In two hours' time she would be getting ready to confront the world again. But how could she do that? Where could she hide? She couldn't even face her children when they came home for the weekend. She hadn't seen them for a month yet she knew they couldn't help her. Her life was an absurd thing, she thought to herself. She was an ignorant, silly, fool who was trying to count her blessings but could find none to count.

When her sobs finally subsided, she lay on the bed in the dark and tried to clear her mind. 'I need to tell someone,' she thought to herself, 'but who?'

Arabella would be no help with her moralising. Rachel might be sympathetic – but no, her advice about Hugo had simply been wrong. How could she have just turned a blind eye when Hugo had behaved so scandalously? She instinctively felt that Ann knew more than the others, but didn't that make her the most dangerous of the three?

She thought of the lunches she had with her friends. They were full of gripes about their husbands: they fell asleep too early, they demanded a clean shirt every day, they spent too much time with their male friends playing sport and not enough time with their kids. We all love confessing, getting things out into the open. It's why we're friends, a little betrayal does us and our marriages good. But Hugo's sins are too vast. They wouldn't laugh at those. They wouldn't know where to look. We wouldn't be invited anywhere again, they would just wait until we got divorced and then start matchmaking. And what about me? What about my sins? How would I confess to those? 'I'm in love with a boy from Hounslow West whose mother's younger than me.' How much sympathy would I get, exactly?

She tried to imagine life beyond Hugo. She had every reason to divorce him. Yet the memory of him pleading his love for her in his underpants at one in the morning moved her. He was a good dad, a good husband. And even though she was rather disenchanted with her Clapham life right at this moment, wasn't that rather short-sighted of her? What sort of life would she have with Jed, after all? It was an absurd idea. Where would they live, to begin with?

Then, just as she was about to see sense, another truth dawned on her: 'Why would I care where I live? I could live in a caravan with him!' In fact, she was quite resolved to do so when Hugo came home with a small, wrapped present for his tear-stained wife. He kissed her and whispered, 'My life belongs to you. I love you more, Laura, than I have ever loved any woman in my life, or ever will love. Your sweetness, your generosity of spirit, your unremitting kindness to me and our children. I am so, so sorry.'

Then Laura began to cry all over again, and they made love like never before.

By half past eight Laura was clean and ravishing and wearing a bracelet from Tiffany's in gold and jade. She wore a plain wool dress in indigo blue with a white collar to set it off, all very demure. Hugo was dapper in a claret moleskin suit and grey nubuck shoes. They decided to walk to Ann's house – it was only two streets away, after all – and Hugo told Laura that the new faux fur coat she'd bought in the Browns sale was the sexiest thing he'd ever seen, as he put it on his wife for their evening's walk.

'I am a truly lucky man,' Hugo declared, 'to even *know* you, to even have the privilege of calling you by your Christian name.'

'And you, darling Hugo, have a way with words, and I don't trust you an inch.'

Nonetheless, Laura was comforted, and she pulled herself together. They made their way to Ann's house as an impeccable couple.

❖

'Laura, you're looking stunning!' Patrick said, as he welcomed her and Hugo into his home. 'Come in, both of you! It's bitter out there, come in! Here, let me take your coats. What a beautiful coat, Laura. I'm sure you won't mind, Hugo, if I kiss your wife?'

Laura thought, uncharitably, 'Of course he won't. Look at that paunch of yours which even a cashmere jumper won't hide!' but then Patrick had always been the butt of jokes, the country bumpkin of Clapham.

Patrick planted a single kiss on Laura's cheek and made a strange high-pitched sucking noise as he did so.

'Let me get you a drink,' he said, and disappeared with their coats.

Laura saw to her horror that Arabella was there. Hugo was already kissing her, as though she were his favourite person in the world. She suddenly remembered how she'd cancelled lunch on *that* day and had never bothered to apologise. Oh, how she loathed gossip! She dreaded to think who Arabella had been on the phone to. Ann for one. 'I hate them,' she thought to herself, 'I hate them all. Why on earth had she ever told them about Hugo? Why had she sought their idiotic advice in the first place? Well, she would show them. She was going to put on the performance of her life; she was going to prove to them quite how happily married she was. How dare they pity her?

Patrick was back with a glass of cava in his hand.

'So, Laura, how are things? You get younger and more ravishing every day. How do you do it?'

Laura beamed. 'Patrick, you always say the sweetest things,' she said. 'Quite honestly, this January has been rather a flat month. But I always find Januaries flat, after the hectic lead-up to Christmas and the New Year.'

'Those fireworks were splendid this year, weren't they?'

'Were they better than usual? Did the twins enjoy them?' Laura feigned interest. She was watching Arabella hover near her, but she wasn't ready for her yet. She was determined to give Patrick her exclusive attention.

'Do you know what? Becky and Sal are four now. And they were so entranced by the fireworks that Ann and I think they will one day count as their very first memory. You know they've started school, just in the mornings?'

'Yes, Ann told me. How's that going?'

('Arabella's looking a real fright,' thought Laura. 'She's wearing that ghastly pinstriped trouser suit again. No wonder she can't find a boyfriend. Why doesn't she wear make-up, for God's sake?')

'The headmistress is a real gem. Mrs Steed. Did you have her when your kids were there?'

'No,' said Laura, absent-mindedly.

Patrick began to tell Laura all about her, and he waxed lyrical about the twins' form teacher, and the twins' paintings, too, all of which they called 'Fireworks', and they really did show a great deal of talent, though he was naturally biased, being their dad.

The expression on Arabella's face (raised eyebrows, sideways look) said: 'So, how are things? Am I to feel sorry for you or angry with you? You default on your lunch, and then, not a whimper. Friend or foe?'

'That trouser suit,' thought Laura, and blushed. Once she had gently teased Arabella about her choice of clothes – Why all these trouser suits, Bella? –'You know why,' she had thundered back. Laura cringed at her faux pas.

'I'm boring you, aren't I?' said Patrick.

'No, no; no!' insisted Laura.

'Are we standing too near the fire? Here, let me get you another drink.'

Patrick took Laura's empty glass and disappeared before she could ask more questions about the twins' school, and she felt bad.

Arabella moved into the vacuum. Again, that look: am I to be angry or forgive you? Justify yourself!

Laura responded with an anxious smile – please be my friend, it said. But if it's the truth you want, I'm still not ready to give it to you.

Arabella kissed her on the cheek. It was more than a social kiss, and Laura tried hard to fathom it, while Patrick thrust a glass of cava into the hands of each of them.

'So, Laura, tell all. Where have you been all these weeks?'

Patrick tactfully left the two together, and Laura missed his gentle neutrality. The way Arabella was looking at her was awful. Where was she nowadays, her best, most darling friend, from whom she swore she would never keep a secret? Her first kiss had been with this girl, her only kiss with someone of the same sex, though it had been passionate enough. Long before she'd lost her leg in a skiing accident, and her unborn child, and her husband, too. She was once all mellow and giggly, and her hair was wild and long. But who was this spiky woman before her now, who spread malice?

Laura managed, 'Hold on a moment! I'm the one who's been trying to get hold of *you*!' (It was true. Laura had rung her once the previous week, while waiting for Hugo to get home.) 'I promise,

Arabella!' she repeated. 'I've been longing to see you, and there's so much to talk about. It's you who's been working far too hard!'

'January is always a miserable month for divorces. I'm up to my neck in some horrible cases. God, people are vile about each other! I suppose Christmas is always the last straw, the last pretence. How was yours? Did you go down to Dorset?'

'We had a wonderful time! We always do. Dad took Hugo shooting, which he adored. It rained all the time, but that didn't dampen our spirits at all. And we went to see my grandmother, who's ninety-two and going strong, and she and Jemima got on famously. They made a pact. Jemima is going to make her a great-great-grandmother before she dies.'

Laura realised Hugo was eavesdropping. He'd often accused her and her friends of being disloyal to their husbands at a drop of a hat. But Laura felt confident. Betrayal was the last thing on her mind.

'When families work, they must be great,' conceded Arabella. She looked her friend straight in the eye. Laura didn't flinch. 'I think it's bothered my mother more than myself that I never had children.'

'Oh, children! They are so overrated!'

'Come on, Laura, you don't mean that. You sound like a rich man saying that money is overrated. Your children have been your life.'

Laura hung her head in shame. Arabella held her hand out to her and said, 'Laura, I'm over that now, I promise.'

Arabella's voice was so tender Laura felt like bursting into tears. She felt guilty now for thinking her anything but noble and strong. How tragic it was that her own happy marriage had driven them apart, forced them into parallel lives.

'I've never understood how someone as attractive as you are …' began Laura.

'Don't give me that shit,' said Arabella, snatching her hand away. But when silent tears began to fall down Laura's cheeks, Arabella suddenly embraced her friend and said, with feeling, 'Why can't we talk any more?'

'I'm a useless friend, I know I am,' began Laura, but then she didn't know what else to add. She could see Hugo watching them, and she gave him a little flirtatious wave, which came from nowhere, and immediately began showing Arabella her bracelet. Hugo took a while to be satisfied that all was as it should be, and the two women retreated back into themselves.

Ann came round with the canapés. 'Honestly, she looks more mumsy by the day,' thought Laura uncharitably. 'You can't wear a belt round a dress when you have no waist. How can she not know that?'

Ann spoke loudly and publicly: 'Laura, I'm so pleased you made it! Arabella, it's been too long! Have a little *foie gras,* you two!' But then she whispered, 'Oh my God, Laura! Where the hell have you been? We've been worried sick about you.'

The word 'we' cut Laura to the quick. How she loathed being the subject of their chatter.

'I went down to visit my parents, that's all,' shrugged Laura.

Both looked at her in disbelief.

'No, I didn't go to the Caribbean, Ann.'

'And you didn't go to your parents either. I rang them.'

'Ann, how could you?'

'I was worried. You weren't at home. I rang every day for a week, not a murmur. I even looked in your dustbin, Laura, to see if you were putting out the rubbish.'

'How could you ring my parents? You must have worried them sick.'

Hugo was on full alert. Their nickname at school had been the 'the witches'. Hugo often teased them about it. Quite charmingly, of course. But now his look was almost thunderous, and Laura could see he was on the point of coming up to them.

Ann came to the rescue. 'Arabella, take round the canapés,' she instructed. 'Laura, I need you in the kitchen,' and Laura was relieved to follow her there.

'Hugo won't like that, you know. He'll think you're up to something,' laughed Laura anxiously.

'Don't worry about him. Do you hear the doorbell? There's a

rather lovely-looking doctor Patrick is going to introduce him to within a few moments. He'll have other things on his mind.'

'Oh God, do you really think of Hugo like that?'

'We all know what Hugo is like! He's an outrageous flirt.'

Laura wanted to say, 'But do you think he's more than a flirt? Do you think he acts on his flirting? Was Hugo's behaviour a surprise to you that dreadful day?'

But she was all confused, confused about everything. The old Laura would have offered to help, but she was dizzy with not-knowing and found a stool to perch on. God, Ann's kitchen was tiny. She was always struck by the fact that there wasn't even room for a table in it. You could just about walk up and down the middle of it and do your business and then get out as quickly as possible. There was nothing of any charm to hold you there at all, unless you counted the magnetic numbers and letters that were strewn over the fridge, and on which the twins had made their mark with a few random words like 'hedgehog'.

Ann was getting homemade ice cream out of the freezer. Laura wondered whether she regretted her comments about Hugo. How odd it was to be sitting in this confessional chamber and be incapable of confessing. She couldn't decide whether to defend Hugo or lambast him. She wanted to tell Ann she liked her earrings, simple pewter hoops, but she was so brimming with poison that the words (which in another mood would have come so naturally) remained trapped inside her.

Ann was trying to break up the frozen ice cream with a wooden spoon in a large glass bowl. 'Come on, Laura. Don't be naïve.' There was a note of irritation in her voice.

'Hugo likes women. It's not a crime, you know. Most men do.'

Then Ann tried a knife, stabbing and stabbing at the ice cream, but still it resisted her. In the end she gave up, covered it with cling film and tried to find a space for it in the fridge. 'Damn,' she said.

But then Patrick came in, full of beans. 'Gloria's just arrived. More cava!'

Laura watched the couple crouching together by the fridge, rearranging things to make room. She noticed Patrick kiss his wife affectionately on the cheek, and her hand slipping into his. These gestures were so quick, so habitual to these two that Laura almost missed them, and it would have been better if she had. She felt herself slouching on the stool, and had to consciously raise herself up again. Then Patrick gave Laura a sympathetic smile that said, 'I know your marriage is going through a rocky patch, not to worry. Good to see you two friends talking again!' and disappeared again, opening another bottle of cava as he did so.

Then Ann turned round to pay full attention to her friend. Her face was open, gentle, full of genuine concern.

But Laura would not crack.

'Gosh, Ann, you are so *good*.'

'Good?' queried Ann. 'I don't quite get you.'

'Good to have a young family *and* give a dinner party.' That sounded pretty feeble, thought Laura.

'For God's sake, Laura! What are you hiding? You know why I'm giving this dinner party, don't you? When you never answered the phone, yes, I imagined you'd gone away, as we'd planned. I wondered how Hugo was coping. I hoped he'd ring me. I wanted to talk to him. I even thought I could be of some help. So one evening I phoned him.'

'You seem to have phoned everyone,' said Laura, bitterly.

'What did you imagine I'd do? We've all been worried sick about you, Laura!'

'Who else have you told, then?'

'*You* told Rachel, *you* told Arabella. And of course I told Patrick. He's my husband, of course I'd tell him.'

'And you told my parents.' Laura hid her face in her hands in utter despair.

'I did not tell your parents! I rang them. Perhaps I shouldn't have. I thought you might have gone down there, I know how close to them you are.'

'They adore Hugo. They'd be the last people I'd tell.'

'Anyway, we had a nice chat, and they suspect nothing.'

And it was true. Laura had spoken to her parents at least three times since getting back from the Isle of Man. At least they believed her lies, with no quibbling. They bought 'the skiing holiday with friends' version of things at first airing.

'So how was Hugo, then? How did he cope without me?'

'Rather too well, is the honest truth. He told me you were at an NSPCC meeting, and he'd get you to call back. And of course you didn't call back, so three days later I tried again. I can't even remember his next lie, but he still sounded perfectly cheery. This time I could tell he wanted to see whether *I* knew where you were. Well, I didn't know. It was easy to feign innocence. He asked me if he could leave a message for you, as you weren't going to be back till terribly late. This dinner party is the result of me thinking on my feet. Anyway, it was about time we gave one.'

'So Hugo didn't seem to mind? Not at all?' Why did it hurt so much to hear it, when she more or less knew that already? Laura could think of nothing to say. She suddenly felt a desperate yearning to go home and hide herself away.

'You seem to be managing all this terribly well,' said Ann.

Laura wanted to be light, she wanted to be able to say, 'What's there to manage? Look at my beautiful jade bracelet from Tiffany's. Can't you see we've made up?' But she couldn't say a word.

Ann began rummaging around in her fridge again. 'The cheese,' she murmured. She found four neatly wrapped packages and put them out on the counter top.

'It was a bad episode, I admit,' said Laura, at length. 'But it's over.'

'"It's over"? Is that all you're going to give me?'

'Quite honestly, I don't know what else to say.' Laura felt as vulnerable as a squid.

'Okay, old friend, tell me. Where did you go? You're looking beautiful as always, Laura. I'll grant you that. You didn't go to the Caribbean, and you're not tanned, so you didn't head south to warmer climes. Do I have to keep on guessing?'

'In actual fact I went to the Isle of Man. I booked into a B&B and went on long solitary walks in a biting wind.' Laura looked so pitiful that it was hard not to believe her.

'I'm so sorry,' said Ann. Then it was her turn to be on the spot, and fumble her way through a hard conversation. 'Would you say you're getting on better now? Is he ... is he over her, do you think?'

'Who knows? Sometimes I wonder whether they aren't still seeing each other. He seems so absent from me.'

'But you're going to give your marriage a go, aren't you? You're not going to walk out?'

Laura was surprised by the passion with which she defended it.

'We've been married for almost twenty years, Ann! How many have you managed? Less than seven, isn't it? You're still on your honeymoon!'

Laura's tone was harsh: it invited Ann to speak equally harshly.

'Did you ever find out if kissing was all there was to it? Has Hugo actually ever been unfaithful to you, Laura?'

Laura shrugged. 'Men are always unfaithful, that's just who they are. Even Rachel told me that Jerry shags his black models, and she just puts up with it.'

'That's not true!' exclaimed Ann, aghast.

'Oh, probably someone like Patrick isn't,' said Laura, with a dismissive wave of her hand.

'What exactly are you saying?'

'I'm saying someone as good and kind and considerate as Patrick wouldn't even look in the direction of another woman,' said Laura, correcting herself. 'Why do we all insist on fidelity, anyway? There's been no period in history when men have been faithful to their spouses. They're made differently to us.'

'So you're just going to forgive and forget, are you? Or it seems, you already have forgotten and forgiven. Lucky Hugo, is all I can say, to have such an understanding wife.'

'We're working things out.'

'Well, I'm pleased to hear it,' said Ann coldly. 'I am not the enemy, you know. Let's go back to the party!'

Laura wondered how she was going to face three more hours of this. Patrick was now chatting to Arabella. Both looked animated. She fancied he was saying, 'Poor old Laura, what a loser! She does nothing all day but shop and hang around her house that's far too big for a family of four let alone two! And she pretends she does work for charity, when all that consists of is lunching with her dull, dull friends. Now you, Arabella, have a proper job, a proper life! Tell me, didn't I see your name in the papers some weeks ago? Didn't you get an extraordinary settlement for someone or other?'

And Hugo was talking to a black woman in silver. His back was to her. But she was flirting with him, goddammit! She was loving the attention he was lavishing on her. Imagine wearing a silver lamé dress to a Clapham dinner party. Who did she think she was? The Queen of Sheba?

Ann took Laura to meet another couple, who looked dreary enough. She tried to think of one thing she might have in common with them. The man was thin with glasses. He looked serious and clever. Probably an accountant, thought Laura. His wife was mousy and freckled, and very small. Nonetheless, a size 14. Laura couldn't understand why anyone above a size 12 didn't keep themselves permanently on a diet. Patrick was calling them to the dining room. She'd be interested to observe if this woman ate a second helping of ice cream.

'Robert and Pandora, our new neighbours! Meet Laura, who's married to Hugo over there. She lives a stone's throw away in Lavender Street!'

'Pleased to meet you!' said Robert and Pandora almost simultaneously. It was dreadful when married couples took on each other's habits, thought Laura, uncharitably. My God, what was she becoming? What was happening to her?

The eight of them squashed round a table that would have been happier with six. Nonetheless, Laura liked this room: the fireplace was original, a cast-iron mantelpiece above pretty Victorian tiles, and the walls were painted fuschia-pink. Two single candlesticks lit up the room. There was a vote on this. Patrick thought it was too dark and put on a light. 'No, no, no!' the guests cried. 'Give us back our candlelight! Much more flattering! It doesn't make us feel so terribly middle-aged!'

By now, most of the party were fairly drunk. No one was driving home. Arabella and Gloria agreed to share a taxi at midnight. Even that irritated Laura. They've never met before tonight and suddenly they're best buddies.

Laura found herself sitting next to Patrick and Pandora. 'God help me!' she thought, when she saw the placements. Patrick she knew too well, eternally good-tempered and well-wishing. You might as well be dead when you sat next to him. And as for Pandora, is it possible to be so dull? Why did Ann place her next to *her* of all people? Was it to spite her? While Gloria was cosying up to her husband like they were lovers already. That was also Ann's mischief, she decided.

For their first course Ann gave them cream of celery soup, and Patrick filled their glasses with a 1992 Sancerre Premier Cru, mentioning that the wine had got some superb reviews and he'd be interested to know what they thought.

Everything they tasted got the thumbs-up. The wine was first class, a couple of the women asked for the recipe of the celery soup, and a couple of men asked Ann if she'd made the bread rolls herself.

'I can't make bread!' she laughed. 'M & S half-bake. There, the secret's out!'

But the conversation really began to get going over the ragout of lamb and the Châteauneuf-du-Pape.

A film had come out recently, and it seemed that everyone had seen it. Everyone, that is, bar Laura and Hugo. It was called *Carrington*. And the subject of it was: What happens when you love more than one person at once?

In Dora Carrington's case, a *menage à trois*. Marry one, and have the other as your lodger. And have the lodger (Lytton Strachey) fall in love with your husband (Ralph Partridge).

The question that little dinner party addressed was: 'Were they right to act as they did?' Should society condemn them, or praise them as being free-spirited?

Hugo was the first to condemn them. He believed in marriage, he said. He believed it was sacrosanct.

He spoke with such eloquence that Laura felt momentarily proud of him. 'That'll keep the gossips quiet,' she thought.

But Ann and Arabella were looking at each other, sceptical as ever, and even Gloria looked astonished.

Laura leapt to his defence. 'I agree!' she said. 'Marriage is surely about exclusiveness. Why get married if you don't intend to be faithful to one another?'

'For money,' said Arabella. 'Or some marry because they want a child. Or do you think, Laura, that all marriages have to be based on romantic love – haven't you just had your night of a hundred roses?'

'I got *one* rose this year,' laughed Laura good-humouredly.

Ann and Arabella caught each other's eye, and Laura wanted to hit them.

Pandora asked, earnestly: 'How important do you think it is, Laura, to keep the romance of a marriage alive?'

Her husband, Robert, was hanging on his wife's reply. He took off his glasses and wiped them with his napkin.

Laura was caught off guard. How happy she would have been to have given Pandora an effusive 'Yes!' with some tips on how to do so. But everyone was looking at her. Finally she said, looking at Hugo, 'It's terribly important, isn't it?'

Hugo said, 'When the romance is gone, and I suppose it must go eventually, what else is there?'

'Wrong reply, Hugo!' said Patrick. 'Are you saying that marriages die when you're too old for romance? In my experience, a marriage gets *beyond* romance. Romance is just the first stage. Though we all laugh at habits and slippers, time itself glues you to each other, irrevocably. As time passes, in my experience, the bond gets stronger.'

'But you've only been married seven years,' said Laura. 'I've been married twenty.'

'You mean, darling,' said Hugo, '*we've* been married twenty years. And no, in case any of you are wondering, I don't have slippers yet, God forbid.'

'He doesn't even wear pyjamas!' laughed Laura.

'Well I do!' said Patrick. 'And perhaps when you're my age, dear Hugo, and have a belly like mine, you might resort to them too.'

Laura thought furiously: 'Hugo will never have a belly like yours! Hugo exercises!'

'Patrick, darling, you are not an OAP,' said Ann.

'But too old for a *menage à trois*, I fear.'

'Regardless of how old you are, I say it's impossible to be in love with two people at the same time,' said Hugo.

'So damn you, which of us are you actually in love with?' thought Laura.

'I've managed it!' said Gloria.

Laura watched Hugo's eyes light up.

'Or at least, there've been times when I've been in love with two people at once. Hey, everyone, I'm divorced by the way, don't follow my example!'

Hugo was looking at her admiringly, Laura noted. What an idiot woman. But he wasn't quite drunk enough to switch points of view, at least, not in public.

'But what about jealousy?' asked Ann. 'Even if you can rationalise things, even if you can say, well, let my husband have his strawberry ice cream if he wants it, he'll soon tire of it – even if you're strong enough to say that – well, I can only speak for myself, I would find the whole business inordinately painful.'

Laura didn't look at her, but dipped a little mashed potato in some gravy and tried to eat it.

'I am the child of a *menage à trois*,' the mousy Pandora suddenly declared. 'I loathe romance. I distrust it from the bottom of my heart. One day I learnt that our lodger, a man I didn't even like, was my father. This invader of our family life was my dad! My two sisters, and we were a real gang of three, were only half-sisters. I took my revenge by driving this man who gave his sperm to my mother out of the house. I was twelve. I wanted my father dead, and told him so.'

'But surely it was your mother you were angry with?' asked Arabella.

'It's the man who penetrates the woman, *always*. It's the man who does the deed,' insisted Pandora.

'What about the man you thought was your dad?' asked Laura, genuinely concerned.

'How weak is that to put up with your mother's lover? I lost all respect for him, of course I did. I pitied him. But that's not exactly a relationship, is it?'

Arabella retorted, 'So, Pandora, you don't think a woman wishes to be penetrated? Well, I do. Not a day passes when I don't think, I want to be penetrated.'

'Oh please, please don't tell her about your leg, not now, not here!' thought Laura. But then more charitably: 'I had no idea how much you needed to be loved!'

Pandora's poor husband looked mortified, but said nothing.

'There is always power play between the sheets, Pandora. Sex and feminism just don't fit,' said Gloria. 'I wouldn't have it any other way.'

Hugo was looking thoroughly smitten. Laura laughed and raged inwardly, all at once.

'Isn't that what happened to Angelica Garnett?' interjected Arabella, regretting, perhaps, her outburst and trying to get the conversation back on to an even keel. 'She found out that Duncan Grant was her father when she was seventeen. But unlike you, she was delighted, as she'd always found the father she thought was her father, Clive Bell, rather distant. What would you have felt, Pandora, if you had actually preferred your lodger to the man you took to be your dad? If he'd been the one to bring you little presents, and spent time with you playing Snakes and Ladders?'

All the party were hanging on Pandora's reply.

'A child shouldn't have to make that choice!' she said with passion. 'We have two kids, I'm their mum, Robert's their dad. We make things safe for them. We make boundaries for them. I had none of that when I was growing up. My mother lived in her own self-centred world and we were outsiders to it. How I loathe bohemianism! How self-adoring that crowd were.' And then, with a terrible voice, that sad, drab woman, daughter of two free spirits, began to parody them: 'How clever we are to break free from tedious convention! Oh my, how creative we are, look how well I paint! Look how well I write! We don't have to be stuffy and have those dull things called nuclear families. No, we believe in sex and freedom, and the more we have of each the better!'

That shut the party up for a few moments. Then Pandora looked straight at Gloria and asked: 'Have you got a child?'

Gloria shook her head.

'Well, you can do what you like, then.' Suddenly, Pandora was done. She immediately picked up her fork and began to eat voraciously, as though she'd been hill-walking all day and was home at last.

But Gloria felt insulted and would not let the matter lie.

'I take it you're not into sex,' she said.

Poor Robert flinched.

'I can take it or leave it,' said Pandora.

'How does Robert feel about that?' pursued Gloria.

Now all eyes were on her poor husband. Even in the light of two candles he blushed puce.

'I take it!' he laughed.

Pandora, regretting the outburst of honesty that had just slipped off her tongue, sent Robert a grateful smile and said, 'I suppose I present myself as the antidote to this sex-obsessed society of ours. We present it – the media presents it, doctors present it, even governments present it, as something healthy and good. But sex is an animal instinct, it's not glorious. Freud ruined it for us all when he said: if you're not getting the sex you want, you're repressed. Next stop, mental illness, hysteria. In France a woman gets therapy on the state if she feels she's not getting enough orgasms. It's pathetic.'

'So would you put the clock back to the Victorian era, Pandora? Lie back and think of England and all that?' It was Patrick who asked the question. Laura thought him very bold.

'Victorian women enjoyed sex too little, I admit. But we've gone too far in the opposite direction. Modern women enjoy sex too much.'

'You can't be serious!' exclaimed Gloria. 'Can you really enjoy sex too much?'

Hugo was impressed. So was Patrick. Ann looked at her and wondered for the first time whether this new GP that had so delighted Patrick might actually be a threat to her.

'Oh, you most certainly can!' answered Pandora. 'Sex is like a drug, you get addicted to it. And like drugs, only the most illicit, after a while, seem attractive. Look at Fred West. Sex is about power. Ultimately, when you've tried everything else, sadism and masochism come into their own. To cause the death of another becomes erotic.'

'That is quite the most depressing thing I've ever heard!' ventured Hugo. 'Robert, have you ever had fantasies about killing your wife while having sex?'

Robert said, 'I'm not allowed to become addicted!'

Pandora looked hurt.

'The ice cream!' remembered Ann, and leapt up to dash to the kitchen.

'It's not just men who wield the power in sex,' said Gloria.

'I'm quite sure you have men eating out of your hand,' said Pandora.

'And quite right, too,' said Hugo, drunkenly.

Laura cringed and looked down at her plate.

But he went on: 'Who around this table thinks sex, really good sex, with someone quite amazingly sexy, is the best experience life can offer us?'

'Oh Hugo, don't be such a jerk!' said Laura, in such a tone that they all felt jerks.

Ann walked into the dining room holding a large green bowl of pistachio ice cream in her arms.

'What is everyone doing sitting in the dark?' she said, turning on the lights.

This time, no one objected.

4

Laura and Hugo didn't say a word to each other on the way home. They might have had a row about Gloria, but Laura simply didn't have the spirit. Watching Arabella and Gloria getting into a taxi together as though they were already bosom friends had somehow disorientated her. But she was too tired to work out why, too thoroughly emptied out to bother to attach words to so many conflicting emotions.

When they got home they made straight for the bedroom. Laura briefly wondered whether submitting to Hugo's amorous advances might ease an overwhelming sense of loneliness. Then at four in the morning Laura woke up and unaccountably began to weep, copiously and silently.

They stayed in bed till midday on the Saturday morning. Laura lay with her cheek on Hugo's chest, and his arm enveloped her. But what did that mean? Guilt? Hope? They ignored the telephone, had desultory sex, and were incapable of getting out of bed. Their normal routine on a Saturday in term time (of which they were both rather proud) was to enjoy a large cooked breakfast at 10 a.m., Laura having run four miles, Hugo, a manly eight. When the routine lapsed, Laura didn't even mention it. She wouldn't have known where to begin.

It was remembering their children that finally nudged them into getting up. They hadn't seen them for three weeks, Jemima and Leo preferring to party than to spend quality time with their parents. The Bedales train would deliver them at Waterloo at 2.28. In a happier frame of mind Laura might have jogged to meet them at Clapham Underground Station, and even carried their overnight bags while they walked home over the common, chatting about school and friends. Normally, it was a good moment in the week, one which justified Laura's very existence. But a lethargy had descended upon Laura, and a deep sorrow she couldn't make sense of. She only knew she had lost something dear to her: whether that was her marriage or Jed she couldn't fathom; or perhaps her greatest loss was her innocence.

So Laura got up and tried to spring into action. For God's sake, she hadn't even cleared out the children's rooms since they'd gone back to school after the Christmas holidays. In happier times she could barely have waited to bring order back to her beloved house: the Monday after their return to school would have been spent tidying, cleaning, re-arranging her children's bedrooms, finding places for the stocking toys she had so lovingly bought for them over the preceding months. How happy she had been last June to find a yoyo for Leo that chimed when you put it through its paces! Now she found it under his bed, several knots in the string. At least he had taken it out of the packet, she sighed. Unlike the origami paper. Unlike the small wooden case of top quality acrylic paints. Unlike the artists' charcoal, which she'd bought at a Christmas fair from a terribly nice bearded man, who'd made it himself in some forest somewhere, though she couldn't quite remember how, while his girlfriend had woven the hessian bag it came in.

When Leo had been at nursery school, how artistic he'd been! Other mothers and Leo's teachers were always telling her so. Laura had had several of his early efforts framed: now they hung in the kitchen and the hall. Wonderful abstracts in orange and teal, lemon and lime green. How she'd nurtured Leo's talent over the years, only to watch it fall away like so many milk teeth. What happens to children, she mused. This year she'd given him a beautiful red leather Filofax from Harvey Nichols. At first she'd bought him a green one, but after Leo had chosen a red jumper to bring to school with him, she'd even bothered to go back to the shop and exchange it. When she saw it lying discarded on Leo's desk, she'd felt hurt that he hadn't taken it back to school with him – she'd even bought some fact-finder cards and a school timetable to file in it, along with the diary and address section. Now when she opened it she noticed he hadn't even filled in the first page: no name, no address, no blood group, no next of kin.

Leo had the only single bed in the house and he often complained of it. He said it made him feel like a kid. Laura changed the bed linen: toucans for Indian elephants, but thought of Action Man and Jed. She soldiered on. Her body felt weighted down. Even fetching the hoover from a cupboard on the same floor seemed to require more will than she had ever needed to diet or run.

Laura tried hard to shift her mood. While tidying away fashion magazines in Jemima's room she noticed a picture of a palm tree on the back of one of them, with a wide expanse of white sand and a turquoise sea. How she yearned for that sea, that horizon. She had always taken for granted that she was free and had barely bothered to ponder the question. Now she knew that she was not.

People said of Jemima that she was Laura's double. Certainly she was as slim and tall as Laura, but she had a superior, bored expression, and a way of raising her eyebrows as if to say, 'What now? Typical!' Despite being only sixteen years old, she took at least an hour putting on her make-up: foundation, blusher, thick kohl round her eyes. While Laura had a wholesome air about her, Jemima looked like she badly needed a few months living rough in the country. She was over-civilised, self-conscious, faddy about her food and fearfully left-wing.

'Nothing is ever good enough for her,' thought Laura, as she grudgingly put on a clean *broderie anglaise* duvet cover. 'All her life I've handed myself over to her every whim. But not any more. At her age, she should be putting on her own bloody duvet covers.' Laura took one look at the make-up on her dressing table, and with an angry swipe put the whole job lot of lipsticks, scents and moisturisers into the front drawer.

At 2 p.m. Hugo and Laura had a little lunch together. Laura put an array of cheese, taramasalata and hummus on the kitchen table and opened up a pack of pre-packed salad leaves. They said little.

'I can't remember where the children have been these last two weekends,' said Laura.

'Leo's been staying over at Barnaby's,' said Hugo.

'I don't like Barnaby,' said Laura.

'Jemima's been partying.'

'She shouldn't be going to parties during term time. It exhausts her.'

Hugo shrugged. 'You can't exactly ban her if all her friends are going.'

'I certainly can!' declared Laura.

Hugo laughed good-humouredly. 'I love it when you get tough, you sexy minx. Let's go back to bed.'

For want of anything better to do, Laura followed him upstairs.

Hugo undressed her, and Laura didn't resist. 'I've only had my clothes on two hours today,' she thought to herself. 'How can he keep doing this, time and time again? What a very odd thing sex is.' Yet the act's very strangeness was a relief to her. What else was there to do with her body? So she gave herself to Hugo not half-heartedly but with no heart, and desire (for what?) crying out for satisfaction.

When the doorbell went two hours later, Laura jumped out of bed and got dressed as fast as she could. Hugo thought it all very amusing.

'The new Laura! I like her!'

Laura was thinking to herself, 'The old Hugo, why did I ever like him?' and rushed downstairs to meet the children.

'Why did you take so long? It's freezing out here!' said Jemima, striding into the house.

'Why didn't you come to meet us at the station?' asked Leo, walking a step behind his sister.

The bags thudded to the floor.

'I'm starving. What's there to eat?' asked Jemima.

'I haven't seen you for three weeks!' said her mother. 'Don't I even get a peck on the cheek?'

'You might have done if you'd bothered to meet us at the station. We were waiting for ages. It's the coldest day of the year and my ears are completely numb.' Jemima disappeared into the kitchen.

'Well I'm sorry,' said Laura, genuinely repentant. 'I had to help your father with something. It couldn't wait.'

'It was all my fault,' said Hugo, good-humouredly, as he came down the stairs into the hall. Leo was kissing his mother. Hugo gave him a manly hug.

'Are they working you hard this term, Leo? How are things going?'

'Dad, you know it's my birthday coming up?'

'Not for two months!' said Laura.

'Six weeks,' corrected Leo.

'What do you want this time?' said Hugo, indulgently.

Laura gave him a look as if to say, 'Haven't we already spoilt our children to death? Are you just going to let him have exactly what he wants every time?'

'A PlayStation. At least half my friends got them for Christmas. Barnaby did. Oh my God, it's just so brilliant, and you, Dad, you would just love it, too! It's like you're really driving a car, it feels that real …'

Hugo noticed his wife's reprimand and said, 'If you do quite staggeringly good work between now and then, and overwhelm your teachers with your incipient genius, I don't see why you can't have one of these PlayStations. What do you think, Laura?'

'He'll do medium-good work, with promises of better to come, and you'll give in. Then he'll play on his PlayStation every weekend, and homework will become a distant memory. Look how Leo got fixated on his Nintendo! If it hadn't broken when it did I would have destroyed it with my own fair hand.'

'You are so violent, nowadays, Laura!' said Hugo, impressed. He gave Leo a wink as if to say, 'Don't you worry! I have your mum under my control!' and took him into the kitchen for a sandwich.

Laura stayed where she was in the hall. Did she want to hear news of Jemima's bitching friends, lost sports fixtures, complaints about the housemistress who punished them whenever they were found in the 'boys' flat' after 9 p.m.? Did she want to hear about essays unfairly marked, postponed music exams because Jemima hadn't even taken her clarinet out of its case over the Christmas holidays? How much interest did she really have in Jemima's rants about girls whom she had never met? As for Leo, he didn't seem to remember anything about school life at all, besides the occasional fire practice. Even the occasional scandal – sex, drugs, expulsions – washed over Leo's empty head.

Laura slowly began to walk upstairs, but amongst the ten bedrooms and the nine double beds no sanctuary awaited her. Where could she go? Where could she be at peace? There was nowhere. So she sat slumped on the staircase, incapable of choosing an upward or a downward path. She wanted to cry, but the tears wouldn't come. Perhaps this was why people took to drink, Laura wondered, to ease the flow of life, to break down this sense of being blocked up.

Then a thought occurred to her. Or rather, an impulse. Laura needed to stir the becalmed sea that was her heart and soul. For one thing was for certain, she couldn't go on like this. She was going to do something impossibly, recklessly brave. Yes, she was going to *make something happen.* She was going to walk upstairs and book a hairdressing appointment with Toni & Guy.

She did it quickly before rational thought could intervene.

Laura held the phone tight to her ear, as though that might steel her resolve. 'I'd like Amy, please, to cut my hair,' she said to the receptionist.

It was like throwing herself off a precipice just for the fun of it. One, two, three! She heard her own voice sounding ordinary and friendly. And when the appointment was made – Tuesday morning at ten – she saw that she was shaking and felt giddy, and that it was quite the right thing to have done.

On the strength of that decision, the weekend passed pleasantly enough and the children never suspected for a moment that their parents had moved on in life, and were inhabiting a new world that barely contained them. Laura consented about the PlayStation, because she was too tired to resist and Leo's voice was beginning to irritate her. She finally gave Jemima the gym shirt she'd so lovingly washed and ironed before she'd gone back to school, only to learn that she'd outgrown it and bought another at the school shop. By four thirty in the afternoon it was dark and the four snuggled together into their vast Conran sofa to watch *Journey to the Center of the Earth.* Both Jemima and Leo fell fast asleep, and Laura stroked her son's hair with tenderness, half-checking for nits as was her maternal custom. Jemima lay her head on her father's shoulder, and Laura and Hugo gave each other looks as if to say, 'How precious they are!' And they went on watching, because while it lasted, everyone was safe.

On the Monday, when the children were back at school and Laura's thinking space was her own once more, she spent most of it on the problem: should she, or should she not, have clean hair when she confronted Amy? For Laura's hair was magnificent when clean: it was both thick and silky, with a lovely swing to it. However, her hair rapidly became lanky and dull. Ideally it was washed daily with a light shampoo. But it would do her hair no good at all to be washed twice in a single morning! The problem exhausted Laura. She lay in her bath on the Tuesday morning, her head above the water, unable to act. She had never felt so ugly, so powerless. And what would Amy be thinking now, how had she been planning her self-defence? Perhaps she had cried off sick.

In the event, even if she had wanted to wash her hair, time ran out and she found herself on the common flagging down a taxi. Amy, for her part, hadn't bothered to check her appointments. She had had five minutes precisely to compose her thoughts, and none to run away.

'Mrs Glass!' greeted Amy, as though it were a genuine pleasure to see her. 'Coffee?'

It was by now three weeks since Amy had run off, caught in a half-naked clasp with her husband. If Laura's hair was lank, Amy had cut all hers off. Amy's bob was a regular haircut on a regular face, quite pretty, but nothing to write home about. No more glorious blond locks for Hugo! Just a few mousy tufts. Laura felt a surge of relief.

'You've cut off your hair!' said Laura.

'All for a good cause,' said Amy. 'They're making a wig with it for a young girl with leukaemia, who's been coming here since she was a toddler.'

'What a very good person you are, Amy! I'm impressed.'

Amy raised her eyebrows in surprise.

'You know I'm not *that*, Mrs Glass. If you've come here for an apology, I'll give you one. I'm an idiot.'

'Hugo's the idiot,' said Laura, with feeling.

Laura sat looking at the mirror. 'I look a wreck,' she thought. 'I look like I haven't slept for weeks. I wish I could go to sleep and never wake up. I wish the floor would open up under me and swallow me whole.'

Amy stood behind her, comb in hand. She was wearing a black velveteen top that hugged her nubile figure. Laura found it hard to share the frame of the mirror with her. It occurred to her that she yearned for another life, any life, to the one she had. She wanted to be Amy, even, young and fresh, who'd had her hair cut for a good cause, and who had her whole life in front of her. How can you think you're living well when you're living a lie?

'Your hair,' Amy said, 'it's so knotty today. Perhaps you'd like to comb it yourself while I fetch you a cup of coffee? White, no sugar, if I remember rightly? It's been a while since I cut *your* hair, Mrs Glass.'

Amy handed Laura the comb and disappeared into the kitchen. Everyone else in the salon seemed to be laughing. In the chair next to hers a woman of about thirty was recounting the story of a blind date that went horribly wrong. 'My God, his *breath*!' she overheard. She closed her eyes and caught straggles of conversations, restaurants being recommended, skiing holidays being planned.

'Your coffee!' said Amy.

Laura opened her eyes and apologised for having made so little progress. For some reason she couldn't put her finger on, she felt angry with this girl for not combing it herself.

Amy laughed and said, 'No worries. I just didn't want to hurt you, that's all.'

'You've just been smoking in there, haven't you? I can smell you!' said Laura, aggressively.

'It's not against the rules, you know,' Amy retorted.

Neither spoke for a full five minutes. Amy kept her head down and concentrated on her task, occasionally spraying on conditioner when the knot refused to yield. Then Laura's neighbour was summoned to the sink to have her hair washed and the coast was clear.

Amy spoke first. 'Perhaps you'd prefer to go to a café or something after work if you want to talk about …'

'No, I'm quite happy here, thank you,' said Laura.

'It's just I thought you might want a little privacy.' Amy spoke quietly but with confidence. Damn her confidence!

'I didn't think you cared about privacy! That you should trot off quite happily to your lover's *home?* To *my* home?" Laura felt her voice rising, despite her best intentions.

'At least you can't shout at me here. It's safer for me.'

'How often did you see Hugo?'

'Can't he tell you that?'

'I just want to know if your stories tally, that's all. When did you start seeing him?'

Amy was quiet.

'So when?'

'I don't know what you want me to say.'

'Look, I'm not blaming you, Amy. I'm on your side. You're just a girl, half his age.'

'I'm twenty-two.'

'Half his age exactly.'

'I'm not good at this.'

'Good at what?'

'You shouldn't ask these things.'

'I can ask what I like.'

Laura could see that Amy was on the point of giving up and getting someone else to cut her hair. So she softened her tone and said, 'I have a lover, too, remember. I believe you met him.'

'That blond bloke.'

'I'm still seeing him, Amy. We're still lovers. Are you still seeing Hugo?'

'What are you playing at?'

'I just want to know. Have you seen him again?'

Amy shook her head and gave Laura's hair a tug.

'Ouch!' she cried out. 'Has he contacted you, Amy?'

'I don't need to answer you.'

'Amy, I don't *care* if he has. I'm not going to make a scene. I just need to know.'

'What does Hugo say?'

Even the word 'Hugo' tripping off this other woman's tongue so familiarly stung her.

'Hugo says he hasn't seen you but he has phoned you.'

'There you are! You have it!' said Amy, with relief.

'What did he say to you?'

'You should know.'

'He said, in so many words, that he couldn't see you any more but that what you had was really special and he missed you.' Laura was becoming a good guesser of men, or at least her man.

Amy looked close to tears.

'He told you that?' she said.

'We share everything, Amy, I told you. But he really loved you in his way. Don't look so upset.'

'Why did you come here? To tell me that?'

'I came to say Hugo's missing you. He was much happier when he was seeing you. I'm living with half the man he was. I miss the old Hugo.'

'Are you saying you want us to get back together?'

'There's so little love in the world we should grab whatever we can get, that's what I think. Do you still love him?'

Amy looked close to tears and couldn't speak.

'You sweet girl!'

'Hugo was always so kind to me, Mrs Glass!'

'Call me Laura, please!'

'Laura, I'm so grateful!'

'And Amy, I've been thinking.' (This was untrue. The thought had just come to her.) 'We're rattling around in our house now the kids are at boarding school. Come and stay whenever you like!'

'What are you saying, Laura?'

'I'm saying, *stir once, stir twice, turn it into something nice.*'

'I don't know what you're saying.'

'Some rhyme I learnt at school once.'

'What does it mean? What are you saying?'

'What I'm really saying, Amy, in the biggest possible way, in great big capital letters, is SO WHAT? The milk is already spilt, we may as well lap up what we can.'

'Are you a witch, Mrs Glass?'

'I am the opposite of a witch, Amy. I look for the good in all things. In Hugo, and in you. You are my husband's mistress. I am his wife. Those roles have to stay pretty intact. But we have to live for the day, don't we? We have to snatch at joy when we can. Come and stay with us, Amy!'

'I don't think I should …' began Amy, looking seriously distressed.

'What have you got to lose? Could things be any worse than they already are?'

'What does Hugo say?'

'Ring him. He'll be so delighted. He misses you so much.'

'Perhaps I will,' said Amy, earnestly.

'Or why don't you come to supper tonight and surprise him? I could make you two a little supper and run away, go to a movie or something. I don't want to get in your way.'

'Why are you doing this?'

'Why not, Amy? Why should I cling to a life that's so empty of life? I know Hugo too well. I know every movement he makes, from the first moment he wakes up and turns on the power shower while he pisses, to the moment he smells his socks before he goes to bed.'

Amy looked alarmed.

'Doesn't he smell his socks when he's with you?' asked Laura, gently.

'Why does he do that?'

'So he can give them to me to wash if they do.'

'Oh,' said Amy.

'But you will de-domesticise him. You will restore his sense of the romantic! Has Hugo ever given you flowers?'

'Yes,' said Amy quietly.

'Hugo likes flowers, doesn't he? Has he ever given you a hundred roses all at once?'

'No,' said Amy.

Laura couldn't have taken it if he had. She would have broken.

'Promise me you'll come to supper, won't you? There'll be no more secrets between us, will there?'

'No more,' said Amy, almost at a whisper.

'Well,' said Laura, satisfied. 'I think you've managed to unknot my hair!'

An hour and a half later Laura was swinging her glossy, trimmed hair down Oxford Street. She was trying to work out what had just happened. In an attempt to make things seem more real, to restore some edge to her life, things felt less real than ever.

Then she understood: she had given herself permission to see Jed again. If things had been all square before: airless, claustrophobic, predictable and dead, Laura had created movement. She was in no mood to follow the tracks that other people had set out for her to follow. She didn't wish to grow old and dull without having tasted something different. How bored she was being nice! What satisfaction had she ever got from it? Was she going to be content to live and die with a sealed-up soul that just wanted to be safe? Today would see the birth of a different Laura who would live dangerously.

Laura didn't want to go home, so she sat in a coffee shop to muse. Instinctively she felt that returning to Hounslow right at that moment was premature. After all, she'd only seen Jed four days ago. But she would go back there. Next time she'd just take him away from that horrible place. Her dream was to go to one of those five star hotels by Heathrow Airport. She should find out the name of the one with the candlelit swimming pool one of her friends had told her about. Perhaps they could all come to some arrangement, such as 'Wednesdays, I'm out. I'll leave supper in the oven'. Hey, why should I make Hugo supper? They can go to a restaurant, if they want something fancy. But what if someone sees them? Perhaps I should make them supper, just to show this is all okay by me. Or what if Hugo doesn't fancy Amy without her hair? That would be a joke. God, men are so shallow.

Imagine that. She'd just invited her husband's lover to supper. Even to stay the night. Isn't that what bohemians do? Isn't that what artistic people do? She tried to remember whether she had been any good at art at school. She hadn't been stretched exactly. All those vases of flowers she had to draw, all those bowls of old fruit. Perhaps she should go to a life-drawing class. She had seen one advertised in Battersea town hall. The classes were held in the daytime, too, when she was beside herself with boredom. And she could take up pottery. She'd always wanted to throw a pot on a real potters' wheel. She should stop willing Leo to draw with charcoal when *she* was the one who should be drawing with charcoal. How hadn't she realised it before? Soon she would go home and draw, just to prove it.

Then Laura went home to cook supper for the three of them. Something homely, like a shepherd's pie, just to prove how abso-lutely normal everything was. Why was she so happy? She couldn't wait to see Hugo's face when he saw how Amy's glorious golden plait had been cut off, and how ordinary she was looking.

So then, wondered Laura. What if Hugo resisted Amy's remaining charms and pleaded lifelong devotion to her? Wouldn't that plunge her straight back into a nowhere land, where nothing ever happened?

And then a sick-making thought came to her. Was it just possible that she didn't love Hugo any more? But Hugo had been her life for twenty years. Do you fall out of love with the speed of falling in love? Falling out of love at last sight, which was, in Laura's case, the sight of Hugo burping in front of the bathroom mirror and wiping off the condensation with his sleeve. Did she still want that person in her life at all?

No one would have suspected that Laura, as she fried onions and carrots on her Aga wearing a pretty spotted apron, was anything but the good and kindly wife and mother she'd always been. But a madness was brewing inside her, something uncontained. The last time she'd made a shepherd's pie, she'd measured out the Worcester sauce with a teaspoon. Now she threw it in with abandon.

By four in the afternoon the pie was ready. And suddenly all the energy that had deserted her these last few days was back. As she took off her apron, she found herself singing a song she had forgotten since her schooldays, 'The Logical Song' by Supertramp. Now Laura hadn't sung for years, and half the words she couldn't even remember, but she didn't care.

She looked in vain for the original LP, but found others in a cupboard in the attic: Genesis, Bob Dylan, Led Zeppelin. She never realised that you could feel *hungry* for music, and how she had been so starved of it. It was always Hugo who chose the music, who always insisted they listen to jazz. Hugo had made her feel her own taste in music had been arrested at the age of seventeen, had even mocked her for it in public. She had come to believe him. A few years ago Hugo had bought a new CD player. Laura had barely complained at the time, she'd been too busy with the kids ever to listen to music anyway. But now she suddenly recalled the brutality with which he'd unwired her old record player, calling it clutter, telling her to take it to the tip. Well, she hadn't taken it to the tip. She'd wrapped it in a blanket and put it on the top shelf of the linen cupboard. Now she was going to bring it down again and re-instate it, and if Hugo didn't want it, tough.

When Hugo came into the house at seven that evening he found his wife lying on the sofa in the dark singing along to 'Stairway to Heaven'.

He came in, turned on the light, and said, 'What the fuck do you think you're playing at?' He shoved the stylus to one side but the record went on spinning round.

Before Laura had a moment to answer him, he went on: 'How dare you go and make that girl cut your hair this morning? What do you think you're playing at? How do you think you made her feel?'

'I was just being friendly. I wanted to surprise you, Hugo. Put my music back on!'

'You actually invited her here, you invited her to share our lives, Laura!'

'She already is sharing our lives. I know you think of her. I know you ring her. And I know you miss her. Now put my music back on!'

'Here's your fucking music!' Hugo picked the record up and threw it at her. Laura hid her head in a cushion and took cover.

Then Hugo ran upstairs. Laura could hear him shouting, 'Damn her! Damn her! Damn her!' and even two floors up she could hear the bedroom door slamming.

All was still. Laura hugged the cushion that had so protected her from her evil husband and tried to work out how to react. A part of her wished Hugo had drawn blood. Then at least things would have been clear: she would never forget her husband was a wife-abuser and she would never, ever forgive him. But as things stood, why, was that guilt she felt? Was it possible that Hugo was just a tiny bit right? Had she behaved badly?

Laura wondered how she was ever to get up from the sofa. Well, perhaps she wouldn't. Perhaps she'd bed in there for the night. The idea of ever setting eyes on Hugo again appalled her.

Yet, again, something Hugo said had touched her, something in the way he had said her name, like a plea. He wanted things back the way they were. He didn't want Amy as part of their lives. He wanted her.

It was while Laura was tossing to and fro between love and loathing that the doorbell rang. She jumped up and smoothed down her clothes. In the hall, she turned on the light, took a quick glance in the mirror, adjusted her hair and her expression, and answered the door.

It was Amy carrying a large suitcase. She looked so small and defenceless standing there, like a war evacuee. She'd dyed her hair black since the morning, it was now spiky and dishevelled. Annoyingly, it rather suited her. Her face was pale, her lips painted plum, and round her eyes was a thick band of kohl.

'You said to come, Mrs Glass,' she said, pathetically.

'Come in, Amy!' Laura said generously.

'Amy?' called Hugo from the top of the stairs. 'Amy?' he said again as he rushed down. 'What are you doing here?'

Hugo's tone was so genuinely solicitous that Amy burst into tears and diluted kohl ran down her cheeks in dark streams.

Laura stood by to watch Amy burrowing herself into her husband, and saw how tenderly he stroked Amy's shorn hair – exhibiting no surprise that the fine golden plait had disappeared. Had she warned him? Was she always dyeing her hair? To her horror, it occurred to her that they had already seen each other that day.

'I like your hair,' said Hugo, 'it suits you.'

Laura felt that her one and only missile had landed in the wrong field.

'Ian came home early,' cried the girl. 'He found me in floods of tears. I told him everything, Hugo. He was so angry, I've never seen a man so angry. I told him it was finished, I told him that I would never see you again, but he didn't listen. And now he's chucked me out!'

'You mean, you have a boyfriend?' asked Laura.

'No, not any more!' blubbed the girl. 'He was so horrible to me! He said such horrible things!'

Laura wanted to say, 'What, you mean, just because you were shagging someone else's husband? How terribly unfair!'

But instead she said, 'I'm sure he didn't mean it! People just say things sometimes, without thinking.'

'But he did mean it, Mrs Glass! He meant every word. He opened the cupboard and began throwing all my clothes at me, throwing my shoes at me, my boots, too. I thought he was really going to hurt me.'

'Poor Amy, love,' said Laura. 'I know just how that feels. I'll tell you what, Hugo can pour you a drink and I'll put a shepherd's pie in the oven.'

'I can't believe how understanding you are. You are so kind, Mrs Glass!'

'Please, call me Laura. If you're to move in with us for a while, and it looks like you are, you have to call me Laura.'

Hugo shot Laura a look as if to say, 'What are you playing at? Amy's not moving in!' But it only fuelled her.

'Let me show you your bedroom, Amy. I'll carry your case,' said Laura, graciously.

'Oh Laura!' exclaimed Amy, flooding with emotion, as she followed her hostess upstairs, 'I've never met anyone like you. My mum used to shout all the time. I've not seen her in five years. She doesn't even remember my birthday. She ran off to the US with her bloke when I was only sixteen. I wish you'd been my mum!'

'You have to think of me as your friend, Amy,' said Laura, firmly. 'I'm not your mum. Here, this is your bedroom.'

While Amy stood satisfyingly speechless at the door of her new bedroom and bathroom *en suite*, Laura called downstairs, 'Put the oven on, Hugo!'

'It's amazing, Laura. It's a palace!'

Laura felt a surge of pride and a sense of her own good fortune. It occurred to her that she couldn't remember the last time she had a guest to stay and a person to whom she could show off this exquisite room. Rachel and Jerry had come up from Somerset over a year ago, had stayed with them for four days, but had said not a word about the Liberty lawn curtains in a pink and turquoise stripe, the 100 per cent wool Wilton carpet in fawn, and the French wallpaper she had found in Pimlico.

Now Amy was stroking the curtains like she had never felt the sumptuous cool smoothness of lawn in her whole life, and it gave Laura the satisfaction the happy owner of a puppy might feel on introducing it to the wonders of nature for the very first time.

'I'll help Hugo with the supper, Amy. You make yourself at home and unpack,' said Laura, but then a great desire came upon her to show Amy the bathroom and witness her delight afresh, so she said, 'I'll just check you have fresh towels and a new soap.'

Laura spent some five minutes fiddling in the bathroom waiting for Amy to follow her. From where she stood, she could see the girl touching the shiny teal phoenixes that stood in bas-relief on her wallpaper. She half wished to call out, 'Please don't do that, not before you've washed your hands!' but the half of her that delighted in Amy's admiration of her house won the moment and she resisted.

Laura was pleased she waited. Amy had never seen such a huge bath and confided in Laura that she couldn't swim, and was so small she thought she might sink. Amy actually meant what she said, but Laura laughed. Amy still hadn't mentioned the ravishing Moroccan tiles behind the sink, butter yellow with a floral pattern in cerulean blue. Laura had to gently nudge her.

'I'm not sure about these tiles,' she said.

'They're just beautiful!' said Amy, right on cue. 'And the pink blind! I love pink!'

When, at last, her taste had been sufficiently admired, Laura said, 'I'd better give Hugo a hand then. Supper will be in about twenty minutes or so.'

Amy looked like she would burst into tears with gratitude. Laura considered giving her a peck on the cheek, but decided that might be construed as maternal, so she gave her a little wave and ran downstairs to the kitchen. The double doors that separated their vast kitchen from the hall were rarely closed, but on this occasion they most certainly were.

'What the fuck have you been doing up there?' hissed Hugo. 'What do you mean, inviting her to stay? So that you can keep an eye on her? So that you can win her over to your cause?'

'She has nowhere else to go!' said Laura defensively. 'Were we to send her back out there into the street?'

'You are playing at something so toxic! So unremittingly spiteful!'

'I absolutely am not! Hugo, you should know me after all these years. I don't have a spiteful cell in my body.'

'Know yourself, Laura! You are plotting!'

'What am I plotting, then, clever clogs? What could I possibly *be* plotting? I am simply being kind!'

'If you want to be kind, why don't you go and make soup for the tramps under Waterloo Bridge? And haven't you got about fifty blankets hanging around in the attic now you've filled the house with goose-down duvets? Why don't you take them with you and hand them out?'

'Those are good-quality blankets, Hugo!'

'All the more reason to give them away to those who need them!'

'I thought you liked sleeping under a duvet. You said you did.'

'You spent two grand on duvets!'

'You always say to get the best of everything!'

'The blankets were fine. You got the best of those, too, if you remember.'

'Shh!' Laura said suddenly. 'I hear her coming downstairs. For God's sake, Hugo, you didn't even put the pie in the oven.'

'Nor did you!'

'That's because I thought you had!' Laura hurriedly slid the pie dish on to the top shelf of the Aga and turned towards the door to receive her guest. The door handle began to turn tentatively, and Laura called out, 'Yes, Amy, we're in here!'

Amy looked so pretty, so demure, standing there in the doorway. She had washed her face, and hadn't bothered to re-apply her make-up. Her short, black crop made her look like a waif, and indeed, thought Laura charitably, that's exactly what she was.

But Laura didn't like it when she saw that Hugo's face was also brimming in sympathy. He looked far more concerned than when Jemima had broken her elbow skiing. Nor did she like the look Amy gave Hugo in return, a soupy darling-are-you-pleased-to-see-me? sort of look. Laura was strong, however. She invited her to sit at their kitchen table and then found a cushion for her to sit on so she wouldn't look so short.

'Have a drink!' said Hugo. 'What can I get you?'

'I should love a cup of tea, if you don't mind,' said Amy, politely.

'Have something stronger than that!' insisted Hugo.

'After all you've been through today!' gushed Laura, equally insistent. 'I notice you've even dyed your hair.'

'I'll get you a whisky!'

'I don't know if you have a Babycham?' asked Amy, shyly.

Laura and Hugo never realised anyone actually drank Babycham.

'Don't we have a dessert wine, darling, we could add some soda to?' Hugo suggested.

'I'm sure we have!' enthused Laura, barely able to withhold a grin.

So they mixed some fine vintage Sauternes Château Suduiraut with soda water in a jug – Laura fetching the wine, Hugo fetching his 1950s silver soda syphon from the drawing room – and they made Amy a tall glass of it.

'Drink that down,' Laura said encouragingly. 'Drink that down and tell us the whole story!'

Amy looked at Hugo for permission to begin. Hugo gave her an encouraging nod.

'I don't know where to start!' she said, sipping at her drink.

'That's a really good wine! What do you think of it?' asked Laura.

'Oh, it's great, thanks,' said Amy nervously.

'So, your boyfriend's just chucked you out of his flat,' Laura reminded her.

'Well, you see …' Then Amy stalled again and continued to drink.

'Remind me of his name?'

'Ian,' she said. She looked like she was going to burst into tears.

'How long have you been going out with him?' Laura asked, gently.

'I've been living with him for nearly two years.'

It was Hugo's turn to look jealous.

'Has he been a good boyfriend to you?' asked Laura.

'Oh yes! He's always been so kind to me, and he loved me so much!' cried Amy.

'And did you love him back?'

'Oh yes!' exclaimed Amy.

Hugo couldn't help himself. He said, 'Did you?' and looked hurt.

Laura leapt up to find two more glasses for her and Hugo. The shepherd's pie was beginning to smell sweet and she noticed she was ravenously hungry. As she came back to the table she saw Hugo and Amy giving each other an intimate look, which was hard to stomach.

'Do you like peas?' asked Laura. Her voice was bright and shrill.

'Yes,' said Amy. It was unclear whom she was answering.

Laura went to the chest freezer in the pantry to fetch the peas and momentarily slumped over it. The day had been long and she needed to sleep. In fact, she didn't know what she needed.

'So how did you meet this Ian?' Laura asked, as she came back into the kitchen.

'We were at school together. He was two years above me. He said he loved me from the moment he caught sight of me, when I was only eleven and he was thirteen.'

'That's so romantic!' said Laura as she poured the peas into a saucepan. 'Where were you at school?'

'Holland Park Comprehensive.'

'Gosh, isn't that quite a tough school?'

'Not if you had good friends. I had good friends. It was a laugh.'

'Do you think you might contact one of them in the morning and tell them what's been going on?' asked Hugo, drinking back the sweet wine and soda like it were beer.

'What do you mean?' Laura looked accusingly at her husband.

'I'm thinking about where Amy can live, in the long term,' explained Hugo.

'Well, why doesn't she live here, Hugo? We've got enough space!'

Amy looked at Hugo as if to say, 'Can't I? Please?'

And Hugo, knowing exactly the pain he would cause his wife, picked up Amy's small, slim hands and said, lovingly, 'Of course you can!'

Hugo and Laura were to outdo each other in their kindness towards Amy that evening. Laura deemed her too young, too innocent, to understand exactly what they wanted from her.

And what exactly was that, by the way? As Laura tossed in bed that night, aware that Hugo was equally restless at her side, she tried to make sense of the day's events, and tried to remember why having Amy in their home had ever seemed a good idea.

Then deep in the dead of night, Laura inadvertently held her hand towards Hugo's for reassurance, and Hugo squeezed it. For a few fleeting seconds Laura was happier than she'd been for a long time.

5

The following Sunday afternoon Laura sat with her cheek slumped on the kitchen table and realised she didn't like the new arrangement of things at all. Occasionally she could hear a shout of glee or despair emanating from the sitting room where Hugo, Amy and the children were playing Monopoly together.

Of course, they'd asked her to play, too, pleaded with her, even. But Laura hated competitive games and was no good at them. She told them she was going on a run, something she'd been neglecting to do for days and felt the worse for it. She'd only popped into the kitchen on autopilot, there was always a surface to wipe down or something to put away, but the sound of those four having such good fun without her irked her, and she had collapsed like a little child in some foreign country who only wants to go home.

Anyway, realised Laura, there wasn't even a spoon to return to its sugar bowl in that immaculate kitchen. So happy was Hugo, he had spurred 'his troops' into action like never before. Amy had scoured the roasting tin, despite Laura's instruction to 'leave it to soak'. Leo, reeking of Lynx aftershave, had insisted on standing by Amy at the sink with a tea towel. Jemima had put the leftovers neatly into little bowls and covered them with cling film. Hugo loaded the dishwasher and not only cleared the kitchen table but spent a few minutes rubbing at a stain of red wine, and when he successfully removed it was so delighted he kissed his wife on the cheek.

Amy was irritatingly happy. The fact that her boyfriend had chucked her out of her flat less than a week ago already seemed a distant memory, and even when Laura would occasionally remind her of that fact, trying to sober her up, as it were, Amy would flick her hand at the wrist and look dismissive, as though it meant nothing to her.

How could she seem so at ease with herself? How could she walk around their home, as she did, with bare feet? She was like a young animal, setting out on real life for the first time, enjoying every adventure that came her way. She was living in a ten-bedroomed house crammed with beautiful things, with a man she loved and a mum-surrogate. Why shouldn't she be happy?

At lunch, she had never stopped chatting. 'If I had a mum like you I'd never have been a hairdresser. I wouldn't have settled just for that. Jemima and Leo tell me they're going to university. I would give anything to go! Anything! All these dreams I had when I was a kid, making movies, travelling the world, where have they gone to?'

'But being a hairdresser is important,' Laura had insisted. 'And creative!'

'My only realistic hope is that one day I'll own my own salon. Hugo said he'd help, you know!'

Hugo hadn't even looked embarrassed, but caught Amy's eye, light and guiltless. No, he had nothing to hide now. Damn him! Damn him! And Amy, oh Amy! Just who have I brought into my house, so young and fresh? What was I thinking? I'd hoped I would demystify her, domesticise her, humiliate her, be in control of this wretched business. Even my kids adore her, even my kids think she's been chucked out on the street by her nasty boyfriend and want to look after her. And what part do I have to play? My whole life is slipping away from me. I can't hang on any more.

Laura didn't even know whether Hugo was actually having sex with her. At eleven at night, when the three of them went up to bed, Hugo would make a point of having 'a little chat' with Amy in her bedroom. Laura couldn't help but time him – he would take between twelve and fifteen minutes. Well, anything might be happening. And though it crossed her mind to ask Hugo directly, she knew that she simply couldn't bear to hear the truth.

A week later, when Arabella asked Laura to have lunch with her at a fine fish restaurant in the city, Laura sought every reason not to go, but Arabella fended off her feeble excuses like an able tennis player at the net. Laura was just about managing to keep her life on an even keel. She found that if she kept her head down and she didn't question things too much, she could get through till the end of the day. She didn't fancy an hour and a half of being lectured. She didn't have the strength to undergo further cross-examination on the subject of her husband and his wandering eye. In short, she didn't want to divorce her husband. Despite everything, she still loved him. She still wanted her marriage to work.

'You look terrible!' were the words that greeted Laura when she finally found her friend in a back room of Whistler's fish restaurant. 'And you're late!'

Arabella was already a glass into a bottle of rosé which stood in a large ice bucket on a stand beside her. 'I took the liberty of ordering for you, dish of the day, poached sea bass on spinach. I have to be back in an hour. A new client. Her husband's made a fortune in bathrooms. There'll be some settlement there, I can tell you.'

'I'm sorry,' said Laura. 'There seem to be half as many buses as there used to be. And it was pouring with rain.'

'Can't you stretch to a taxi nowadays? Actually, stop there. I don't want another speech on the merits of public transport.'

'I just like feeling part of things, that's all. I hate living my life in a bubble of privilege.'

'But you do, nonetheless, my dear girl. I hereby award you the title of my most unworldly friend. You haven't lived!'

'You always say that.'

'Now, we mustn't be at risk of repeating ourselves. So little time, so much to get through! Here, let me pour you a glass of rosé.'

But just as Arabella took hold of the neck of the bottle a waiter took it from her and gave Laura a glass himself.

'Some canapés for you ladies?' he asked in a French accent.

'No, we don't want canapés,' said Arabella. 'Just our lunch when it's ready. And you don't have to worry about filling our glasses with wine every other minute. I can do that myself.'

The waiter gave a polite nod and left them.

'You don't have to be so rude!' Laura said.

'And you don't have to be so polite! Polite people get walked over. You get walked over.'

'I do not!'

'Hugo walks all over you and you know it. And your children do!'

'I thought this was why you wanted to have lunch with me.'

'So that's why you've been avoiding me, is it? You don't want someone to spell out the truth!'

'Why are you being so aggressive?'

'All right then,' said Arabella, gentler now. 'You, dear girl, are the best friend I ever had. And one day my best friend rings me in hysterics of tears to tell me her husband has been snogging a young girl with a golden plait, remember? This is over a month ago, Laura! First you cancel lunch and then you seem to disappear off the face of the planet. You never answer your phone! It crossed my mind … well, no matter what crossed my mind but put it this way, I was concerned enough to call round during the week and the house was as lifeless as a tomb.'

'I would never kill myself!'

'And then that debacle of a dinner party! I still don't have any real idea what's going on in your life, Laura. You seemed sad, my heart went out to you, and then you lie! What are you hiding? And you now have fifty-two minutes to put me in the picture. You and Hugo are still together, I see.'

Laura said nothing. She searched the restaurant for her new ally, the waiter, but couldn't see him.

'Laura, look at me! I am your friend! I only want what's best for you, you know that!'

At last Laura spotted the waiter coming out of the swing door from the kitchen carrying two plates. She noticed the spinach and prayed to God that this kind waiter would rescue her, which he did.

A minute and a half's reprieve: she savoured it, smiling at the waiter in gratitude.

'This looks delicious,' she said.

Arabella marched on. 'Okay, it's the ninth of January. You ring me in hysterics. Hugo is having an affair. I tell you to divorce him, pretty harsh words I know, but I've had nearly twenty years' experience of this sort of thing, don't sniff it. Then I hear not a whimper from you ever again. Did you confront Hugo when he came home? How did he take it?'

'It's all so boring to me now!' sighed Laura with feeling. 'Yes, I was upset. I wanted to get out of the house. My parents were busy, they needed notice, they said. So I went to stay with an old friend in Northamptonshire for a few days. I'm surprised Ann didn't tell you that, as you two always seem to be on the phone to one another.'

'Funnily enough, we were on the phone. Ann told me you went to the Isle of Man. But it would be great if you had been able to tell me that yourself.'

Laura had completely forgotten anything she'd told Ann in her horrible kitchen at her horrible party and blushed scarlet.

'Forget where you went, you went somewhere,' said Arabella imperiously. 'Anyway, if you had a friend in Northamptonshire, I'd know about it.'

'You don't know everything about me, you know,' said Laura.

'Are you saying that's a good thing?'

Laura looked so close to tears that Arabella softened her tone.

'Let's go back to the beginning. My question is, did you have it out with Hugo before you left?'

'God, you sound like you're in court.'

'Forty-two minutes,' said Arabella, looking at her watch.

'I took the cowardly way out. I just set off. Left a note.'

'Did he know where you'd gone?'

'I obviously didn't tell him that.'

'How hard do you think he tried to find out?'

Laura shrugged. The sad truth was, he probably hadn't tried at all.

Suddenly Arabella laughed. 'Honestly, "an old friend in Northamptonshire" indeed. You are such a bad liar, Laura. I know all your old friends.'

'You don't. I have lots of friends you don't know. You don't own me.'

'Silly me! I am unbearably presumptuous, aren't I? Now, why did you go to the Isle of Man? That is where you went, isn't it? Ann's right, isn't she?'

'I can't talk about it here,' said Laura, lethargically moving her fish about the plate.

'You mean you won't talk about it here. Or anywhere, for that matter. Am I right?'

Laura lifted her fork as though it weighed a hundredweight and put a couple of leaves of wilted spinach into her mouth.

'Rachel told me she advised you just to put up with Hugo's infidelities, like she puts up with Jerry's. But has she heard a word from you since you sobbed down the line at her, too? Not a murmur.'

'I hate the way you all gossip,' managed Laura.

'But what I don't understand is this. What you can possibly be trying to hide? You're the victim here, you're the goodie! You could have bonked your way through a rugger team and you're still the goodie! Hugo betrayed you first. I can see from your face that I'm getting warm, aren't I? You have a secret. You are hiding something from us, aren't you? You have a lover! Or rather, you had a lover because if he was still around you wouldn't be looking so sorry for yourself. I'm right, aren't I? You had a short affair and for some reason he's no longer around. I'm right, aren't I?'

Laura looked down at her plate and said, 'Yes.'

'If I thought you were happier about it I'd say "yippee!"'

Laura didn't look up. Her face betrayed no emotion whatsoever. Even her fork was still.

'Does Hugo know about it?'

'Yes,' said Laura.

Arabella smiled. 'At least there's some poetic justice in the world, then. That must have hurt him.'

Laura made some strange expression with her mouth, which seemed to suggest it had been water off a duck's back.

'Is Hugo still seeing Miss Golden Plait, do you know?'

'I don't think so,' said Laura.

'So you see yourselves as being back together, all square, as it were.'

'I suppose so.'

'Although I hate to say this, it's not going to be all square for much longer.'

Laura looked up.

'I went home last week with that black woman dressed in silver. Gloria, I think her name is. Your husband had written his phone number on her arm. He said he wanted to play squash. I thought I'd tell you.'

'Is that what you wanted to tell me?' said Laura, bitterly. 'It's unbelievable. She's a doctor, goddammit, going to a dinner party in Clapham, dressed like an ageing pop star. She looked completely ridiculous.'

'Why should you have to dress dowdily if you're a doctor?'

'Her dress wasn't even in fashion! God knows where she found it.'

'Come on, Laura. The old Laura would have had a good laugh.'

'The old Laura would have had something to laugh about.'

Just then, the French waiter came to take their plates away. 'Would you like to see the dessert menus, ladies?' he said.

'No, we wouldn't,' said Arabella brusquely.

'Yes, please,' said Laura.

'Well, you'll have to eat it alone because I'm off in ten minutes.'

The waiter looked at Laura for confirmation.

'Get me the most chocolatey thing there is, please.' And when Arabella looked at her, furious, Laura said to the waiter, 'And a small glass of limoncello.'

Arabella looked at her watch and sighed. 'I can see I'm not being much help to you, am I? I'm going to go now. Ring me, Laura dear, if ever you want an honest chat. Something you're probably not quite ready for, yet.'

Arabella got up and left a twenty pound note on the table.

'I shall kiss you farewell,' Arabella said. She leant down and planted a condescending kiss on the top of Laura's head. 'And I mean that in the old-fashioned sense. Fare-thee-well, dear Laura.'

In spite of everything, Laura quite enjoyed her chocolate cheesecake and liqueur. She ate slowly, drawing out the taste of every mouthful, fancying that the waiter was watching her out of sentiment, when in fact there was a queue of people at the door waiting for her to finish. It was only when she passed their curious and angry stares on her way out forty-five minutes later that she realised her mistake and blushed to the core.

As she left the restaurant, Laura didn't know where she was going. Her home was abhorrent to her. Her home was where Amy and Hugo had stolen kisses. Her friends had deserted her, even her children. It's official, thought Laura as she raced down the streets without looking where she was going, everything that has ever made my life sweet has gone.

I'm drowning, thought Laura. I don't know who I am any more. She tried to earth herself, think of good things. She passed by sandwich shops, exclusive city boutiques, small and sleek. She passed by a luggage shop, a handbag shop, a man's shoe shop. She passed a shop called Feather and Fin for hunters and anglers and thought of dead birds and dead fish. And then a vision of her first pony, Adam, popped into her head, the pony her dad had given to her when she was six. 'You can't call your pony Adam!' said her mum. 'Oh yes you can!' said her dad. How many gymkhanas she used to win, row upon row of rosettes stuck to the wall above her bed! Her dad had been so proud of her, taking her to every event himself. Now, that was something she was good at. Why ever did she stop riding? Boyfriends, of course, parties. If her dad had been disappointed in her he had never let her know.

Onward she tramped. She was leaving the city now, marching down High Holborn. Computers, technology, hi-fi. She paused only to look in a cake shop. Laura had never been one to comfort eat, had never really understood what it felt like to *succumb*. A pretty china plate brimming with chocolate cupcakes held her attention. She briefly wondered whether she might buy the lot of them and find a niche in a park somewhere and work her way through them. She remembered making cakes with her mum to take to her granny. Heavy, black, treacle cake. On she went, down Holborn, along Tottenham Court Road. That cake. So heavy. So black. She had never even liked it, had never even learned to associate the word 'cake' with 'tasty'. For Laura, 'cake' represented something overwhelming, hard to digest. She walked on.

As she neared Oxford Street, she stopped again outside a shop selling negligees. Nothing fancy, nothing tempting. In fact, Laura wondered whether she would ever be tempted again. Temptation belonged to the world. Temptation was healthy. It was when you wished to be part of the world, to dress up for it, to join it in its aspirations. But Laura realised she no longer gave a damn about anything. If her entire wardrobe went up in flames she would scarcely care.

And then she thought of Arabella. Arabella was her first love. Expelled from her London day school for reasons no one ever found out, there was always a hint of the mysterious about her. Her flaming red hair down to her waist was the most exotic thing Laura had ever encountered. In Arabella's arms she lay, sixteen years old, among the ruins of an old priory in the grounds of their boarding school, all their lives before them, their white nightdresses resplendent under the moon.

They were a foursome once. Charlie was Hugo's best friend. They used to go to restaurants together, and then go on to dance till four in the morning at all the trendy nightclubs from Annabel's to Tramps. Arabella and Laura were married within a few months of each other, were even pregnant at the same time. Then Arabella took a wrong turning on a ski slope when she was twenty-three. That's all it took: a moment of inattention. A common mogul sent the lovely Arabella flying, and she landed, crash, on her leg.

Arabella had been unremittingly brave. Laura told her so all the time: 'Brave' is such an easy word. A much harder word is 'baby' as in 'lost baby'. The best Laura managed was to ask Arabella to be godmother to her own. Arabella had declined, brusquely.

Months later, when Arabella took off her prosthetic leg before going to bed, she had asked Charlie to make love to her. He had said to her: 'Do you know, it's oddly erotic fucking a woman with only one leg!'

Now the tears came. 'Is that all I am to Charlie?' Arabella had sobbed. 'A woman with one leg? Is it *odd* to fancy me?'

Charlie had gone even before she could chuck him out. Men are like that, thought Laura. Hugo would have left me, too. Arabella's right. Men are all the same. And now, thought Laura, she was the one who was going to get bitter. She was feeling it right now in her heart, the coldness lurking there, the steel. Arabella had had her test in life and had passed it admirably. She had done something with her life. Now it was her turn to prove herself. But she would fail. She would be exposed for the empty, useless person that she was.

When she saw to her horror that New Oxford Street was turning into Oxford Street proper, and that Toni & Guy was a mere two hundred yards away, Laura turned a sharp left into Wardour Street and ended up at Piccadilly Circus.

Now what?

The place was thick with humanity going about its business. The vast moving billboards above her told her to wear deodorant and buy a new Volvo. The buses invited her to enter them, offering destinations in the suburbs of London that she had never even heard of. 'Archway, Archway,' she muttered to herself, but she yearned more for a seat and a quiet place than a new adventure. She looked out for fellow drifters, people whose eyes and bodies weren't set in a particular direction, people who weren't going anywhere much and were just whiling away the day. Her only kindred spirits, she found to her dismay, were tramps. On any other day, on a *normal* day, she would catch someone's eye and smile, but it was as though she had lost the knack. Perhaps there was a new smell about her, she considered. Perhaps people realised she was dangerous, or worse, irrelevant.

Going back to Hounslow West was not a conscious decision. She knew she looked a wreck – Arabella had already told her so – and she didn't even bother to put on make-up. It was more to see if she was totally dead inside or whether some surge of adrenalin might resurrect her. In fact, the final push was not the desire to see her lover but the realisation that it was the Piccadilly line that would take her direct to his door. And it was true, something did rise in her as she abandoned herself to the rhythms of the train, her eyes closed, breathing deeply, as one might in sleep, conscious only of the screeching of brakes, the stopping, the starting, and the gathering speed. That something was hope.

When she emerged from the tube station it was pouring with rain. But that was good! she thought. Something had shifted, the dam had burst. Ten, fifteen minutes' walk at most. The lights of the oncoming traffic blinded her, but she wove her way through it, horns blaring. Hug me, Jed, please hug me. Do anything you like with me. Kiss me, hold me, take me away from all this. I'm ready for you now. I give myself, every part of myself, to you, my love.

Then Jed wasn't there.

A small part of Laura was relieved. A very small part, called pride. Standing in front of his door, shivering, her thin wool coat and hair wet through, she knew she'd cut a sorry figure. Instinctively, she knew that Jed wasn't the pitying kind. Nor, it turned out, was his mother.

'He's not here,' she said. She stood with her hand on her hip, superior. Above all, dry and warm.

'Do you know when he'll be back?'

Jed's mother shrugged. She was the queen of her doorstep, standing tall.

'The heat's getting out,' she said, poised to close the door.

'Can you just give me a vague time or something?' asked poor Laura.

'How the fuck should I know?'

'I just thought …'

'I haven't seen him for days, madam.'

'Has he moved out?'

'Who knows?'

'He must have told you something.'

She shrugged again.

'You must have some idea, though!'

'I can't help you,' said Jed's mother. 'You see …'

'Yes, yes …?'

'I thought he was with you.'

Laura's heart danced when she said that, at least until the moment she realised that he hadn't been with her at all but had been, most probably, with someone else.

Laura crumpled and went on her way.

It was now six in the evening. Anyone who watched her would have thought she was drunk, as she swayed to left and right. How ironic it was, that the only person left in the world who still esteemed her was her husband's lover. Was that absurd or what?

Laura waited at a bus stop a while. If she had been strong for all of two weeks, there was now not a whimper of strength left. She was emptied out of reason, of feeling, of any human emotion whatsoever. When those about her got on to a bus, and she could find a seat on the bench in the shelter, she sat, bent double, with her cheek on her knee. No one asked her what was wrong. No one gave a damn.

Where oh where could she find oblivion, a rest from being her?

At seven o'clock she decided to go home, and was back on that wretched train she had come to loathe.

An hour later she was walking across the common. She thought, 'This is what it feels like to be no one. But I am no one. My crime has been to have ever thought I mattered. None of us matter. We just soldier on, that's what we do in life. And then we get old. And then we die.'

An icy wind chilled her to the bone. Her coat was still damp and she started shivering. She considered running to warm up, but she couldn't muster the spirit to run. Anyway, she considered, she might get ill. She would like that. She could lay low for a while, drifting in and out of sleep – she was so tired! Hugo could bring her a tray with hot soup and a little posy of flowers in a cup when he came home from work, and tell her how much he loved her. She'd like that. Or more likely, Amy would bring her the tray, and with bright and breezy manner ask if she wanted white or brown toast.

Hugo and Amy would both be at home by now. Amy got home at half past six, except on Thursdays, when she worked late. Hugo, well, he was more variable. She hadn't even considered what to give that happy threesome for supper. Why, why had she invited that idiotic girl into their home? Perhaps she should come clean that evening and say it wasn't working. Or perhaps she could say she wasn't feeling well, and leave Amy with some pasta and a frozen Bolognese sauce and tell her she was in charge. Then she could slip into a hot bath and be free of them.

Then it occurred to Laura that she might spy on them. She could sneak in and sit on the top of the stairs. If the kitchen door was open, wouldn't she be able to hear what they said to each other? They didn't exactly flirt with each other in a sexual way, not when she was around, anyway. But there was a certain intimacy between them that disturbed her. Revise that, an intimacy that had become intolerable. What might Hugo and Amy talk about, anyway? What could they possibly have in common? Amy wasn't the mother of his children, after all. She couldn't imagine Hugo being enthralled by Amy's tales of perms and haircuts. But then again, what did *she* talk about with Hugo? The kids. Where to go on holiday. Domestic things. What do married people talk about anyway? Hugo already knew everything there was to know about her. Parents who loved her, a gentle, ordinary life. Amy probably had a violent stepfather who got into bed with her when she was fifteen. Amy probably had stories to tell. Laura had none.

In fact, the most extraordinary thing that had ever happened to her in her forty-one years she had to keep secret. So secret, it was beginning to disappear. Just for a few moments, she had lived life as it was meant to be lived.

At least Amy was one of many. At least Amy meant nothing to Hugo.

As she approached the house, she could see that the lights of the front room were on and the curtains were closed. The last time she'd been in that room, she'd caught Hugo on the sofa with Amy. She felt sick at the memory of it, but bored by the prospect of a repeat performance. Those idiots can do what they like. They couldn't touch her any more. Their cosy little threesome was over.

But the man sitting demurely on the sofa next to Amy, a mug of tea in his hands, was Jed.

Laura could rely on her social graces to get her through even this. She walked into the room and said a warm hello to them both, and when they stood up to greet her, there were kisses all round. Amy then told her that Hugo had phoned to say he wouldn't be back till half past eight, and she'd bumped into Jed on her way home. Even the word 'home' didn't grate on Laura like it might have.

'I'm drenched through,' she told them. 'I'm taking a hot shower and warming myself up. Amy, why don't you find a bottle of wine in the pantry and pour yourselves a glass?'

'There's not any of that delicious mixture you made the other night, is there? Like a Babycham? Jed, would you prefer a beer?' On any other night, Laura might have considered it *her* role to offer Jed a beer. But such was the strength of her dominant emotion – a ludicrous, childish thrill which utterly suffused her – that she said, 'Amy, the house is yours! Take Jed into the pantry and show him everything on offer!' Then she gave the pair a little wave and went upstairs.

Upstairs, in the privacy of her bedroom, Laura rid herself of her damp, dark clothes. Despite a hundred anxieties that kept trying to present themselves upon her – as in, she now recalled that Jed's biker boots had left black footprints on her cream carpet, and Amy had been sitting cross-legged and bare-footed on the cream damask sofa when she'd come in, and worse, Hugo would be home soon – she relished the *joie de vivre* that was flooding into her once more. Hot water poured down her naked body, as she held her face inches from the nozzle of her power shower. And having washed away the misery of those last few weeks, and enjoying afresh that at long last Jed was coming to see *her*, that Jed was in her house because he missed her in the way she missed him, she almost danced towards her wardrobe. Her better, soberer half told her to slip on some jeans with a cashmere jumper, something she might normally wear for a kitchen supper. But then she noticed a dressing gown Hugo has bought her several Christmases ago, a ravishing thing made of antique Indian silk in teal, turquoise and fuchsia pink stripes. She remembered she had spent the whole of that Christmas wearing it, Boxing Day, too, but then had never found occasion to wear it again. Too smart for a kitchen supper *à deux*, too eccentric to wear for dining with friends. But now she lay it out on the bed in delight, wondering whether she should wear her nightdress under it. Of course she shouldn't! How absurd it would be to own such a ravishing garment and not feel the silk against her naked skin! And perhaps she should follow Amy's example and have bare feet, in which case she should paint her toenails red.

It was while Laura was stark naked painting her toenails that she heard the front door open and Hugo come in. She could hear him mumbling something to Amy and Jed and coming upstairs with a heavy tread. If it hadn't been for the wet nail varnish, she would have hidden herself under the covers, turned out the light and pretended to be ill. As it was, she put the nail varnish to one side, threw the dressing gown on to the chair and lay on the bed as though waiting for Hugo. She turned off the main light and half-smiled in the warm yellow glow of her bedside light.

'Darling,' she said, as Hugo came in – it was the only word she'd had the time to practise – 'you're so late tonight.'

But Hugo was in no mood to be seduced.

'For God's sake, Laura,' he said, turning on the main light. 'For God's sake, what are you playing at, you idiot?'

'I didn't invite him!' she pleaded. 'He just came!'

'Well, get rid of him!'

'At least let him stay for supper,' said Laura, leaping up from the bed and putting on her dressing gown.

'God, you make me sick,' said Hugo.

'I promise you I didn't invite him!'

'I suppose you've been having a sex fest all afternoon ...'

'That's not true! He was here when I got back ...'

'Back from where, Laura? How do you fill your days anyway?'

'I had lunch with Arabella.'

'Lunch with a girlfriend! Of course! How stupid I am! How busy you've been. And then, I suppose, you did a little shopping. Or did you go on a run, Laura, or have you had a game of squash, perhaps?'

'Shut up!'

'You look great in that dressing gown! Is that for my benefit?'

'I haven't worn it for ages, I just thought ...'

'For God's sake, you lie, you lie, you lie, don't you hear the lies just tripping off your tongue? You had sex with him in this bed, didn't you?'

'I did not!'

Hugo stripped the bed looking for tell-tale signs.

'Even if I had had sex, do you think I'd be stupid enough to have it in our bed? Do you think I'd stoop that far?'

'Ah, so you're confessing now ...'

'I am not confessing! I only got back half an hour ago!'

'You liar!' said Hugo. 'Or do you want to tell me you were still enjoying a post-prandial coffee with your good friend at 6 p.m.? At least Arabella works for a living.'

'You guessed right, I went shopping.'

'You liar, Laura! You liar! Show me your parcels then! Show me the shoes you bought, the lacy blouses, the scents, the lipsticks! You didn't get anything, did you? And why not? Because you were here fucking Jed!'

'That's not true!' said Laura, weakly, beginning to break down.

'I'm getting myself a drink,' said Hugo, and he left her sobbing on the bed.

Yet still the idea of her lover so close to her was, at that moment, the dominant one. Hugo's words would come to haunt her at another time, she knew that. But now she concentrated on how to see Jed, alone.

Laura pulled herself together and quickly chose a plain, grey serge dress with a red velvet collar much admired by her friends. The dressing gown she put away. She tied her hair back and put on a little make-up, not enough to be noticed, but enough to make her feel herself. Everything was silent downstairs: she imagined Hugo sitting at the kitchen table, a bottle of beer beside him, doing *The Times* crossword, glasses on, shutting out the world which so displeased him. She wondered whether Jed and Amy had heard any of their argument, but reassured herself: the house was a solid one, and their bedroom was two floors above the sitting room rather than the 'drawing room' where the two were sitting. Then suddenly she heard Hugo striding through the hall and calling out: 'Champagne everyone! Who's for champagne?'

Once in the drawing room, he shut the door. This was Hugo's idea of a game, she realised. No eavesdropping allowed by her. He was going to get to the bottom of what went on that afternoon. Well, let him. She was innocent. Even Jed didn't know her whereabouts that afternoon.

The thought gave her courage. Hugo would realise that he had misjudged her. She would go to the kitchen, and start cooking spaghetti Bolognese: the sauce was frozen but would take as long to melt as for the spaghetti to cook, and there was a delicious slice of Parmesan in the fridge, even enough lettuce to make a salad. She could do it: their supper would be as friendly and normal as the night Amy arrived. She was a woman in charge again.

Laura laid the table and opened a bottle of Chianti. She noticed that her hand was shaking as she did so, and was reminded that the champagne party might not be going well. Once the pasta was in the boiling water and the sauce on a low heat she dared go out into the hall, to see if she could gauge what was going on. Suddenly Hugo bounced out and exclaimed: 'Goodness, Laura, how your friends knock this stuff back, I'm going to fetch another bottle!'

Laura managed to walk into the drawing room as though nothing untoward was going on in her life at all. She smiled graciously at her two guests, whose champagne flutes – Venetian glass – were almost empty. Jed had taken off his boots and was smiling at her affectionately – how she fed on that warmth! Amy looked as happy as she always did.

'I hope Hugo remembers to bring me a glass!' she laughed, and watched them to see if they gave her any pitying glances. Thank God, they did not. What a great house it was to keep privacy intact! Oh thank you, Victorians, for building it so well!

Hugo did bring her a glass. Laura knocked back her first glass of champagne almost in one. Amy clapped her hands in admiration.

'Go, Laura, go!' she exclaimed.

'Another, Hugo, dear,' said Laura.

'Coming up!' said Hugo, as he poured her a glass.

Laura sipped at her second glass, looking about her for evidence of betrayal. She saw none.

'Here's to all of us!' she said, raising her glass.

'To all of us!' said Amy and Jed.

Laura watched for the anger in Hugo's face and saw it.

'To all of us, to us happy four,' said Hugo. His sarcasm was only noticed by his wife.

'Let's have supper, folks!' enthused Laura, and they followed her into the kitchen.

What followed was the kind of cosy kitchen supper commercials dream of, all beautifully lit up by the porcelain pendant light which hung over the table. Both Hugo and Laura pulled off an exemplary double-act as the perfect host and hostess: Laura managed to get all the frozen bits out of the Bolognese sauce, and the spaghetti was a perfect *al dente*. Jed told jokes about Hounslow West, about how the airport was built so that everyone could make a fast exit. Amy told jokes about her ex-boyfriend, about how boring he was and about how he was more like fifty than twenty. She told them how he put Brylcreem in his hair. She merrily told them about their sex life, how absurdly shy he was about his body and how he had red pubic hair. Jed laughed. Jed laughed for all of them because Hugo and Laura were giving each other looks that said, 'Poor man, to be pilloried like this.'

'So Jed,' asked Hugo, 'what line of business are you in?'

Laura had naturally assumed that Jed was unemployed but Jed met Hugo's eye and said, 'This and that.'

'Lucrative?'

Jed looked puzzled.

'Does it pay well?' Hugo clarified.

'I know what "lucrative" fucking means,' said Jed. 'I just thought that was a question posh people like you didn't ask.'

'I'm not posh, Jed,' said Hugo. 'I'm just curious. What kind of line are you in?'

Jed shrugged.

'Ah, drugs, you push drugs!' prompted Hugo, with a little clap.

Jed didn't even bother to reply. He told Laura she was a fucking good cook.

'I'm not naïve. Now, Laura, as you might have noticed, is naïve.'

'I'm happy to do what I do. No one forces me.'

'Taxidermy! That's it, isn't it, Jed, you stuff dead animals, don't you?'

'Wrong again,' said Jed, coolly.

'Do you have your own place in Hounslow?' persisted Hugo, topping up each of their glasses with Chianti and stretching over towards the wine rack to get another bottle.

'I want to move on, as it happens,' said Jed.

'Another homeless youngster!' said Hugo. 'This won't do at all, will it, Laura? But we've got a great big house with bedrooms galore and if you want a room …'

Laura looked horrified.

'Laura, what about the room opposite Amy's? The bed's only a small double, but it's *en suite*. You'd like the shower.'

'Would anyone like a yoghurt or a piece of fruit?' asked Laura.

'No thanks, Laura,' said Amy, in a tone which was infuriatingly familiar.

'No thanks,' said Jed.

'Here, Jed, let me take you to your room,' said Hugo. 'Personally it's my favourite. I think Laura decorated it with a view to entertaining her bachelor friends, isn't that right, Laura? There's not a single speck of pink in it, not a single bloom. And the wallpaper's from France, isn't that right, darling? Could you enlighten us?'

'Yes,' said Laura.

'It's rather cartoonish, I'd say. Hunting scenes. Men with guns and horses. They're rather into their hunting in France, aren't they, darling? Come on, Jed, see what you think of it.'

Jed dutifully followed his host, and Laura tried to catch Jed's eye, but he didn't look round.

When the two had gone, Amy said, gushing: 'Oh Laura! You two just have the most amazing marriage. You two are just the most generous people I have ever known. And Jed, oh my God, Laura, Jed is so cute! But what I just can't get is why you're not jealous. If I were you, I'd just be so jealous all the time, but you're not one bit, are you?'

'Why should I be jealous?' asked Laura. 'I am Hugo's wife, after all. I'm the number one!'

'Well, most wives, let me tell you, would be wanting to throttle me. They'd see me as such a threat. But the only vibe I get from you is … is … well, we get on so well, don't we?'

'We certainly do,' said Laura.

When Jed and Hugo came back into the kitchen, they were both smiling. Kissing his wife on the top of her head, Hugo said, 'Jed simply loves his new bedroom, don't you, Jed?'

'Thank you,' said Jed. 'It's good. But could you give me a key to your house? I'm working tonight.'

'Working? At this time?' asked Laura, horrified.

'Perhaps Jed sells house keys for a living!' laughed Hugo.

'That is not funny!' said Laura, indignant.

'I thought it was quite funny,' said Jed. 'But I won't sell your house key.'

For the first time since Jed had entered her house, Laura looked him in the eye. Jed was beautiful, but completely impossible to read. He held her gaze, and opened his mouth ever so slightly. Laura looked hard for a secret message. She fancied he might be saying, 'I've come for you! I didn't let you down!'

But then he said, 'You don't happen to have a spare key, Laura?'

'I'm afraid I've lent my spare to Amy. But I don't see why you can't borrow mine. I don't know what your plans are exactly, but if you're going to stay longer I'll get another one cut. I go out on a run at 7.45 but I'll be back by half past eight …'

'I'll be back by then,' said Jed, in a matter-of-fact way.

Again a pause.

Everyone was waiting for some kind of explanation.

Jed raised his eyebrows and looked at Laura as if to say, 'Well?'

'I'll get my key,' said Laura uneasily. Hugo was watching her, but made no attempt to intercept.

Laura went upstairs to fetch it. Gone was the skip of a couple of hours ago. As she sat down on the bed, trying to extract the damn key from a bundle of others on a key ring and failing again and again, she was suddenly overcome with exhaustion, her delight in Jed now coupled with the realisation that she had never quite trusted him. She wondered briefly whether that was why she loved him, why she wanted him. She lay her head on a pillow for all of a few seconds to ask herself the question, 'Do I still want him? Who is this man, exactly, who is now living under my roof?' Then she went back down to the kitchen, defeated.

'Let me help you, darling,' said Hugo, and took the keys from her.

'There you go, Jed,' he said, victoriously handing him the key within a few moments. 'Have a good night. See you tomorrow evening, I hope.'

'Thanks,' said Jed. 'You've got a good set-up here.'

'That's just what I said, Jed!" said Amy. 'You've come to the most loving, generous, biggest-hearted family in all London!'

Hugo and Laura looked at each other and at Amy. Was she being serious?

'I can tell,' said Jed. 'Thanks again.'

And he disappeared into the night.

Laura was lying in the dark at seven in the morning, the curtains still closed. Hugo had just left her a cup of tea and kissed her cheek, before setting off for work. She felt the imprint of it and smiled. The previous night he'd come back from his visit to Amy's bedroom full of desire for her, and she was trying to work out why. Was Jed's arrival in their house an aphrodisiac? There was no question now, in her mind, that full-blown sex was part of Amy's goodnight package. Amy more or less thanked her for the privilege of borrowing him, while their own sex life had gone down to zero. So, perhaps they'd had their very first argument. Or perhaps Hugo's desire for Amy had waned now that he had competition for his wife. She couldn't help feeling pleased. Or at least curious.

So, Hugo had ended up inviting Jed to stay with them. Was he setting her a test? Had he realised that the household was becoming rather lopsided? But his spirit had been vengeful, not generous. Well, not exactly vengeful. Rather, controlling. Hugo wanted to prove something to her – that Jed was an idiot she'd soon tire of if he lived under their roof. And he'd been so affectionate in the night! Asserting his ownership over her. She had to confess, she was pleased.

No, 'affectionate' was the wrong word, she decided. In fact, while making love to her, he'd actually told her that he hated her.

Laura's mood as she waited for Hugo after his little sorties into Amy's bedroom was never good, and Hugo's treatment of Jed had been so patronising she'd felt like hitting him. She'd been waiting for a row, stiff as a ramrod, but somehow Hugo had pummelled her into submission. And while they were having sex, she'd shouted out, 'I love you!' though who she loved she couldn't tell.

So Laura lay with her hand on the cheek that Hugo had so recently kissed and tried to get her emotional life in some sort of order. She was yearning to see if Jed had got back, yet just imagining their first intimate time together here in her own home terrified her. Wouldn't it feel sacrilegious somehow? She'd had the foresight to leave the door of Jed's bedroom ajar, so now she crept up to see if he'd come home yet. When she peeked in and saw the bed was still made and that he'd taken his rucksack with him, she panicked that he'd never come back, and not because he still had their front door key.

Back in her bedroom she began to pace, trying to remember what Jed had told her. Suddenly she remembered she'd said she went for a run at a quarter to eight and perhaps they would meet on the common. The only problem was, he had her key and Amy had the spare, so if they didn't meet she'd be locked out of the house. There was nothing for it but to get into her running gear and wake Amy.

Amy's bedroom door, dead opposite Jed's on the first floor of their home, was still shut. Amy usually left the house at about half past eight. She wasn't sure whether Amy would still be asleep, and wasn't it a bit mean to wake her? It occurred to Laura that she'd never even once gone into this spare bedroom since Amy had appropriated it, not even to snoop, not even to make sure she was keeping it clean. Of course, it was absolutely reasonable she should knock and get her key. She just needed to borrow it now and get a couple more made that afternoon. But she was nervous somehow, for reasons she couldn't quite grasp. Her knock was timid.

'Come in,' said a small voice, so small it gave Laura confidence.

The room was dark, and Laura intuited a deep gloom, which encouraged her.

'I hope I've not woken you,' said Laura, kindly. 'Can I get you a cup of tea? I'm afraid I'm going to take your key off you. I'm going for a run and I've given mine to Jed.'

Laura drew those fine curtains and let a drab morning light into the room. Amy looked terrible. There were dark red rings under her swollen eyes.

'Oh Amy!' said Laura. 'Are you ill? Shall I call Toni & Guy's and tell them you can't go in today?'

'Please do that, Laura. You're so kind to me. I haven't slept a wink. I think I've upset Hugo.'

'Of course you haven't upset him! You know he thinks the world of you.'

'Sometimes I try and get close to him and …' Amy began to sob.

'You dear, sweet thing,' said Laura, soothingly, feeling all the warmth of a deep compassion. 'Men are difficult creatures!'

'Oh Laura, you always say the right thing! I just have to listen to your voice … it's such a lovely voice, so warm. You never get flustered about anything, do you?'

'Oh, I do,' said Laura. 'You just haven't seen me, that's all.'

For some moments Laura sat on the bed looking at the young girl, her hair black and dishevelled against the smooth, ivory-white linen of the pillowcase.

'She looks like an orphan from a picture book,' thought Laura. 'What a sweet, harmless thing she is! And I'm so pleased I got this quilt in blue and not bronze. Blue is such an innocent colour!' In fact, she was so happy with the bedding that she sat down on it, and the one hundred per cent goose down did not disappoint, but was as soft as air.

She looked down at Amy in the way a mother might her child and said, soothingly: 'You must think of me as your friend, Amy. Something happened last night, didn't it?'

'Oh yes, it did, Laura!'

'Something really upsetting. Poor child. You can talk to me, you know.'

'I'm not sure that I should, really …'

'It's about Hugo, isn't it?'

'Oh, Laura, it was terrible! I'm such an idiot!'

'Hugo's the idiot, dear Amy.'

'Oh no! It was completely my fault. I'm such a blabbermouth. I just like to tell him everything about me.'

'That's what intimacy is all about!'

'I thought he'd think it was funny. I told him …' Amy paused, unable to continue with her wretched tale.

'What did you think was funny?'

'It was just a funny thing about Ian. I know he's a bit jealous of him so I told him about the way I used to spy on Ian when he was in the bathroom. He's got these horrible spots above his ears. They were little pustules which exploded when he squeezed them.'

Laura laughed! How she laughed, imagining Hugo wishing to make love to the girl …

'You see, it is funny, isn't it?'

'It's very funny, Amy. Sometimes, that man in our life just has a sense of humour failure, that's all.'

'But he's such a hoot sometimes. He's always making *me* laugh. I just don't seem to be able to make *him* laugh.'

Laura thought, 'Hugo never bothers to make *me* laugh,' and made some sort of grimace.

'Don't look like that, Laura. You're married to the kindest, most generous, most wonderful man in the world! He's in a completely different class to Ian. Ian was …'

Laura looked at her watch.

'Hey, I must go!' she said.

Amy grabbed her hand.

'Laura, you've really cheered me up, you know. You are just so kind.'

'The key,' she said, taking her hand back rather too quickly.

'The key's in the pocket of my jeans,' mumbled Amy, suddenly sad again.

Laura picked them up off the floor and wondered why Amy couldn't use a chair. She found the key in a back pocket.

'Thanks, Amy,' she said. 'I'll get a couple more made this afternoon.'

'Would that be all right if you phoned Toni & Guy for me?' said Amy, pathetically.

'But you look so much better!'

The idea of Amy loafing around the house all day when Jed was finally hers appalled her. 'If you're still in bed when I get back I'll ring them then,' she added brightly.

Amy said, 'Thanks,' and turned over on to her side.

The day was dull, but Laura thought she saw a pearly light waiting to break through the clouds and it uplifted her. For the first time in weeks, she waved at her admirers in Lavender Street as they set off to work, and remembered to put the rubbish in the bin. As she ran, she considered why she was so happy. There were crocuses sprouting through the frost, the air felt clean and cold and new. Today, Clapham Common seemed such a *good* place: the cross-section of paths where men and women, rich and poor, black and white, young and old rubbed shoulders with one another while going about their business. Wasn't that how the whole world should be?

Everyone who popped into Laura's head while she ran her circuits suddenly became the object of her absolute benevolence: how happy her children had seemed over the weekend, Jemima was growing into such a beauty, and she was quite certain that Leo fancied Amy, that dear, sensitive girl who'd been weeping all night because she thought she'd upset Hugo! And even Hugo, how lucky she was to have married him. How handsome he was still at forty-four! How pleased she was that he'd kept his body in such good shape! And if the penalty for that was that other women found him attractive, how could she blame him for simply following his male instincts? After such a wonderful night with him she knew her friend Rachel was right: what did it matter whom he slept with as long as he went on loving her? Because the odd thing was, despite his protestations of hate, she had never felt more loved.

But of course, the real source of Laura's joy was the thought that at any moment she might meet her lover, that they would go home together and spend the morning in bed. And Laura was not disappointed. At precisely 8.25, a few minutes before the end of her run, Jed caught up with her and began to run at her side.

Laura stopped dead in her tracks. If she'd been cooler, she would have carried on, lackadaisical, and Jed would have got a half-smile at most. But Laura was not cool. She had never been so overjoyed in her whole life, and the joy brimmed over.

Jed kissed her cheek straight off and seemed ready to kiss her like the first time they met, but Laura said. 'Not here, Jed! Are you coming home, then?'

Jed took her hand, but Laura took it back. She quickly looked round to see if anyone noticed.

'Everyone knows me here!' she said.

Jed looked around at the dog walkers and the mums. 'That baby's waving at you,' he said.

'Oh Jed! You know what I mean, people talk!'

'What would they say, Laura?'

'I'm a married woman!' whispered Laura to her lover.

Jed had one more go and slipped his arm around her waist. Laura giggled and said, 'Wait, wait!'

Laura almost kissed the red door of her house as she entered it. Even Amy had done the decent thing and set off for work. The house and Jed were hers alone.

'Coffee?' she asked Jed, politely, once safely in the hall. But she didn't mean it. She had no interest in going into the kitchen at all.

'You've got to be joking. I need to go to bed.'

'Oh Jed, haven't you slept all night? You poor thing! Where have you been, Jed?'

But Laura had as little interest in her question as Jed had in answering it. He sighed wearily. Laura kissed his cheek and grabbed his hand.

'We're going upstairs,' she said.

Laura took Jed into his new bedroom. She couldn't remember the last time anyone actually slept here. Perhaps no one had. It crossed her mind that the sheets on the bed might have lain undisturbed for years. Would they still be clean after so long?

Jed lay on the bed first.

'Come here, Laura,' he said, arms outstretched.

'Would it be all right if I had a quick shower? I've been running and …'

'You come here!'

But Laura had smelt the faintest whiff of sweat emanating from her armpits, which she hadn't written into the script at all.

'I'll be two minutes,' she said. 'Wait for me.'

But Laura took five. By the time she came back, clean as a whistle and wrapped in the ravishing silk dressing gown she'd so yearned to wear the previous evening, Jed was fast asleep.

Laura's day was spent waiting for him to wake up again. After the initial disappointment – for the sight of her own naked body in the shower had taken her desire to a new crescendo – she found the act of gazing upon her lovely Jed in her own home to be exquisite. Never for a moment had she imagined things might turn out like this. It was like capturing a rare bird in a tropical forest – no, better! 'The rare bird has come of its own accord and is sitting on my shoulder,' mused Laura.

The first time she came to watch her sleeping Jed, she lay beside him, leaning on an elbow, for a full hour. She noticed a little scratch beside his left eye, newly made, the scab not yet formed. It crossed her mind that Jed had been in a fight. Perhaps Jed was a bouncer at a club. She looked for signs of bruising but found none. She felt both disappointed and relieved.

Laura spent a good few minutes studying Jed's mouth. She

remembered it on her body in the Hilton: herself raised up on pillows, yielding. She closed her eyes and thought of his tongue darting over her clitoris; then she studied his fingers and imagined them prising her open. So aroused was she, it occurred to her she was within moments of orgasm. Was it possible to come, she wondered, without being touched? By just thinking about what it might be like to be touched?

Laura thought it would be unfair to wake him and decided to get dressed and go about her ordinary life. Bills and letters lay unopened on the desk in the sitting room, and she spent a moment or two trying to pay attention to them. But if she'd had too little energy before, she now had too much. Oh look, the Led Zeppelin album Hugo had thrown at her was still not back in its sleeve! Thank God, it was barely scratched. She imagined listening to 'Stairway to Heaven' with Jed later. Oh, the bliss of it! Just being able to introduce him to all her old favourites. So happy was she that she opened a pack of new dusters and a jar of virgin beeswax from Fortnum's. She had long since dispensed with a cleaner: housework was a positive pleasure when done as a little dance routine to music. Laura's guilty secret was to listen to Radio One or Two on her large Roberts radio and make up dances. That morning her body had never felt more lithe, more nimble. She found a feather duster and stretched upwards to the corners of all the downstairs rooms in time to 'My House' by Madness.

Laura's heart and mind had never felt more in tune with her body. She had always been rather baffled by her friends when they talked about yoga being 'holistic'. In fact, Laura thought the word began with a 'w' and it was about feeling 'whole'. She had never been sure whether she did feel whole because she had never felt anything different: even when Ann dragged her to a yoga class, suggesting she should learn to truly relax and become one with her body, she dutifully went through the exercises – which she could do rather better than most of the others, she noticed gleefully – she was still Laura, doing what she was told, obedient and eager.

'If only Ann could see me now!' she thought. 'I could dance forever. My body and soul are finally in perfect sync.'

From time to time she would creep upstairs to see if Jed was waking up yet. She gazed at him with the adoration of a mother who has just given birth, and holds her baby in her arms for the first time. He was all hers, lying on a bed in a room in *her* house! My God, what a god-like creature he was! And he was *hers*!

Laura knelt on the carpet next to him, and lay her head on his pillow, a mere six inches from his own. She could feel his breath on her, wet and warm. So here he was, at last more than just a figment of her imagination, more than an object of longing … a real person who would any time now wake up and talk to her, hold her, hear her, love her. Yes, when he woke up he would kiss her, and the kiss would last for hours. She would get up on to the bed and lie next to him, she would stroke his hair, his face; she would slip her hands under his grubby T-shirt, feeling the smooth skin of his young body underneath it.

When he finally did wake up at 2 p.m. it was almost as good as she had imagined it would be.

Perhaps it was wrong of her to even try and start a conversation with him. Talking always spoiled everything.

She had the terrible feeling that despite her best intentions she had woken him up. She wondered whether you could wake someone up just by looking at them for a long time.

'Hello, Jed,' she whispered. His breathing was different, his eyelids were moving. He was surely just about to open them now. But when he didn't respond, she wondered whether he had been dreaming.

Then, after some minutes, Jed's whole head turned away from her, and she briefly felt the weight of his rejection.

Then his head turned back towards her again, and his eyes opened.

'Jed!' exclaimed Laura warmly. 'You've been sleeping all morning!'

Jed looked at his watch. 'Five hours,' he said, slightly irritated. 'You've given me five hours.'

'I didn't wake you though, did I? I've been so quiet!'

'Come here, Laura,' said Jed.

Laura climbed up on to the bed and lay next to him.

'Closer!' demanded Jed.

'I can't get any closer!'

'Take your clothes off and lie on top of me.'

Though Laura had been rehearsing all morning for this moment, she suddenly felt shy.

'Aren't *you* going to take your clothes off, Jed?'

'Come on, Laura, lie on top of me!'

She did, fully clothed. Jed didn't even kiss her.

'Not like that,' he said.

'Okay then,' laughed Laura, and she stripped naked. Jed wasn't watching her, though. His eyes were shut. She was worried he was falling asleep again.

Nonetheless, Laura gingerly lowered her body on to him.

'You're squashing me ...'

Laura blushed, and rolled off him.

Jed laughed. 'That was a joke, Laura.'

'Look, I'll let you get some more sleep ...' said Laura getting up, but Jed pulled her back and made her lie down again.

Jed, fully clothed, eyes shut, began to feel the naked body beside him.

Laura surrendered to being felt. She breathed slow and deep, yet was conscious of her heart beating fast.

But then Jed stopped feeling her and she wondered whether she'd done anything wrong. When she looked at him his eyes were closed and he seemed to be falling asleep again.

'Jed,' she whispered.

'Mmm?'

Why did she say 'Jed', goddammit? Laura couldn't even think of a question. She wondered whether she might apologise for Hugo's aggression the previous evening, but then she thought that in Hounslow West he'd be used to far worse and the last thing she wanted was a conversation. Then she wondered whether she should ask him to take his clothes off, but exactly how should she ask him? What should be the tone of it? Should she ask him politely? (But their relationship was anything but polite.) Or humorously? (But their relationship was surely too intense, too passionate for humour.) Or should she command him, 'Take your clothes off!' But that was Jed's style, he wouldn't like that, he wouldn't just obey her. In the end she said, 'You know, Jed, I don't even know your surname.'

Jed said nothing.

Then he said, 'Do you need to know it?'

He propped himself up on an elbow to survey her.

'You are so, so sexy,' he said.

He ran a finger from Laura's lips, down her chin, her neck, drawing a line between her breasts, over her belly button and all the way home till it rested inside her. Then he made love to her, half-clothed. Laura wanted their lovemaking to go on all afternoon; in the event, it was all over within a few moments.

Laura wanted to say, 'Oh Jed, all you have to do is touch me one more time and I shall come!' but she held back.

Jed fell back against the pillows and was asleep again.

Laura crept away, somehow disappointed. She showered and dressed. It was still only half past two. For some time she lay in bed, trying to rest, but her mind was still racing.

'I've got to get those keys cut!' she suddenly remembered, and jumped out of bed.

'There will be four of us now with a front door key. What a very odd arrangement that will be.'

Nonetheless, she was pleased with herself. She felt she was breaking free of a life that had held her down, that hadn't allowed her to flourish. She put on a pair of knee-high boots – Cognac leather, buckles at the ankle, three-inch heels – tied her hair back, and slipped into her faux fur coat. She strode down the road to Clapham High Street, greeting everyone she passed, helping old ladies with their shopping, waving at the children who were coming out of school. Life was splendid indeed.

6

Laura's happiness was infectious. Gone were the sullen ways of her children, and Hugo took to singing in the bathroom. One month on, despite the irregularity of things, despite the fact that Hugo spent longer and longer with Amy before he slept beside his wife – and yes, there were certainly moments when Hugo was in the shower at midnight and Laura paused to wonder at their situation – life was beginning to seem *normal*.

There was even a routine, of sorts. Jed worked four nights a week, Monday to Thursday, leaving the house soon after supper and creeping back into the house about the time Hugo was getting up. Often the men would exchange a few polite words as they passed each other on the staircase. At two in the afternoon, Laura would come up to see Jed with a cup of tea, and more often than not, they would make love till three. After that, they might lounge around at home listening to music, or take a bus into the middle of town and go to a film or visit an art gallery together. Laura had often regretted not taking up her place at St Andrews to do History of Art: but now she had her very own student, her dear Jed, and it became her mission both to educate and impress him.

Jed went along in good humour. He told Laura that Hounslow West didn't have much to offer in the way of art galleries. He liked the size of them. He had never seen rooms so big. He liked the seriousness of them, and the way people didn't raise their voices. He didn't know much about the lifestyle of women like Laura, and was curious that they should sit in rooms like these for hour upon hour looking at pictures. He neither envied them, nor aspired to be one of them; but that didn't mean he didn't enjoy this new dimension to his life, like a botanist might enjoy the discovery of a new species of plant.

They might be found – Laura and Jed – sitting close together on a low leather bench – in the Turner Room extension at the Tate, for example. Laura would sigh with pleasure.

'You see how Joseph Mallord William Turner has broken free of every convention that might have stifled him. He was the precursor of the impressionists, Jed. Painting for him wasn't just about getting the lines right. It wasn't about getting the lines right at all. It was about sharing his vision with us, taking us into his world with him. They called him "the painter of light", Jed, and when he died, his last words were, "God is light".'

'I thought God was love,' said Jed.

'Light, love,' said Laura whimsically. 'Doesn't it all boil down to the same thing in the end?'

'Would you like to live in a world where everything was light and love, Laura?'

Laura paused. 'I don't think so,' she said. 'If everything was all light and love, it wouldn't mean much. I've spent rather too much of my life bathed in light and love. It can get awfully cloying, you know.'

'No, I don't know,' said Jed.

'You need the dark. I think that's why I love you, Jed. You're my dark side.'

Laura was always slightly worried she'd bump into a friend, so they would continue their conversation somewhere people didn't stare at them. Perhaps they might retreat to the café in the gallery itself or find one in an adjacent street. Laura would always have tea with lemon and Jed hot chocolate.

'I'm not dark,' said Jed.

'Why, yes you are! You come from a dark place!' insisted Laura.

'Is Hounslow West so much darker than Clapham South?'

'In a way, yes. Everyone's quite jolly in Clapham.'

'You mean, everyone's quite rich in Clapham.'

Laura laughed. 'Perhaps I do mean that.'

'But rich people can be dark,' suggested Jed.

'No one knows I have a dark side but you, Jed. Not even Hugo. Not even my closest friends. But I make sure I don't act on mine.'

'You being here with me, that's fucking dark, isn't it? Me being from a dark place and all that.'

'Dear Jed, it's the very opposite! To take you to these places, to show you how much beauty there is in the world … I think of myself as taking you *from* the dark *to* the light.'

'I don't know what kind of life you think I've had.'

Laura immediately thought of that horrible house and Jed's single bed in a row of four.

'Tougher than mine. And anyway, I'm not naïve. I don't know what you do at nights. Whatever it is, I can't imagine you paying tax.'

'Tax? What's tax got to do with anything?'

'Don't worry, I won't pry, I know you'd hate that. But just answer me straight, yes or no. Do you pay tax?'

'No,' said Jed immediately.

Laura looked victorious.

'What, I'm a dark person if I don't pay fucking tax?'

'It means you're not a regular guy. A Tory voter. Someone who cares what his taxes are being spent on …'

'What do you think I do at night, Laura?'

'Answer me this. Has anyone ever hit you in the middle of the night?'

'If I told you I'd been hit would I be dark?'

'I would say, yes.'

'That's ridiculous, Laura. Do you think old ladies who get mugged on their way home are dark?'

'Getting mugged is different from getting into a fight. And you, Jed, I suspect, get into fights.'

'I don't,' said Jed. 'Or not much.'

'I wasn't born yesterday, you know. Hugo says he bets you push drugs. And I confess, when I wash your clothes I sometimes smell them. And I absolutely know for a fact you've had cannabis in a pocket of your black jeans.'

'You look through my pockets?' said Jed, irritated.

'Not in a nosy way,' said Laura defensively. 'That's what you do, when you wash clothes, you take all the stuff out of the pockets, otherwise …'

'Okay, okay,' said Jed. 'I don't want you to wash my clothes any more.'

'But …'

'Forget it.'

'Oh Jed, what I meant is, I don't care what you do, it doesn't bother me! You know the question I hate most at dinner parties? "So Laura, what do you do?" I don't even feel I can say I'm a mum any more, now the kids go to boarding school. I don't want to be defined by what I *do*, I want to be loved for who I *am!* And I don't care what you do! I love you for who you *are!*'

'This dark side you love … You think I'm rough. You think I'm common. I don't deny it. I don't go to your fancy dinner parties. I don't say, "So, Laura, what do you do?" I think that's why you love me.'

'Of course I don't love you because you're common! What an awful word "common" is! Of course I don't. But it's true I love you because you don't label me. You let me be myself. If I were the most successful career woman who ever lived, I still wouldn't want to be defined by that.'

'What if I were a cashier at a bank and had a flat and a mortgage and was doing well for myself – and those are all things I might want, Laura, one day – you wouldn't love me then?'

'But you wouldn't want to be a cashier at a bank! I know you wouldn't!'

'Laura, I'm twenty, I have years to live. What do you want me to be?'

'Well!' said Laura, enchanted, looking at her lover square on. 'I imagine you doing something artistic. You know what? I think you'd make a fine sculptor! Have you ever in your whole life had a moment when you thought you might be a sculptor?'

Jed grimaced. 'Not this again,' he said. 'Why a fucking poncy sculptor?'

'Don't look like that! You must have played with Plasticine when you were little, and made little men with fat tummies and thin legs …'

'Laura, *you* made little men with fat tummies and thin legs. *I* fucking didn't.'

'That's probably because your mum didn't buy you Plasticine.'

'And you know what, if she had, I would have made planes and motorbikes …'

'There you go, Jed! I always knew you were creative.'

'Laura, *you* are the creative one, not me!'

Laura laughed it off, but thought to herself, 'Perhaps he's right.'

'Perhaps we should join an art class,' said Laura. 'It would be such fun, you and I!'

'Fuck, no,' said Jed.

'Or there's a series of lectures on the Bloomsbury Group, Tuesday lunchtimes, I noticed, running at the Tate. We've only missed one.'

'*We?* We're not a fucking *we*, are we?'

'You really are so marvellous, Jed. You're far better than any of those fey people in that ridiculous social set. No, we're not a *we!* I am an *I* and you are an *I*. Isn't that a wonderful thought?'

'Then you being an *I* should go along and enjoy yourself,' said Jed.

Laura was hurt, but managed to laugh. Nonetheless, she thought she might just go along.

Jemima and Leo thought their new lodgers were just the best. No longer did they spend their weekends at 'gatherings' at their friends' houses, no longer did they mooch away the hours doing nothing, sighing, moaning, the implication being that 'it's just so dull here!'; rather, the first question they asked when they came through the door on a Saturday afternoon was, 'Are Amy and Jed here?'

Laura had told the children that Jed was a friend of Amy's, not a boyfriend, but whose mum had thrown him out of their home because there was just not enough space for her new family. Both Amy and Jed were staying there 'temporarily' while looking for new places to live, but Leo and Jemima were always saying to them over Saturday suppers and Sunday lunches, 'Why don't you just live here forever?'

It was quite obvious that Jemima fancied Jed like mad and Leo was completely smitten by the lovely Amy. Hugo and Laura could even laugh about it together. They had found the recipe for parenthood: if you want your teenagers to behave well, shower often, watch their language and even be helpful in the kitchen, get yourself some good-looking lodgers.

On Saturday afternoons they would happily leave 'the young' snuggled up on the sofa together watching musicals starring Fred Astaire and Ginger Rogers. They would have a cup of tea together in the kitchen, and enjoy one or two of Laura's raisin bran biscuits – for Laura, among other things, had taken to baking again – and reminisce about when they were teenagers themselves. Hugo told Laura about the time he had lost his virginity to his thirty-year-old matron at school.

'Oh my God, what happened? Was she just incredibly sexy?'

'She *would* have been. She had this most amazing body. But she had a harelip. She tried to kiss me, but I wouldn't let her. That would have been horrible.'

'That is so *mean*, Hugo.'

'I suppose it was. But in a way, we were both doing each other a good turn.'

'Did you go on sleeping with her?'

'Right until I left school. I had other girls in the holidays. Nothing too exciting. A couple of girlfriends even, lasting about three months each, which is a lifetime when you're seventeen. But no one as good as Shona.'

'I can't believe you never told me about Shona.'

'Well, I'm not particularly proud of Shona. I think she loved me, in her way. It's quite brave to be a matron in a boys' school when you have a harelip.'

'God, how awful! Weren't the boys merciless?'

'We called her "Lippy" behind her back, which of course she would have known, and probably expected. But it was sexy, you know, Laura, sexy and sweet. Surgery closed at a quarter to two. If there was no one there and no one watching I slipped in and we just locked the door. There was a proper surgical couch. The first time I was still in my football kit with this bloody knee and she washed it clean. Then she put her hand down my shorts …'

'That's child abuse!'

'It was the most erotic thing that had ever happened to me. When she locked the door I knew just what would be expected of me. She let me undress her. In fact she let me do everything. Previously I'd been lucky to be allowed into a girl's bra. But she let me touch her all over, put my fingers up her. God, you have no idea what that feels like when you're fifteen! Talk about premature ejaculation.'

'You don't think Amy would ever …' said Laura, suddenly alarmed.

'Oh, God no! Amy's a nice girl. She's our guest, after all. Take my word, she wouldn't dream of it.'

'Well, that's a relief,' said Laura. 'More tea?'

'Yes, please,' said Hugo happily. 'Amy's thinking about having a tattoo. She can't decide between a dragon on her shoulder or a snake at the top of her thigh. She says she'll do what I tell her to. I like that in a woman. But perhaps I'll suggest what you think. You're a woman of superlative taste, darling. What should I tell her?'

'The snake on her thigh. Her inner thigh.'

Laura's tone was light but a wave of nausea rose up in her.

Hugo said, 'I never realised what a remarkable woman I've

married. Twenty years of bliss. Weren't we supposed to be renting the town hall this year for the jamboree of our lives? Don't tell me we completely forgot!'

'We did,' said Laura. It was all she could do not to be sick.

Hugo took her hands in his and said, 'Let's go to the George Cinq in Paris instead. Far more romantic.'

'Great,' said Laura, trying to sound keen. 'That would be really great.'

Then she told Hugo she was going to take a bath and ran away upstairs.

It was by now the middle of March and Laura was beginning to miss her old friends. Since that abysmal lunch with Arabella, she hadn't heard from anyone. She had just assumed that Arabella would have telephoned Ann and Rachel to tell them all about it, quite how miserable she was about Hugo, and how she'd had an unhappy love affair of her own.

Laura couldn't bear to be on the receiving end of others' sympathy. Her role in life, rather, was to give it. No friend could have been more loyal, more loving, than Laura when Arabella had lost her leg in the skiing accident. When Ann's twins were born, and Laura's own children were at school, she was there for her, helping her feed them, bathe them, and play with them when they got a little older. But being pitied made her feel like a victim. And she wanted to put that right. The Glass family had never been happier: that's what she wanted to show the world, and that's why she decided to plan the dinner party of dinner parties. She would invite Rachel and Jerry up to London for the weekend, and give a dinner party for all her closest friends. And this time, she wouldn't tell her children to keep out of the way, but show them off. Jed and Amy would be guests of honour. Mix the ages, mix the social classes, let everyone breathe the same sweet fresh air as the Glass family! The party was also a sort of revenge for their ever having doubted her.

If Arabella hadn't already poisoned Rachel against her, she was quite sure she'd be the most sympathetic. After all, on the day her life changed forever, Monday, the ninth January, hadn't she made it clear that Jerry was sleeping with the black models he used in Senegal? And that she didn't mind because she knew that Jerry still loved her? Mightn't they therefore be the very couple to take into their confidence? For Laura was longing to share her discovery with the world: nuclear families were dull, they festered, their ordinariness killed them.

When she rang, Jerry picked up the phone.

'Jerry! How lovely to hear you,' Laura enthused. 'You're back at last from your travels.'

'I am,' said Jerry.

Laura wanted to say, 'Is it true you sleep with your models but that only makes your marriage the stronger?' but actually said, 'Have you had a lot of snow this winter? My parents were saying they've been snowed in.'

'A fair bit,' said Jerry. 'Enough for a toboggan run or two.'

'Oh Jerry, have you been out tobogganing? You lucky thing!'

'Rachel, too. We've been having a rum old time. I finally got round to making an old design of mine, complete with metal runners.'

'Oh Jerry! You are *so* clever with your hands! When did you get back from Senegal?'

'Six weeks ago now. And I have an exhibition in another six.'

'Tell me, Jerry, do you pick your models because their faces are interesting or beautiful?'

'What is interesting *is* beautiful, don't you think?'

Laura wanted to ask: 'What, do you make love to *old* women, too?' But said, 'Oh Jerry, you are so wise. And reassuring for those of us who are growing older by the moment. And I am just *longing* to see you. Would you and Rachel be able to come and stay in two or three weeks from now? Say, the weekend of the eighth?'

'Not me, I'm afraid, I won't have the time. Rachel's not here at the moment. But I know she'd say yes. I'm not good company when I have a deadline. I'll get her to ring you.'

When they had said their goodbyes, Laura thought to herself, God, Jerry, you really do have your cake and eat it, don't you! All those women. And the thought of Hugo being *normal*, being just as nature intended, pleased her. She never did bother to go to the Tate lectures on Bloomsbury, but she'd read through the brochure many times and understood this: they lived their lives authentically, not as convention would have them live it. And if they loved, they didn't resist, whatever the consequences.

Jerry was right, Rachel was overjoyed to be coming up to London, not least because her daughter Clara was on her way home from Manchester for the Easter holidays, and Clara could catch up with Jemima. When Rachel had lived in London as a single mother, their daughters had been best friends despite their three-year age gap.

'What a relief it'll be to talk to someone who will actually *understand!*' thought Laura. 'At last the time has come to confide in a wise and trusted friend!'

But while Rachel, she was sure, would enjoy discussing all her new bohemian ideas, Arabella and Ann were a different matter. They must never learn the truth. Amy was the children's hairdresser, fallen on hard times. Jed was her friend. Well, these straight types must be fed a straight story.

Laura hadn't spoken to Arabella since their lunch together two months previously. She sat by her phone, took a few deep breaths, and dialled her number. She apologised for not being in touch sooner, but then didn't let Arabella get a word in edgeways. How busy she'd been! How many galleries she had visited! She had rekindled her love of art, and was reading some really good books on the subject. Anyway, she had suddenly realised how badly she had been neglecting her old friends and was determined to put it right. Could she come to dinner on the eighth of April? Rachel was coming up from Somerset, Clara would be there too, she hadn't phoned Ann yet but hoped that the whole gang would be there together …

Arabella asked how Hugo was and Laura completely ignored her, or rather, she didn't even hear the question. She went on and on, how she was in such a 'good space' at the moment, how happy she was 'in her skin'. ('*Dans ma peau,* as the French say, Arabella.')

Then when the conversation was at an end, she was conscious that Arabella had been rather frosty towards her. These bitter types! There was no pleasing them. But at least Arabella said she could come, that was one thing. If only she could find a *man* for Arabella, how she'd tried over the years! Perhaps Ann knew someone she could invite. And at least, one could rely on Ann to be friendly. Having paced her kitchen a couple of times, she dialled again.

'Ann!' she gushed. 'It's been *ages* since we saw you. We had such a lovely dinner party with you at the end of January, and I don't think I ever wrote to thank you. I've been feeling terribly guilty, you know …'

'Please don't worry about that, the important thing is you enjoyed …'

'Now, Ann, we were wondering if you and Patrick could come and have dinner with us on the eighth? And also the glorious Gloria in the silver dress. Hugo was quite taken with her. Do you think she could be persuaded to wear it again? Doctors aren't what they used to be, are they? I think I shall surprise Hugo, I won't warn him. Do you have her telephone number, Ann? And do you know any bachelors? Any age. Did I tell you that my party is for all ages? Actually, your children aren't quite old enough …'

'Are you all right, Laura?' said Ann.

'What do you mean, am I all right?'

'You're speaking so quickly. You're not on any …'

'Of course I'm bloody well not taking pills! You always think I'm drugged up, don't you?'

'That's not fair, Laura!'

'Well, can you come or not? And are you going to give me Gloria's number?'

Ann made a note to warn Gloria and gave Laura her number. But she told her that Arabella had gone through her list of bachelors one by one and now it was her turn to find Arabella a mate. Then she hung up, only briefly thanking her for the invitation.

Laura paced again, infuriated. Then she phoned Ann again. Engaged. She rang Arabella, just to check. Engaged. For God's sake, what was wrong with these friends of hers? How she loathed this back-stabbing they insisted on indulging in. She was beginning to feel she could trust nobody.

But the show must go on. Rachel at least would be coming to support her. Who else could she invite? She certainly wasn't going to invite any of those awful women she had lunch with. They were such sticks-in-the-mud! If Ann wasn't going to come up with any bachelors, well, then she must find some herself. She decided it was about time to approach her admirers up and down the street. For the next few days she was all smiles at a quarter to eight in the morning. She went up to every fan in turn and said, 'Isn't it about time we met each other properly? We're having a dinner party on the eighth of April. Incidentally, are you married?'

In the end, Ronnie the accountant couldn't come, nor could lanky Mike, but George could, and that was the important thing. Mid-thirties, IT, average height, brown hair which was slightly receding (but never mind). Room for improvement but definitely worth the investment. Then there was a couple in their fifties. Not that she'd known Mark was married when she'd invited him. For an older man, Mark was rather attractive, she thought. A solicitor. Well, who knows? Perhaps he had a dumpy wife and would hit it off with Arabella. For generous-hearted Laura wanted everyone to know the delights of love, and even when she rang Gloria, she praised George as though they had been best friends for years, saying, 'Gloria, you really must meet him!'

Laura consulted recipe books for days. She was beginning to love cooking: it made her feel creative, useful, loving. At first, she wanted an Indian theme, and set about buying the ingredients for a Goan fish curry: fresh ginger, chillies, garlic and coconut milk. But she found so many recipes that by the time she'd plumped for one, the fish had gone off and she had to start again. Then she decided to keep it simple: a slow-cooked Bolognese sauce with fresh pasta quills. But no sooner was the sauce made than she thought, 'I don't look like I've tried hard enough!' and she put it in the freezer. Finally she decided on a selection of Moroccan dishes: homemade hummus, tagine of lamb and tabbouleh with fresh mint.

Laura was quite determined to be the queen of the occasion. The hours she'd spent trying on more than twenty dresses that hung in her wardrobe! And she wasn't thinking of Jed as she did so. She knew Jed loved her, she had nothing to prove to him. Oddly, the woman who had been obsessing her wasn't even dear, pretty Amy, so anxious to please. It was Gloria, the woman who had so upstaged her at Ann's dinner party in a silver dress. Gloria, who was purportedly a doctor! Gloria, on whose arm, according to Arabella, Hugo had scribbled his work number angling for a game of squash. A game of squash! I'll give her a game of squash.

It's strange, thought Laura, how you do things and you don't even know why. If Gloria hadn't accepted her invitation – 'to meet someone I think you'd love' (though poor George had barely dared smile at her since he'd agreed to come), Laura would have dressed down (a skirt, perhaps, with a linen shirt) for Rachel and Clara's sake. But there was an argument still to be had on the Gloria front; there was something she had never settled. Laura's worst instinct won through: she would so outshine this silver woman that Hugo would wonder why he'd ever even given her a second glance.

'Why did I invite her anyway?' Laura mused as she put on a dress that was straight out of a children's illustrated book, perhaps something that Guinevere might wear while out flirting with Lancelot. In fact, the dress had been made for her for her wedding day, in keeping with the May Day theme. She'd worn it when she and Hugo had been driven away in a horse-drawn carriage to begin their honeymoon. For some reason, it had always seemed a little *de trop* for Laura, and she had never worn it since. But now it seemed to her that her life was beginning again, so why not celebrate by wearing something completely unsuitable?

The dress was close-fitting, in turquoise satin. No, she hadn't put on a pound since she was twenty-one. The sleeves were like large bells rimmed with rabbit fur, as was the square neckline, also edged with fur. It was so long that Laura had to wear her highest heels to make sure the fur hem kept well clear of the floor and didn't get ruined. Again, she felt anxious that it was just too over the top, but only for a moment or two. It seemed to her that life was this exquisite thing that you should grasp, while you still could. Her new motto would be 'why not?' And Laura danced in front of the mirror in her Guinevere dress and sang out, 'Why not? Why not?' And that, without a drop of wine.

There were other, more wicked ways, in which Laura conceived her party. It was not as innocent an occasion as she pretended. Wearing a pretty dress was one thing; Laura was always one for pretty dresses. But if Laura had been honest with herself, which she wasn't, she would have understood that she wanted to hurt Amy even more than she wished to upstage Gloria. In her ingenious seating plan, she had put Gloria next to Hugo (who was at the top of the table) but opposite poor Amy, who'd never done any harm to anyone, but who would watch as the love of her life made eyes at someone else. And she had put Jed next to Rachel, because no one else could possibly understand what a gem he was.

But Laura did not know herself as well as she might. Laura saw herself as the Great Equaliser, creating a space where young and old, rich and poor would gather together and *party!* Of course, she had to reign supreme, though even this she didn't quite acknowledge. But her guests were equals, she would make sure of that. She was through with the boxed-up existence of forty-one years, where everyone lived to a pre-ordained script. Behave, work hard at school, work hard again, be a perfect wife and mother all within the tiny perimeters of your social class, and be faithful till you die. What kind of an adventure was that? This party was the trumpet call: Laura Glass has broken free!

❖

Laura never realised that no one was looking forward to her dinner party but her. Hugo always dreaded these dinners and kept a low profile. Rachel had been promised a dinner 'with the whole gang' but had been given no idea of Laura's grandiose plans. Gloria said that she was 'delighted to accept' and Laura saw no reason to disbelieve her. George's greetings in the morning were less effusive than they used to be: his natural shyness was slowly and surely giving way to abject terror. Mark tried to retract and explained to her one morning that his wife Sarah had wanted them to go up to Northumberland that weekend to visit a dying aunt. But Laura had said, 'Why don't you bring her along, too? Everyone's welcome!' and then promptly forgot that any conversation had taken place. Amy confided in Laura that she was worried she wouldn't be able to keep up with the conversation, and Jed was the most difficult of all of them. Jed needed a whole afternoon to be persuaded that the house wouldn't be invaded by 'twats'.

It was the Friday before the party, a couple of hours before Laura would be heading up to Bedales to fetch the children for the Easter holidays. The house was still, they had been making love, and sunlight was streaming through the window. They lay in each other's arms, but Laura's bliss was tempered by anxiety.

'I'm sorry you have to go up to the kids' floor,' she said. 'But it'll just be for a couple of nights. You will just *love* Rachel, I know you will. She's my oldest friend, and she has a lovely daughter, Clara, who's a good friend to Jemima. But they're going on Sunday, and then you can come back here again.'

'No problem, Laura,' said Jed, stroking her hair.

'But Jed, will you be all right? There's only one bathroom for the four of you.'

'Of course I'll be okay,' said Jed.

'You like tartan, don't you? The bedspread's tartan, and the curtains are tartan.'

'I like tartan.'

'And you know it's incredibly important that the kids don't find out about us. You know how brilliant you are with them at weekends?

That's what it's got to be like for three weeks, Jed. No flirting allowed! Not a wink.'

'I know that, Laura. We've been through that.'

'I shall miss you, you know.'

'And I'll miss you.'

Laura relaxed a little, and snuggled into Jed's side. 'I know you don't want to go to this dinner party tomorrow,' she said, tentatively. 'But it would make a real difference to me if you came.'

'I'm no good in company,' said Jed.

'But I'm sure you are …'

'I don't like company.'

'But you like people! They're only people!'

'I don't like people. I like you, Laura, I really like you. And I like your family.'

'I know it sounds ridiculous, Jed, but it matters so much to me that you come. And Jemima's going to kick up a terrible fuss if you're not there.'

'I'll think about it,' said Jed.

Then Laura disentangled herself from Jed's arms and knelt on the floor beside him.

'I beg you,' she said.

'I can't promise, but I'll try.'

'*Try?* Are you going somewhere?'

'Hugo said to avoid you on one of your party days.'

'Hugo did? Are you really getting on that well with him?'

'He's a decent bloke, Laura. I like him. You fucking married him. You should know that already.'

'I tell you what. We're sitting down to dinner at nine. Will you be there for that? Please promise me!'

'I can't think why you want me there. You'll see for yourself what fucking lousy company I am. I'll be there for you and Jemima. I promise.'

Jemima and Leo were furious with their mother for completely spoiling their first weekend of the holidays when all they wanted to do was eat pepperoni pizza and watch *Ghostbusters* with Jed and Amy. They had a difficult journey home, complete with the sulks and tantrums that Laura had hoped were a thing of the past.

'I've been telling you about this party for weeks,' said Laura. 'In fact, in a way I'm actually giving the party for *you*. Haven't you always hated it when I tell you to keep out of the way, when I tell you to keep in your bedrooms, when I forbid you even to watch TV? Now, you're old enough to join us. Think of it as a coming-of-age party. And Clara's going to be there. And Jed and Amy.'

'Jed told me he's wasn't coming,' said Jemima. 'He says he hates that kind of thing. And so do I.'

'Jed told you that, did he?' said Laura.

'Thank God the children are both sitting in the back,' she thought, 'or they'd notice how I'm trembling. Keep calm, keep calm, keep your eye on the road!'

'Jed hates it when people get together,' continued Jemima.

'Come on, Jemima, you love parties!'

'When it's with people of my own age, Mum. When there's good music. When there's dancing. Not with a whole load of boring farts like you.'

'So you think Clara's a boring fart, do you?'

'No, she's not. But she'll think you are.'

'What if I promised you that you'll sit next to Jed?'

'He's not coming, I told you.'

'Well, he promised me this afternoon that he would.'

Jemima was finally silenced.

'And I was thinking, why don't you four go off this evening and see *Star Wars*?'

'Yes!' exclaimed Leo.

'And by the way, Jed and Amy will be joining you on the third floor tonight.'

Laura saw in the car mirror her children doing a hi-five.

'Disaster averted,' she thought, happily.

Laura wasn't surprised that Hugo had warned Jed to give her a wide berth on her party days. The occasional dinner parties they gave had never been much fun for either of them, and they often wondered why they bothered. At other times, Laura took on a party as though it were a salaried job and her assessment was due. Laura's fridge would turn into an uber-efficient filing cabinet: the top shelf for a starter, two middle shelves for the main course, and pudding on the bottom shelf, all of which were safe and sound under cling film at least the day before. Even the vegetables were boiled in advance and re-heated in the microwave. But this was a party with a difference. It represented nothing short of the reinvention of the Glass family. Even when Laura had had to abort her Goan fish curry, her good mood remained undented. Rather, she saw it as a lesson: don't live your life for the future, or something will go rotten right under your nose!

Even changing the linen on all the beds early that Friday evening – a task she didn't normally relish – was fun to do with Amy, who was as uptight about the whole weekend as Laura was excited. They chatted about this and that, a difficult customer who'd refused to pay in the morning because she wasn't satisfied with the colour of the hair dye, a new pair of velvet pumps she'd bought especially for the party, that sort of thing. Then they'd ordered takeaway pizzas (that was Jemima's idea) and the young went off to the cinema while Hugo and Laura slumped in front of the TV to watch their favourite sitcom *Men Behaving Badly*, and half of not a very good film, while they waited for their guests to arrive.

When they finally did, it all fell a bit flat. Clara arrived at nine and was disappointed not to see Jemima. She was also slightly concerned that her mum hadn't arrived yet. They all had a hug and Laura told Clara how pretty she was looking and how the stud in her nose suited her so well, and how clever she was to be reading mathematics. Then the conversation dried up and Laura encouraged her to join them on the sofa and watch the film. Rachel's arrival was, if anything, even more of an anti-climax. Laura's greeting to her was utterly heartfelt, of course it was, but after enquiring after Jerry and her studio extension, no one knew quite what to say next. Everything that Laura wanted to say was for Rachel's ears only, and she kept it back. Then when Rachel was hugging her daughter she noticed that her lustrous black hair, for which she had always been so famous at school, was beginning to go grey at the temples, and she wondered whether when they were alone together the next day she might mention it and send her along to Toni & Guy's in the afternoon. Or perhaps there were simply some things you shouldn't say, even to a best friend. It might be that Rachel hadn't noticed. Now that would be embarrassing. Or would it be helpful? Or perhaps she was one of those modern women who just didn't care. The truth was, everyone was tired. There'd been an accident on the A303 and a long and wearisome diversion, and Rachel leapt at the chance of 'an early night' the moment Laura offered it to her.

But when Saturday morning came and the weather was fine, Laura's energy and optimism resurfaced once more, and she didn't give Rachel's grey temples a second thought. When the house was finally empty – Amy at work, Jed and Hugo on their mysterious errands, and the children still fast asleep, Rachel and Laura embraced in their dressing gowns and set about drinking coffee and eating toast.

'Oh my God, Rachel,' began Laura, 'I'm so pleased you were able to come. It was hard enough last night not to spill out all over you. Did you sleep well? I have so much to tell you. I don't know where to begin.'

'Well, whatever you're doing, Laura, it suits you. You look amazing, not a day older than twenty-seven. And I've never known you so … so happy!'

'I don't think I've ever been so happy! But let's talk about you first. How's art restoration nowadays? How's Jerry?'

'Good and good, busy and busy, that's all there is to say about us, Laura. Clara, too, has loved her first two terms at Manchester. But I'm on tenterhooks! What's been going on these last few months? I don't recognise you!'

'Well, you are partly to blame, you know, you and your free-thinking ideas. What if I tell you straight: we are *both* turning a blind eye!'

Laura sat, back straight, head up, proud and joyful.

'Good God, Laura, you don't mean …'

'Yep! Now, you're not allowed to breathe a word of this to Ann and Arabella! I must say, I'm not sure why I invited them tonight …'

'You haven't fallen out with them, have you?' Rachel looked concerned.

'They are such sticks-in-the-mud sometimes. Ann has become *so* conventional, but she has these young daughters and so I forgive her. But Arabella is so angry with me nowadays. I don't know what I've done to deserve it, I must say. She wrenches the truth out of me and then accuses me …'

'What is this truth?'

'Am I getting ahead of myself again? Jed, that fair-haired young man you brushed by on the stairs last night when you went to bed, what do you think of him?'

'Why, what am I supposed to think of him?'

'Come on, you must have had some opinion?'

'Good-looking, I suppose. Young. But then everyone's young nowadays.'

'I thought I heard you wish him "goodnight"?'

'And?'

'And didn't I hear him say, "goodnight" back to you? Didn't he say that?'

'He might have done. But what are you saying, Laura?'

'I hoped you might have been more perceptive than that.'

'What is it that I am supposed to have perceived? Oh Laura, Laura, no!'

'Yes, Rachel, yes!' said Laura triumphantly. 'Jed is my lover!'

'Oh God. Not your lover.' Rachel sighed. 'What, and he lives in your house?'

'But I thought you'd be pleased for me. You said yourself that you'd never seen me happier, and it's true, I can't sleep for happiness.'

'Insomnia's not good.'

'Well, I make up for it in the afternoons. Shall I tell you how I creep into his bed in the early afternoon?'

'No, don't tell me. I'd rather not know.'

'But Rachel, I've just been so longing to tell you! I have to share my secret with someone!'

'Is this why you've fallen out with the others?'

'Who told you I'd fallen out with them? Don't tell me you've been gossiping, too!'

'Arabella suspects something, Ann doesn't. But they are your *friends*, Laura. *Our* friends. It's natural we should talk about you. They're concerned. We're all concerned.'

Suddenly Laura looked as if the sky had fallen in. Rachel took hold of Laura's hand across the kitchen table and said, 'Hugo's a good man, Laura.'

'But Hugo's got Amy!' snapped Laura, taking her hand back. 'Why should I care about Hugo?'

Rachel began to pull at her thick, dark hair, a habit she'd had since her schooldays when the going got tough.

'Amy? Who in the world is Amy?' she said.

But Laura's tone was light and breezy. 'Ah, you've not met Amy yet, have you? You might have spotted her last night when they got back from the cinema. Did you notice?'

'I can't say I did,' mumbled Rachel.

'You've already missed her this morning. She works on a Saturday. She's a hairdresser. Toni & Guy's, Oxford Street. She's terribly sweet and helpful. She'll be back about half past six. In fact, she's doing my hair tonight, and Jemima's, and I'm sure she'll do yours if you ask her, though I'm not sure she'll have time to do Clara's.'

'But isn't Amy the hairdresser who's staying here a while because her boyfriend threw her out on to the street?'

'That's the story, of course.'

'So Jed's not even Amy's friend?'

'Oh, they're probably friends by now. They seem to get on rather well. And that's the point, Rachel, we all get on well here. Even the children, I can't tell you how improved they are. No more grouchy teens in this household, thank God.'

'Whatever happened to the girl with the golden plait? Is she history?'

'That *is* Amy! She's just had a new hairstyle, that's all. But listen, the others don't know that. You, as my privileged friend, get to know the truth.'

'Oh my God,' sighed Rachel, leaning back in her chair and pulling at her hair with renewed vigour. 'But your kids must know what's going on.'

'They certainly don't. Hugo and I completely agree about this: they must never find out.'

'I bet you they suspect. Kids aren't fools, you know.'

'They do not! They haven't an inkling. I wish you could see what good friends they all are … how they sit together, watching movies, playing games …'

'How do you know that's all they're doing?'

'Of course I know! That's obscene what you're insinuating. They're not paedophiles, Rachel. Amy's a sweetheart, Leo's only *just* fifteen.'

'And Jemima?'

'I hate to break this to you, but Jed loves *me!*'

'I'm quite sure he does, Laura. But men are men. Sixteen isn't young for nowadays.'

'I promise you, Jed hasn't even noticed her in *that* way. And Jemima didn't even get her period till last year. She's a babe in arms.'

'If you say so, Laura.'

'Judge for yourself! Amy and Jed will be having supper with us tonight. As will our kids, as will Clara. Young and old together. As it should be.'

'I'm of the old school, I'm afraid. Young and young, middle-aged and middle-aged.'

'I'm astonished at you, Rachel. Didn't you live on kibbutz after you left school?'

'A kibbutz is quite different from what I'm seeing here, I assure you.'

'You told me Jerry sleeps with his models, of all ages, from all backgrounds. I've seen the paintings, Rachel. I've also spoken to him on the phone about it. I asked him whether he preferred to paint faces which were traditionally beautiful, or older faces that were interesting, and he told me wisely that interesting faces *were* beautiful.'

'So do you conclude from that, Laura, that he shags everyone, young and old?'

'Well …' Laura tried to be tactful, tried to find the right words, but then gave up. 'You said it.'

'His models live in Senegal on the other side of the world. And I don't even know for certain that he sleeps with any of them. I don't ask. Perhaps because I don't really want to know.'

'But I think you should know. Be brave, Rachel, find out the truth. You'll only feel closer to Jerry if you do.'

'What's got into you, Laura?'

'We ought to be scientific about this, shouldn't we? If Jerry – who we all think the world of, right? – finds himself desiring women who are half his age …'

'Then that makes it okay for you and Hugo to have lovers half your age, is that the logic?'

'You're the one, Rachel, who made it okay, don't you see that? That great speech of yours about turning a blind eye. Well, I do turn a blind eye, night after night when Hugo creeps into Amy's bed …'

'Oh God, that's awful, I'm so sorry,' sighed Rachel.

'But don't you see, it's not awful, it's liberating. I do so wish you'd got here in time for supper last night, to see how normal and good everything is. Amy is such a treasure. She's so innocent and sweet-natured. She's like the perfect au pair that doesn't get under your feet.'

'And the same girl you found kissing your husband Hugo in a porch in South Molton Street, the girl who reduced you to hysteria?'

'But she's not a bad person, you know. In fact, she cut off that wonderful plait of golden hair for charity. That is exactly the kind of thing she does. Now she has a short black spiky crop. And she's sort of pale and winsome-looking. But what's the point of me describing her when you'll meet her tonight?'

'And what about you and Hugo, how are you two getting on?'

'Well, that's the best of it, never better!'

'I'm sorry, I simply don't believe that,' said Rachel. She broke off a corner of her cold toast and put it in her mouth.

'But you saw us together last night!'

'Well, yes, we all sat on the sofa watching *Newsnight*. I have to say, I didn't notice any startling differences in your relationship, which has always seemed a good one to me. I believe we watched *Newsnight* the last time we came to visit.'

'But that's exactly my point, Rach! We used to watch *Newsnight* before we had children. It's always helped Hugo wind down at the end of a busy day. Even the music has a soporific effect on him. But ever since we had children, particularly when they got to be teenagers and stayed up till God knows when, just sitting quietly on a sofa together is a rare treat. So, Rach, last night our four young people went off to the cinema together to watch *Star Wars*. Isn't that brilliant? Jemima and Leo wouldn't have dreamt of doing that on their own, and anyway, I wouldn't have let them, they're far too young. But Jed and Amy are like the most perfect babysitters. I felt, Rachel, as they trooped off to Clapham High Street, happy as Larry, that we must have done something right. Families can be so *claustrophobic*, don't you find? Certainly ours was, each of us living in our own private bubble of boredom.'

'That's not what it looked like from the outside. You weren't bored. That's never been your style, Laura. In fact, your family seemed perfect in every way. I've often regretted having only Clara in our lives. I'd have loved more, you know.'

'Ah, children!' sighed Laura. She smiled a world-weary smile, as though remembering a time when she was less enlightened. 'They're great when they're small, I'll grant you that. They depend on you for everything, they add purpose to your life. But when they get older and need you less, it's not the same, you know. I wouldn't say you've missed anything, really. But your Clara is a delight, I've always adored her. My favourite goddaughter by a mile.'

'Children broaden you. I don't believe in exclusive love-objects, as though the only thing in your life worthwhile is the romantic love interest ...'

'On that we are in one hundred per cent agreement,' smiled Laura. 'Exclusivity kills life, or at least it dulls it. What a routine, predictable life I've been living until this year. I can't believe that I ever thought it was any fun at all. I have never felt more *full*, Rach. I feel I have arms and legs and fingers and toes and I don't know what I shall do next. In fact, I'm thinking of joining an art class. Remind me, Rach, am I totally untalented?'

'We all have talent,' said Rachel, but without enthusiasm.

'Look, I can tell, you have absolutely no faith in me.'

'I have always had faith in you. We're friends, right?'

'Friends, friends ...' began Laura, dismissively. 'Friends can be tricky, I've discovered.'

'And when they are, you drop them.'

'I do not! My three best friends since the age of sixteen are coming to dinner tonight. Does that sound like I'm being disloyal?'

'You've never told any of us what exactly happened in January this year. We rang each other daily, did you know that? We were worried for you, Laura. But it turns out you were just having sex with a boy half your age. I suppose sex trumps friendship.'

'I never thought I would say this, I, of all people, but yes: the world is right! Sex trumps everything. But that doesn't mean to say my friends are not totally dear to me.'

'Sex has so much to answer for,' said Rachel, sourly.

'Oh Rachel, dear Rachel! I can't tell you how much I used to agree with you. So often sex has seemed a chore to me, something I've gone along with to please Hugo. In a weird sort of way, I used to think it would stop him from being unfaithful. If he were getting his oats at home, I reasoned, he wouldn't be looking to get them somewhere else. And then I discover he's been shagging everything that moves anyway.'

'And if you can't beat 'em, join 'em.'

'But I love Jed,' Laura said, with some passion. Then hearing her own voice resounding rather loud, she looked anxiously at her watch and the kitchen door at the same time. Eleven o'clock: Leo and Jemima would be drifting in for breakfast any time soon.

'So how is good sex different from long-term, married sex?'

Laura paused to think. She closed her eyes and imagined herself lying next to Jed at two in the afternoon, waiting to be transported.

'Good sex is naughty,' she said. 'You shouldn't be doing it.'

'No, you shouldn't,' said Rachel.

When Jemima breezed in, she was looking quite as radiant as her mother. That was because during the film she had given Jed her hand to hold and he had taken it. And better still, he had given her the kiss of her life outside the bathroom at one in the morning. Jemima had known one or two fleeting snogs during the slow songs at friends' birthday parties, but never with someone she fancied like she fancied Jed. They had kissed for a full half-hour, Jed even suggesting she come to his bedroom, or he to hers, but she knew what that might mean and resisted. She hardly knew Jed. Jed was Amy's friend, anyway. Her mother had always taught her, and Jemima believed, that sex was something you waited for, something that happened only when a relationship was well established. If she started having sex with Jed, and her mum found out, her mum would kill her.

Rachel recognised the signs the second she set eyes on her. Jed and Jemima were already lovers. Thank God she lived in Somerset and wouldn't be around to see the fallout when Laura got wind of it. Jemima had grown into a beauty, just like her mother, but there was a youthful, otherworldly glow about Jemima, which was quite absent in her friend. Even *in extremis* Laura was somehow too good to get thoroughly carried away. She wouldn't have let herself, at least not the Laura she knew. Jemima, meanwhile, seemed to be living half in a dream, from which only this boy was not barred.

'Did you remember the Greek yoghurt, Mum?' she said, ignoring their guest altogether.

'Jemima, you've grown so tall!' exclaimed Rachel, standing up from the table to greet her.

'But she's still not *quite* as tall as me, are you, darling?' said Laura giving her daughter a peck on the cheek.

Jemima ignored the peck and said, 'I bet you forgot. You forget everything nowadays.'

'Darling, there are a dozen of us for dinner tonight and I've been cooking all week and will be cooking all afternoon … but I think there's some sort of yoghurt in the fridge …'

Jemima found a pot in the large pink Smeg fridge and said, 'Lucky for you!' She dolloped some into a bowl and began adding a selection of dried fruits, nuts and seeds.

'Very healthy. I'm impressed,' said Rachel when Jemima sat down at the table opposite her. 'Clara still eats Sugar Puffs.'

Jemima looked at her scornfully but said nothing.

'How's school going, Jemima? Have you decided what you're doing for A Levels yet?'

Laura noticed how well they were getting on and went upstairs to change.

'Drama, I should think. English. I want to do psychology but they don't do psychology at Bedales.'

'So you're interested in people, are you?'

Jemima didn't look up from her yoghurt. 'I s'pose,' she said.

'And what sort of people interest you?'

Jemima shrugged but said nothing.

'Are you interested in children?' ventured Rachel.

'Not really.'

'What about madness?'

'Yeah, I s'pose.'

'Do you think people are born mad, or do they go mad?'

Jemima thought for a few seconds and said, 'They go mad.'

'I think you're right. But what makes them go mad?'

Jemima made a strange *prrr* sound and went on eating her yoghurt.

'What about homeless people? Do you think they become homeless because they're mad, or become mad once they're homeless?'

'Hey listen, it's really early for this kind of conversation. Ask me later, okay?'

'I will, Jemima. I hear you're going to be joining us at dinner. There's going to be "young and old" tonight, so your mother tells me.'

Jemima's body slouched over the table in a gesture of superlative boredom.

'I take it you're not all that keen on that idea.'

Jemima looked up, and put her empty yoghurt bowl on one side. She looked like she was trying hard to remember what Rachel was on about, and Rachel couldn't be bothered to remind her.

By eight o'clock that evening, the home team were ready for festivities to begin. Hugo was wearing a lovat-green linen suit; Leo had begrudgingly swapped his filthy *American Dream* sweatshirt for a clean denim shirt with buttons. Amy wore drain-pipe trousers in black velvet and a glittery bolero from the Portobello market. Laura lent Jemima a dress of her own – a sleeveless dress in grey silk with large red roses – and was delighted when Jemima consented to wear it. She did so because the cleavage was low and she wanted to show it to Jed. Rachel didn't dress up at all, complaining she's been led to believe this would be a kitchen supper with her old school friends and she hadn't brought anything smart. Her daughter Clara wore jeans and a white T-shirt, but looked great, her sandy hair tied loosely back and pretty daisy studs in her ears. Laura had offered her goddaughter the pick of her wardrobe: Clara had declined, telling her she would keep her mum company and be low-key.

Laura certainly made an impact when she walked into the kitchen. Only Amy, who'd been doing her hair, knew what to expect. Laura looked around at their astonished faces, which might have seemed threatening if Amy hadn't reassured her that she looked really lovely. She looked at Rachel, whose mouth hung open. 'Just promise me, Rachel, be honest. Is this a bit much?' But Laura was pleased when the doorbell went. She was in no mood for her friend's too sober opinion.

Arabella, Ann and Patrick were the first guests to arrive, and Hugo offered them a glass of champagne from his tray. Laura immediately suspected that they'd been spending the afternoon together gossiping about her but felt sufficiently confident not to care. In fact, she enjoyed the fact that they thought they knew so much about her and yet would have no notion that their hosts' lovers would be their fellow guests. She even looked up at Hugo to smile conspiratorially at him, and Hugo smiled back.

Rachel was so happy to see her old school friends she visibly relaxed. She took them to a corner of the kitchen where almost immediately they fell into thick chatter about everything. Patrick hovered near them, looking rather ill at ease, and kind Laura made a beeline for him with her plate of Moroccan delicacies, before joining her old gang.

'Laura, what a beautiful dress!' exclaimed Ann, generously. 'You look stunning!'

'Isn't that the dress you wore on your wedding day?' Arabella asked. 'And this fur here,' said Arabella, touching Laura's neckline and the edge of her sleeves, 'don't tell me it's real!'

'I'm afraid it is,' said Laura, good-humouredly. 'And I haven't worn it since because I'm terrified of being tarred and feathered for wearing it. But tonight I just couldn't resist. But no one blinked an eyelid in those days, I promise you. Everyone wore fur.'

'So, are you celebrating an anniversary of some sort?' Arabella's tone was aggressive. 'Of course, you've been married twenty years!'

'Not quite,' said Laura, quite unfazed. 'And no, this isn't an anniversary party. Hugo's taking me to Paris in May. This party is celebrating *you*, Arabella, or rather us, our friendship. And Ann, and Rachel. I've been longing to get us all together for months.'

But Ann was kindness itself. 'I can't believe you've not put on a pound since you got married. I still haven't shifted my baby weight.'

'You did insist on having twins!' laughed Laura.

'Does Hugo realise quite how lucky he is?' continued Ann.

'I don't think he's even noticed what I'm wearing! He never does, or if he has he hasn't said anything.'

'How can he not have noticed?' said Arabella. 'He needs punishing for not noticing. Hugo, we need you!'

Hugo was happy to be summoned. He had already spent five minutes with his three neighbours, whom he didn't even recognise when he let them in, and five minutes was already far too long. He glided across the floor, suave and generous, refilling their glasses with champagne.

'Now, we want to ask you,' said Ann. 'Have you noticed how ravishingly lovely your wife is looking tonight?'

'My wife always looks ravishing.'

Laura smiled happily.

'That's not good enough,' Arabella pitched in. 'Have you noticed her dress?'

Hugo looked hard. 'Is that real fur?' he said, eventually, feeling the rim of Laura's sleeve. 'I thought that stuff was banned nowadays.'

'You can't have forgotten!' said Ann. 'Your honeymoon night! Does that ring any bells?'

Hugo did his best to remember, failed, and lied, 'My God, Laura, when we danced to the silvery moon …'

'No,' said Laura, 'when we lay on our queen-sized bed in the Holiday Inn, Heathrow Airport, watching *A Fistful of Dollars.*'

'Great film, great music,' said Hugo, uncertain why this conversation was being had. 'And you were wearing that dress? You mean I didn't rip it off you? Is that what you women are complaining about?'

'We weren't complaining!' said Laura, defensively.

'Well, I am!' said Arabella. 'Are you honestly telling us, Hugo, that you spent your honeymoon night watching a lousy film?'

'We were living together, you know. After a year and a half ...' Hugo stopped in his tracks. 'Anyway, you're all witches and I'm separating you. Arabella, you're to come and meet our near neighbour, Mark, who's a solicitor. You can talk shop.'

'God save me from the legal profession, Hugo. Don't you think I see enough of them?'

'Surely, at your age, you know how to be polite, Arabella.'

Arabella did as she was told – it was not as bad as she feared, Mark was evidently an attractive man – and moments later Hugo had dragged the solicitor's wife back to the other witches and introduced her to them.

'This is Sarah,' he began. 'Sarah's a teacher at the local comprehensive, isn't that right?'

Sarah was a petite and serious redhead, who looked like she'd dressed for a school dance. She looked exhausted. Laura offered her a canapé and thought, 'How does someone so small control a class of thirty? Poor woman, she looks like she'd be happier tucked up in bed than be here.'

Ann said warmly, 'If I were you I'd try a falafel. They're just delicious!' But Sarah didn't know what a falafel was, and took a meatball instead. Laura thought, 'Is she ignorant or is she rude?' But Patrick managed to start up a conversation about education in our state schools today and Hugo managed to escape. Even Laura took sanctuary in her larder, and began to take the bowls of homemade hummus out of the fridge before adding a final flourish of chopped coriander.

After a few deep breaths Laura emerged again to re-join her party. Hugo, blast him, was gone. He only has one task, raged Laura, to keep everyone's glass full, and even that he can't do properly. But Ann and Rachel were talking nineteen to the dozen, Patrick and Sarah were still on the subject of education – should private schools be abolished? – (a bit political, worried Laura) and Arabella was looking more animated than ever talking to Mark. But George (oh poor,

poor George!) was standing near the door without so much as a drink his hand. He looked as forlorn as a dog waiting for his mistress, and when he caught sight of Laura coming out of the larder his whole demeanour relaxed. What more could she do but rush up to him, a plate of goodies in her hand, and bathe him in her good will?

'George!' she exclaimed. 'I am so pleased you made it! I just *love* the jacket you're wearing. And that yellow tie! It's made of silk, isn't it? It's the colour of a cornfield! But hasn't naughty Hugo offered you a drink yet? He really is quite useless!'

George took a mini-meatball as Laura rushed passed him, through the kitchen doors and into the hall. What she found in the sitting room did not amuse her.

Hugo, Amy, Leo, Clara and Jemima were squashed up on the sofa together knocking down glasses of champagne. Leo's arm was draped around Amy who was bearing it good-humouredly, but Hugo's, thank God, was not.

'Hugo,' said Laura coldly. 'What are you doing here?'

Hugo jumped up and looked guilty. 'Just having a little break, that's all. You know how it is.'

Laura didn't know whether to fall into his arms and say, 'Yes, let's just run away together you and I!' or reprimand him. In the event she didn't have to do either because the doorbell rang.

Jemima immediately stood up and looked at her watch, and then stood down again. It was a quarter to nine. 'Poor girl,' thought Laura. 'She really does have a bit of a crush on him!' It was still fifteen minutes till they could expect him. She couldn't imagine him being early.

Hugo, meanwhile, back in host mode and keen to escape any further nagging, went to the front door and let Gloria into the house. 'Oh my God, here she is,' thought Laura, and felt sick at heart. The truth was, what with one thing and another, she'd completely forgotten Gloria was coming. She was wearing a fuchsia pink silk shirt with a black skirt. 'How irritatingly *right*,' she thought to herself. 'How silly I feel in these stupid flouncy sleeves which I've already wet through in the sink, rinsing that stupid coriander. The fur will never be right again.'

Hugo, meanwhile, seemed unconditionally delighted, and ushered her into the sitting room where he'd been hoarding his tray of glasses and the champagne. He immediately gave Gloria a glass and said, 'Laura never told me you were coming! How lovely to see you again!'

She'd wanted Hugo to bring her straight into the kitchen, where she could keep an eye on things, but suddenly everything was too much for her. The minutes were ticking away and she was quite sure Jed wouldn't come. She walked back into the kitchen to the party proper without even reminding Hugo to bring back the champagne, only to find poor George exactly where she'd left him, still without a glass in his hand and looking more pathetic than ever. 'Oh George, this is terrible!' she said when she saw him. 'I'll fetch you a glass myself!' When she went back into the sitting room to fetch the tray, she had some satisfaction however. Amy was looking miserable.

Laura spent some minutes trying to make conversation with George. George merely sipped at his champagne. It had been hardly worth the effort of finding him a glass. Laura made up for it. Usually she barely drank at her own parties, but she was beside herself. One glass, two glasses. George was looking rather shocked at how the champagne was slipping down the throat of his beloved. Five past nine. Ten past nine. She kept looking towards the front door expectantly, only to return again to some laborious description of the company George worked for.

'Are you waiting for someone?' said George, finally.

'I'm afraid he's awfully late,' said Laura, looking at her watch for the nth time.

Hugo dashed back into the kitchen to open a couple more bottles of champagne and quickly filled everyone's glasses. He kissed his wife and said, 'You never said you had invited Gloria!' and promptly disappeared again with a bottle and a skip in his step.

'I hate dinner parties,' Laura thought to herself. 'No one likes them, I can tell. Why do we put ourselves through this torture, slaving away, cooking, polishing, setting out candles? As I look around me no one seems happy at all. Except Arabella and Mark, I suppose. And Ann and Rachel are still chatting. Perhaps it's not a complete failure.' And then she said to poor George, who really was doing his best, 'Would you mind if I waited in the hall? The bell sometimes doesn't work properly, and I'm worried I'll miss him. Why don't you go and talk to that nice man over there? His name's Patrick.' Laura waved at Patrick and more or less pushed George in his direction. Then she went off to pace the hall in peace. It was not a good move.

'So, Gloria, how are you?' she overheard Hugo say. 'How are you settling in to London life? They can't be working you too hard or you wouldn't be looking so damn gorgeous.'

It was obvious from Gloria's tone that she hadn't enjoyed the question. 'So which of these young people are your children?' she asked her host. 'Introduce me!'

'Leo, Jemima,' Hugo began in a voice that was almost bored, 'that's Clara, on the right, who's Jemima's old friend, and Amy's that one, who funnily enough is the kids' hairdresser and who's come to stay for a few weeks while she looks for a flat ...'

Poor Amy, listening to that jerk, thought Laura. She thought of rushing in to protect her. But Gloria saved the day. 'Funnily enough, I was looking for a flatmate,' she said.

'I think she's looking for a flat with people more her age, isn't that right, Amy?'

Laura was pacing in the hall, hands on hips. Hugo was truly abominable. She could bear it no longer. Gone was any sense of victory over this gentle girl, and she marched into the sitting room.

But Amy hadn't needed her. Her rage with her lover was palpable. 'Wow, I'd love to take a look round your flat!' she said, and Gloria gave Amy her phone number.

Laura watched while a remorseful Hugo tried to catch Amy's eye, but Amy resisted. At another time the scene might have sent Laura up to her bedroom in tears, this whole business was too terrible for words. But her desire for order, for normality was too great. She found herself saying 'Hugo, Amy, do you think you could give a hand? We're sitting down to dinner in a few minutes. Amy, do you think you could warm the pitta bread in the oven? Hugo, it's time we moved on to the Sancerre.' Laura spoke flatly, and continued on the same note. 'Hi Gloria, I'm pleased you could make it.'

Hugo laughed. 'She's bossy, isn't she, your mum?' Though in fact he wasn't addressing his children at all, but rather gave a pleading look to Gloria and Amy, which amounted to an apology for his wife's lack of *joie de vivre*.

Gloria was relieved to follow Laura into the kitchen and join the main party. 'Set me to work!' she said. 'How can I help?'

Laura had never seen Hugo look more miserable, more humiliated. That was some solace, at least.

A quarter past nine, it was time for everyone to sit down. Laura was trying so hard to keep chipper. She swore it would be the last party she ever gave. Her placement, over which she had struggled for days, was giving her no satisfaction. Even Mark's evident pleasure in Arabella would go nowhere, a) because he was already married, and b) because even if he wasn't he'd soon discover Arabella had a prosthetic leg. Because the truth was, the romantic, good-hearted Laura could see no good in anything if there wasn't at least the possibility of *living happily ever after*. Nonetheless, they both seemed happy to find their places and be able to continue their conversation.

Gloria and Hugo were sitting next to each other, to Hugo's delight and Gloria's dismay. Laura was watching them, and even felt for her husband when Gloria rather ruthlessly turned her back on him and looked to her right, where she found, to her horror, that she now had to contend with his adolescent son Leo. Laura had thought it would be fun for him to find himself next to a black beauty, but Leo was miserable not to be next to Amy, who was sitting diagonally opposite him, and from time to time he would send her a look of absolute adoration. She watched as both husband and son vied to get Amy's attention: Hugo's efforts were truly pathetic and Amy looked at him contemptuously. Her dear son, Leo, gosh, she hadn't realised how hopelessly smitten he was.

At twenty past nine Laura was sinking into her own private hell: Jed, she was quite certain, would not come. How gullible she had been to believe his promises. She began to wonder what he was doing, who he was with, whether he'd just forgotten about the time, or whether he'd been beaten up. She thought of the knife she'd seen in his room the previous evening when she'd been changing the beds. It hadn't alarmed her at all at the time. It was the sort of knife her father might have owned and used for pruning roses, with a nice wooden handle. But in her mind's eye it was rapidly becoming a flick-blade gangster's knife, and she wondered why she hadn't questioned him about it. No, she knew why not. Jed loathed her nosy questions, that was why. She had learnt not to pry. She had learnt just to let Jed be Jed.

She sat all alone at the head of her table, staring into a bowl of chrysanthemum flower-heads. What was the point of anything? Even her two admirers, who she'd strategically placed to the left and the right of her, turned out to be total duds, absorbed in conversations on the other side: Mark and Arabella were now chatting like old friends who hadn't seen each other in years, and George, it turned out, had taken exactly the same mathematics course as Clara at Manchester, and they even shared a few of the older lecturers.

In fact, Laura mused sadly, no one would even notice if she slipped away to watch a video in the sitting room, or better still go to bed and wash her hands of the whole occasion.

Half past nine. How could he let her down like this? Would she be angry with him? Would she reprimand him in the morning? Or what if he really was in some sort of danger? Or if he'd just decided to move out, because he'd been so irritated by her pathetic entreaties? The place between Jemima and Rachel gaped open. Jemima was looking distraught and said barely a word to anyone. When her neighbour Patrick asked her about school, she answered monosyllabically. Perhaps it wasn't such a good idea to mix the generations.

She could scarcely remember that wondrous time when she had felt so light, so full of joy, so certain of things. When now she felt as good as dead.

Then Jed came.

Jed of the leather jacket, Jed of the mouth that pouted like a cupid, Jed of the blue eyes that looked right through you. All the women looked up when he walked in.

He gave a polite wave, a shy smile.

'Hi,' he said.

'This is Jed,' said Laura, to the party. How hard it was for her to sound normal, but she managed it. 'There, Jed, I've put you between Jemima and Rachel, an old school friend of mine. You're just in time for the lamb tagine.'

Laura was thankful to stand up and be busy. Amy was immediately at her side asking what she might do.

'If you could just clear away the plates. Don't bother loading them in the dishwasher – pile them over there for now.'

Laura took away the bowl of hummus, covered it in cling film and put it back in the fridge. She switched on the microwave to warm the two large bowls of couscous she had prepared earlier. She noticed that people had stopped talking. Everyone was looking at Jemima feeding Jed fingers of her unfinished pitta bread dipped in olive oil.

'Jemima!' she said. 'What are you doing?'

'Jed is starving!' said Jemima.

'Jed?'

'Jemima's right. I'm starving.' Jed was holding his mouth open while Jemima popped the bread into it, finger by finger.

'Couldn't you have waited five minutes more?'

'No, Mummy, he couldn't,' said Jemima.

Some of the other guests tried to deflect attention from the pair by resuming former conversations, but the scene before them was somehow too engrossing.

Then Laura suddenly said, 'Please stop it, Jed, that's enough, the lamb's ready, please stop it.'

The two looked at her, defiant.

The whole party looked up at Laura waiting to see how she would react.

Some seconds passed.

Jemima was holding a bit of bread; she held it, not knowing whether she'd put it back down on to her plate, or hold it up to Jed's mouth.

Rachel gave her a look that said, 'Go on, be a good girl, Jemima, put it down.'

'Please, Jemima,' said her mother.

But Jed opened his beautiful mouth and Jemima popped the bread into it, just like that.

No one said a word. No one even dared look at their hostess, who was evidently on the point of breaking down in tears: one sympathetic look might just send her over the edge.

'I can't take any more of this,' Laura said. 'I'm so sorry.' She left the kitchen and ran upstairs.

Jemima and Jed stopped their game and looked guilty.

Rachel stood up and said, 'I'll go to her. It's been a long day.'

Then Hugo stood up, and said, 'No I'll go.'

Jed said nothing. He left the table and followed her.

When Jed appeared at the door of her bedroom, Laura forgave him everything. He looked so genuinely repentant, it would have been hard not to. Suddenly it was all quite clear: Jemima was a silly thing, Jed was just playing up to her.

Laura had never known Jed so tender. He sat next to her on the bed and kissed her, her hair, her cheeks, her neck, her mouth. He whispered in her ear for the first time that he loved her. Then he lifted the folds of her dress and knelt between her legs, pushing her knickers to one side and licking her there with his beautiful mouth until she came.

'Come on, Laura,' he said, helping her to her feet. 'You've got a party to give.'

By the time they returned to the kitchen Hugo and Amy had already served out the lamb tagine and couscous, and the mood had distinctly lifted.

'She's forgiven me,' said Jed.

That prompted a few laughs.

Laura merely glowed. Some of the party could guess why.

7

Later the same night, Jemima lost her virginity. It was the night every girl both dreads and yearns for, but in her submission to Jed's capable hands, Jemima dreaded little and yearned much.

Her mum and dad were three floors beneath them, clearing up after the dinner party, well out of harm's way. Leo and Amy, Rachel and Clara, had long since gone to bed. The hour they had to themselves, between two and three in the morning, was like an island where nothing mundane could reach them, where there were no clocks or voices or threats or any hint of an existence outside their own.

Jemima had never as much as shown her naked body to a living soul. Her boarding school was co-ed, but that's the trouble with co-ed schools, you're all one great happy family. The boy you like best is someone you know well, not someone you fantasise about. To fall in love, to properly fall in love, there needs to be something deeply unknown about the object of your longing, something you need to unravel, undress.

And that was the thing about Jed. He was the first man Jemima had ever met *from somewhere else*. It wasn't just that he was beautiful: his wavy blond hair, his skin, his sumptuous mouth, even the way he stood with his hands in his pockets, and his chin held high; it was the fact that he was so *aloof* which made him so irresistible to her. Her dorm at school knew all about him, suggested to her that he might be 'the one'. So, while some girls might boast of their loved one's accomplishments, their poetry, their piano-playing, their sporting prowess, Jemima knew little more of her beloved beyond the various parts of his body she had actually seen – his ears, his wrists, his fingers all got a mention. But what is sex but the desire to know and be known? The more Jed remained inaccessible to her, the more she craved him.

They had had banter, of course, snuggling up on the sofa watching repeat episodes of *Star Trek*. She would ask him which film stars he fancied, whether he'd prefer to date Sigourney Weaver or Jamie Curtis, but it was hard to engage him. He didn't really care much for film stars, he said, but then added that if one of them should knock on his door, and say, 'Come with me, Jed!' he more than likely would. She asked him about his family life, if he had brothers and sisters. He said he had two little sisters and a little brother, and when she asked him if he was close to them he said, 'Of course I fucking am. I live with them, don't I?'

'No you don't, you live with us,' said Jemima. But she could see she'd made him angry, and she really didn't want to have an argument.

'What about your mum?' Jemima asked him on another occasion. 'What's she like?'

Jed paused to think, as though no one had ever asked him before.

'Not as good-looking as your mum,' he said.

Jemima laughed, 'Gosh, do you really think my mum's good-looking?'

'Yep,' said Jed.

'I'll tell her next time she complains of feeling fat. That'll cheer her up.'

'She complains of feeling fat?'

'All the time. When she's one quarter of an inch fatter than me, she complains of feeling fat.'

That's when Jed lifted up Jemima's shirt and began squeezing her tummy. When he managed to find a little flesh, he teased, 'Hey J! What've we got here?' Then he slipped his hand down her jeans and went on squeezing.

Jemima re-lived that moment many times.

Sometimes, Jemima would ask Jed what he did for work.

'I'm not sure I'd call it work,' he said.

'Then,' said Jemima, 'what do you do in the middle of the night Monday to Thursday? We all wonder, you know. We guess.'

'And what do you guess?'

'That you're up to no good.'

'I'll take you with me, one day.'

'Will you sell me into slavery?'

'You'll see.'

'I wouldn't want to be a slave, Jed,' said Jemima earnestly.

'You'd make a very bad one,' said Jed.

On the night in question, the night Jemima had fed her beloved fingers of pitta bread dipped in her mother's olive oil, she was ready for anything. Clara had been encouraging her all afternoon. While their mums cooked in the kitchen, the girls had been talking about sex in Jemima's bedroom. Before Rachel moved down to Somerset, they had been like cousins to each other, Clara treating the younger Jemima first as a doll and later as a pupil. Clara had long maintained that sixteen was the perfect age to shed your virginity, so that you could get on with the rest of your life. She knew a girl at Manchester, she said, who was *still* a virgin at twenty, poor thing. Clara was quite certain that sex was always going to be a problem for her.

'Sex is like a sport,' said Clara. 'The more you do it, the better you get, and the better you get, the more you enjoy it.'

'Do you think you have better sex with people you love?' asked Jemima.

Clara thought for a while. 'Bad sex can put you off someone. Good sex is just really mind-blowing. The thing is, Jemima, I'm not sure I believe in love. Love is biological. Love sets the hormones racing. Love is desire, nothing more, nothing less. Why, Jemima, are you in love?'

'I think so,' said Jemima.

'Well that's great.'

'But you don't believe in love.'

'I'm three years older than you. When I was sixteen I thought I was in love. It's a pretty powerful emotion, isn't it, whatever you call it. Who's the bloke?'

'Our lodger, Jed. I noticed you looking admiringly at him last night when we got back from the cinema.'

'Him? He's drop-dead gorgeous, Jemima! Why haven't you gone to bed with him yet? What the hell's stopping you?'

'Mum would kill me! She'd absolutely kill me!'

'Don't tell her.'

'But I always tell her things. We're quite close, really, you know.'

'Why would she kill you, even if you did tell her? She might even be pleased for you. You're sixteen, it's legal.'

'I think she thinks I'm about thirteen. And she'd tell Dad, and Dad would kill me, too.'

'Wrong there. Your Dad would kill Jed. Dads always think their daughters are perfect.'

'Well then, what am I to do?' There was real desperation in Jemima's voice.

'Just don't tell them! It's obvious! Parents are always far too nosy, in my opinion. I tell mine about my maths course, my lodgings, and the food at the cafeteria. About my lovers, nothing, not a word!'

'To think I might have a lover, my very own lover!'

'My advice to you, dear girl: surrender! Relax! Hand yourself over to him, trust him!'

'I will, I will!' said Jemima, happily.

After the guests had gone home at half past one in the morning, Amy was the first to go to bed. She apologised for not helping clear up, but she'd had a hard day at the salon and was completely spent. Leo had wanted to follow her up, but knew Jemima would tease him – he'd foolishly confided to her quite how in love with her he was – so he'd mooched around the kitchen for a while before going upstairs himself. Jemima and Jed were watching things and each other. Clara followed hot on the heels of her mum, giving her hosts a kiss goodnight and Jemima a big grin. Jemima smiled back.

Jemima went up to bed first, while Jed stayed downstairs, humouring her parents. That wasn't difficult, as his humour was particularly good. He had fancied Jemima rotten since the first time he set eyes on her. He enjoyed her surly humour, her spikiness. In some ways, thought Jed, she was just like her mum, but she was ruder, spunkier. Yes, that was J: a rude, spunky virgin. He always knew he was going to be the first into her bed, and tonight was the night. Jed began loading the dishwasher with great verve.

Laura was impressed. 'Look at him!' she thought to herself. 'He can be tamed yet!' Then when Jed had kissed her and wished her goodnight, and set off upstairs to bed, she looked around for Hugo who was sorting out the empty wine bottles in the larder and confided happily: 'My God, that boy has come on, Hugo! You could even think of employing him in one of your shops!'

Jemima was getting into her pink spotty pyjamas from Laura Ashley. It crossed her mind that she should have been wearing a nightdress, but she didn't have one. She suddenly felt nervous. The girls at school said that you break your hymen when you first start using tampons, but then someone had told her that that wasn't true, and that it very definitely hurt when you had sex for the first time. She was frightened of it hurting, but if it did she was determined not to cry out.

She was sitting on the side of the bed when Jed walked in. He sat beside her and kissed her temple affectionately. Jemima hung her head, modestly.

'Have you ever done this before?' she said.

Jed looked puzzled.

'I mean, with someone who's never …' Jemima couldn't bring herself to say the word 'virgin'.

'No,' said Jed. 'But I'm cool with that.'

'Can I turn off the light?'

'No,' said Jed.

They sat on the bed looking at each other, saying nothing, not even kissing. Then after a while Jed began to undo the buttons of her pyjamas.

'You are so beautiful,' he said.

Jemima longed for him to touch her, but he didn't.

When he had taken off her top, Jed said, 'Lie on the bed, Jemima.' He said it in a way that made it impossible to disobey him.

Then he pulled off her pyjama bottoms, not in a sexy way, but an efficient way, like a mother might undress a sleeping child before laying him down to sleep.

Jemima's instinct was to cover herself, but Jed took her hand and said, 'No.'

Jed looked at her. Some minutes passed. Still he didn't lay a finger on her.

Jemima was willing him to undress, too, to lie on her, let her feel less naked, less vulnerable.

At last he touched her, putting his hand between her thighs, prising them open like an oyster.

'Aren't you going to undress?' asked Jemima nervously.

Jed ignored her, and gently put a finger inside her.

'Have you got a condom?'

'Shh,' said Jed. 'Trust me.'

And then, quite suddenly, he took off his shirt and lay on her, and they kissed like they'd been kissing for weeks, with all the longing of young lovers, which is what they were.

In his arms, Jemima felt so safe, so trusting, that when the moment came and she felt her darling Jed penetrate into her very being, the pain was so like joy that it was joy.

'I love you so much!' she said. The words just poured out of her.

Jed said nothing but he kissed her once more on the lips and lay beside her. Soon, he was fast asleep. Jemima just gazed at him for a long time, her heart full to bursting. At last she lifted Jed's sleeping arm and tucked herself under it, and allowed the bliss of the night to subdue her.

❖

Hugo and Laura were so high on the success of their lives and loves that they went on cleaning their kitchen together till four in the morning. He told Laura that he and Amy had now made up, and eventually even Gloria had relaxed. 'And George came up trumps,' he said. 'We might be able to give him our new IT contract. And you, darling Laura, were looking stunning.'

'And you, Hugo, look younger every day!'

'The lamb tagine! The couscous! Laura, you excelled yourself!'

'I've been thinking, Hugo, do you think we could go on holiday to Morocco this year? In our Volvo? We could take a ferry over the Gibraltar Straits and raid the bazaars for exotic furniture and pottery.'

'Why so far? Why not stop at Spain?'

'Well, I've been reading up on the Bloomsbury group. Do you know about them? We really should try and see that film, *Carrington*. Vanessa Bell was married to Clive Bell but loved Duncan Grant who was homosexual and loved lots of other men ... they all lived together very happily, Hugo. And then there was Carrington who was married to Ralph Partridge who was loved by Lytton Strachey who was loved by Carrington. And they were all painters and writers and whatnot, terribly creative, the whole lot of them, and so *free*! But the point is, they used to drive to Europe and pick up total bargains from antique shops in the thirties. Nowadays I imagine we have to go further afield, into Africa. And I just feel so *akin* to Morocco, somehow. I realised that just tonight, that couscous really went to my head. Wasn't it delicious? And when I mentioned it to a couple of others at our end of the table, they said, "Go for it, Laura!" And Ann and Patrick were particularly encouraging. Ann reminded me how good at art I was when I was at school. Do you know, I'd completely forgotten?'

'Well, I hadn't,' said Hugo. 'I've still got some rather charming love letters you wrote me years ago, with little drawings in the margins. You are so talented, Laura! Didn't I try and persuade you to go to art school?'

'Have you really kept my letters? That is so sweet! But I'm sure you never encouraged me to go to art school. You would only have had to say the word and I would have done what you told me to. I only remember giving up my place at St Andrews. History of Art was my passion.'

'Have you ever regretted it?'

'Funnily enough, I've been taking Jed around a few galleries recently. Of course I have to read up about the painter just before I go, but I love it, I completely love it. How wonderful it is just to sit quietly and look at something totally magical right in front of you. And when you know just the smallest amount about the painter, it makes a world of difference.'

'How's Jed been taking to his dose of culture?'

'I told him he would make a fine sculptor.'

Hugo laughed.

'Are you suggesting he wouldn't?'

'Well, honestly! Jed!'

'If Jed had gone to Bedales, he would have outshone everyone. This terrible class system we have, denying half of us a decent start in life. It's scandalous!'

'So, you're becoming political, are you, darling?'

'I am becoming everything, Hugo! You name it, I am becoming it!'

'You're already becoming, Laura. In fact, you're ravishing, and I want to ravish you!'

Within moments, Laura had hoisted herself up on to the kitchen table. She sat there, eyes mischievous, and hitched up her skirt. When the sensation reminded her of her earlier interlude with Jed, it only increased her pleasure.

'Laura!' exclaimed Hugo. 'What's got into you?'

'Something good! Something unconditionally, excitingly, wonderfully good!'

'Oh my God, Laura, you're fucking amazing,' said Hugo, and they had the best fuck of their married lives.

On the Sunday morning Laura was still so full of her dinner party that Rachel's congratulations on 'such a terrific evening' and 'how great it was to catch up with Ann after so long', were not enough to satisfy her. For Laura's burning question was (which she absolutely couldn't ask in front of Hugo and Clara who were having breakfast with them) was, 'What did you think of Jed?' Laura had seen them chatting away, and though she'd strained her ears to hear what they were saying, she'd failed, and now she was longing to ask Rachel what they'd been talking about, and above all, whether she now understood how special he was, and how she was completely right to be so in love with him. But their breakfast together provided no opportunity, and even afterwards, hanging around Rachel's bedroom while she packed, things were more awkward than friendly between them. Soon afterwards Rachel and Clara drove off back to Somerset to avoid the Sunday evening traffic, and the house emptied out.

When the phone rang, she leapt up to answer it, quite sure it would be someone with more pertinent compliments, forgetting that only Rachel knew the whole story of her life and was able to give them.

It was Arabella.

At first her voice was warm and actually sounded happy. Arabella told Laura that Mark was the nicest man she'd met in ages, and they might even meet for lunch some time soon as it turned out they worked in parallel streets in the city.

'Does Sarah know about that?'

'Who's Sarah?'

'His wife, Arabella. He's not single, you know.'

'I'm pleased you're sounding more yourself, Laura.'

'I would never break up a marriage!'

'Nor would Amy, I suppose. I caught her snogging your husband at about midnight last night. Just outside the loo among the coats. Quite passionate, they were.'

'Is that why you phoned? To tell me that?'

'Actually I phoned to say thank you.'

'You have a funny way …' Laura found herself too choked up to speak.

'Is Hugo listening to all this?'

'No, I'm alone.'

'And Jed. That's your bloke, isn't it?'

Laura said nothing.

'He was quite affable, I suppose. So what exactly do young Amy and Jed think of the situation? They don't feel used in any way?'

'Arabella, how could you think such a thing?'

'I shouldn't say these things, should I? It's just that when you start taking the moral high ground it comes tumbling out.'

'We look after them incredibly well.'

'Look after them? You mean, play games with them. Jed and Amy are your middle-aged toys. And it's not going to end happily, you know. One or other of them is going to desert you, then either you or Hugo are going to be miserable. And jealous. Your whole family are in for a fall.'

'The kids love Jed and Amy!'

'Yes, and rather too much. Beware, Laura dear. Don't say I didn't warn you. And thanks again for introducing me to Mark. You did an old friend a good turn there.'

'I'm pleased,' said Laura.

'Say hi and thanks to Hugo for me, won't you?'

'Of course. Bye then.'

'Bye.'

And Arabella hung up, leaving Laura to run upstairs to her bedroom and cry her eyes out.

She lay there for a couple of hours trying to work out why she was so upset. Apart from Jed being late, her party had been everything she had hoped for. Yes, it's true, it had needed a bit of time to get going, but when everyone had relaxed a bit, well, what a lovely glow those Moroccan tea lights had given the room! How could Arabella be so completely horrid? Laura couldn't think why she was still her friend.

No, what had hurt Laura to the quick was the news of Hugo's stolen kiss with Amy. Not the fact that their odd living arrangement would one day come to an end – she wasn't such a fool as to think they'd all grow old together – but that Hugo was still in love with that silly girl. She realised that underneath it all she had been looking for signs that Hugo's ardour was waning, and had found them. She had to face the fact squarely that Hugo might love Amy every bit as much as she loved Jed.

At midday Hugo jumped into bed with the Sunday newspapers and kissed her affectionately. Everything but the sports section was unceremoniously discarded and landed with a thud on the floor. Whatever Hugo was reading was putting him in a good mood. From time to time he squeezed Laura's hand. At last he was done with news of his football team, and snuggled down the bed to join his wife.

'The others are having breakfast,' he said. 'It's a good scene, Laura. You should be down there with them. What are you doing hiding up here, anyway?'

'I didn't sleep much last night. I was too full of it all. It was a great party, wasn't it?'

'And you were the star of it, darling. I'm such a lucky man to have you. The others want to go ice skating in Streatham this afternoon. I thought I might go with them.'

'Ice skating?'

'Well, Jed's never been before. I think Jemima wants to show off to him.'

'But Jemima's not been in years!'

'She used to be rather good at her twirls, I remember,' said her dad, loyally.

'Are you really going to go with them, Hugo? Can't we have our own treat?'

Laura looked at her husband, whose expression was impenetrable. 'It's awfully crowded there on a Sunday. Don't you remember?'

The seconds Hugo took to reply were endless.

'I'll tell you what,' he said. 'Why don't we go to the Ritz for tea? Like we used to before we were married. You look like you could do with a few cucumber sandwiches.'

And that's exactly what they did.

❖

Laura had been rather dreading the Easter holidays. She had grown accustomed to her afternoons with Jed and she hadn't enjoyed the prospect of sharing him with her children. But in fact, for some reason Laura couldn't quite fathom, the household was happier than ever.

Both Jed and Amy told Laura they didn't want to move down to the guest bedrooms on the first floor, even though sharing a floor with the kids meant they had to forsake their *en suite* bathrooms. They said they felt more part of the family upstairs, less like guests, and that suited them seeing as Laura refused point blank to take any rent from them. Laura felt slightly disorientated at first. The first-floor bedroom where she and Jed had spent so many happy afternoons was now possessed of such a *frisson* that she would feel aroused even as she walked by its closed door. But within a couple of days not only had she grown accustomed to Jed sleeping upstairs (their afternoons together were *verboten* anyway, till the kids went back to school) but she grew excited by the prospect of a major refurbishment. She had recently discovered that *real* bohemians didn't have fitted carpets and wallpaper; no, they had murals, floorboards and old oriental rugs. And they filled their houses with beautiful random objects that had no rhyme or reason but were just lovely in themselves. Laura explained this all to Hugo, who loved the idea. Their house was far too polished, he'd always felt that. Perhaps they'd go shopping together in the Portobello market and pick up a few stray and exciting pieces of furniture. Perhaps they'd go to an auction together and bid for old rugs.

'And who shall we get to paint the murals?' Hugo asked his wife.

'We won't get anyone! Let's all paint the walls! I'm sure we have enough talent between us – you and I, Jed and Amy, Leo and Jemima. At least we should have a go. And if we fail, we'll just paint it over and admit defeat. I shall buy us all overalls. We can even start next weekend.'

Laura still went on her runs at a quarter to eight in the morning, but she vaguely noticed that her admirers, after politely thanking her for such a fun party, didn't wave at her with quite the gusto they used to. George had never had quite enough to drink, so his reticence didn't surprise her much. But Mark had had a great time chatting to Arabella, and it rather annoyed her when she felt he was giving her a wide berth as well. One morning she even glimpsed his wife Sarah on her doorstep in a dressing gown on a school day looking very glum. Laura gave her a friendly wave – she was quite certain Sarah had noticed her – but instead of waving back, which would have only been polite, Laura watched as she marched back into the house and (Laura was quite certain despite being a good forty yards away) slammed the door in her husband's face.

Laura was awfully upset for a while. She briefly wondered whether she shouldn't pop round to comfort her (because she naturally assumed that what she was seeing was a jealous tiff) and tell her there was no reason to worry whatsoever. The good-natured Laura wanted to tell her that Arabella was no threat to her at all, because she had a prosthetic leg.

But then she decided that life was too short to get involved in her neighbours' marital problems. Life was far too good to be pulled down like that. She'd recently been to a lecture given by The Arts and Crafts Society in Chelsea, where she'd learnt that her new idols, Duncan Grant and Vanessa Bell, had rediscovered the possibilities of ink. They had used ink to dye linen curtains, as well as quilts and other soft furnishings. The effects had been dramatic.

One night, as they were lying in each other's arms after sex – abstaining from their lovers had meant they had had to turn to each other for satisfaction – Laura said to her husband: 'Darling, I've been thinking! I want to set up a business. I want to call it Glass Inc. Don't you think that's clever? Or perhaps Glass Ink Inc. Or perhaps simply, Glass Ink with a K.'

'Darling,' murmured Hugo, 'you're a genius, I'll invest in you.' And then he promptly fell asleep.

But Laura was in far too good a mood to join him in the land of nod. For a couple of hours, she was thinking where she might source her linen, and where she might find a good ink factory. But then something even more thrilling sprung to mind at about four in the morning. Just as she was finally nodding off to 'Glass Ink, Glass Ink', she woke up again. 'Glass! Glass! Ink is only half the story! My name will be my fortune!' And her mind raced for two hours more, yearning for the dawn so she could tell Hugo all about it.

She lay beside him, waiting for him to stir. And when she thought he had, she whispered, 'Hugo, Hugo, are you awake yet? I have something amazing to tell you!'

Hugo lay an arm on her to signal that she could talk, but was still too sleepy to open his eyes.

'I've got another idea,' said Laura, 'and this one's even better. These bohemians weren't just being rebellious, Hugo. They weren't just flouting all the dreadful Victorian conventions they'd been saddled with. They were being authentic! They were saying to each other and to the world, "This is me! This is what I do, this is who I love! Watch me, I don't harm others. I'm not a bad person. I just want to be allowed to be truly and honestly myself." Do you see what I'm getting at, darling?'

'Yeah,' mumbled Hugo, eyes still closed.

'Well, this is my point. Our family, we have nothing to hide, do we? We can hold our heads high. We are, we are … utterly transparent. Isn't that so? As transparent as glass!'

'"We are as transparent as glass,"' repeated Hugo, to show he had been listening.

'So this is what I thought. Our soft furnishings could be dyed in glorious shades of ink, but our hard furnishings could be made of glass!'

'Hard furnishings?' queried Hugo.

'You know, kitchen cupboards, tables, chairs, wardrobes, you name it. If my wardrobe's a mess, then I should be brave enough to show the world it's a mess. What have I to hide? I'm being honest, Hugo, to myself and everyone else. Isn't that what it means to be authentic? Why should I care if my kitchen cupboards are untidy? Why should anyone care? We are on this earth to *live*, Hugo. We must throw off our Victorian shackles once and for all, we must be *free!*'

Laura spoke from the heart, and Hugo sat up. 'Has anyone ever told you you're a genius?' he said. 'I already invest in a company that makes reinforced glass. We could bring in some of the top designers. Wow, Laura, can we do this one together?'

'You can be my managing director,' said Laura, embracing her husband as though he were her one and only. 'But it's my company, okay?'

'Whatever have I done to deserve you?' said Hugo, and they made love all over again.

Over supper that evening, a Tuesday as it so happened, which meant that Jed would be setting off to work soon afterwards, Laura announced to the family that new times were afoot and they should expect change. Jemima and Leo instinctively looked to their father to gauge his reaction: over the years, they had become used to his casual dismissal of anything remotely interesting their mother had to say. But instead his expression was respectful, and they followed suit. Jed and Amy were simply curious.

'First of all I apologise for being the dullest mother in the land,' began Laura.

'That's not true!' said Jemima. 'You're just a mum, and sometimes mums have to be dull. It's their role in life.'

Laura was touched by her daughter's defence of her.

'But wouldn't you say, Jemima, I'm a tad conventional?'

'That's part of the job of a mum. Mums make kids tidy their rooms, do their homework, go to bed at a reasonable hour, cook their meals, make sure the kitchen isn't infested with germs, that's what mums do …'

'Let's hear what your mum has to say, J,' said Jed.

Some tiny part of Laura was alarmed by the relaxed way those two were talking to each other nowadays, but she was too eager to carry on with her pretty speech to recognise the first stirrings of jealousy. She needed to be certain of Jed's devotion. So she said, 'Jed, you've been here for three months now. You must have thought at some stage, "Laura is so establishment, she doesn't know anything about anything. She needs to be more adventurous, get about a bit more, see the world, be more creative." Tell the truth, Jed, have you ever thought that?'

Everyone looked at Jed.

Eventually, Jed said, nodding, 'Yeah, possibly.'

'You've never thought that!' said Jemima outraged.

'I think you're right, Jed,' said Hugo.

'I don't think so,' said Amy. 'I think you're perfect.'

'Thanks, Amy! It seems that you, Leo, have the casting vote. But I'd be grateful if you didn't cast it. I'm not sure I'm ready for it.' That the two men in her life could be critical of her – even though she invited it, even though she had asked for their criticism and had made a declaration to shed her old self – was nonetheless painful.

Leo couldn't decide whether to make a filial little outburst like his sister's or enjoy the power criticism seemed to have given the men in the household. But Laura didn't let him speak.

'I have long been thinking,' she began rather grandly, 'or at least over the last few days, that wallpaper has had its day and that it's time for a change. So then, I want to strip the wallpaper in the two guest rooms on the first floor and paint two glorious murals instead.'

'You mean you're going to paint?' asked Jemima, sceptically.

'Come on, Jemima, you're my chief ally. And not just me, you're going to paint, too. We're all going to paint them.'

'But those beautiful phoenixes,' said Amy, with passion. 'You can't just strip them. That's such a violent thing to do!'

'The truth is, Amy, I looked at those phoenixes this morning and I thought, "How did I ever love you? How was I ever seduced into thinking that I wanted *you* on my walls?" No, they've had their day, Amy, I'm afraid.'

'Well I can't paint. And Leo can't either. So count us out,' said Jemima.

'Nonsense. Only last Parents' Day your paintings were up in the studio for all to admire. You're doing a GCSE in art. That wonderful portrait you did of an old woman in a red beret …'

'It was a load of crap,' said Jemima.

'Not what your art teacher said, Jemima, when I chatted to her about your progress after your mocks. She's really pleased with you. And as for *you,* Leo, you might not have chosen it as one of your exam subjects but you have within you a rare talent. Amy, Jed, have you ever noticed these wonderful paintings that adorn our kitchen walls?'

'Please, Mum, no …' begged Leo.

'Leo painted them when he was only three years old! Can you believe that? Look at the colours he uses, his brushwork! That's the trouble with school. It educates you out of all spontaneity.'

'Wow, Leo, these are really good, you know,' said Amy, kindly.

Leo slumped and hid his face in his hands.

'Have you got an idea for a mural?' asked Hugo. 'Hey, I think it's a good idea, Laura.'

'Yes, actually, I have. At least for Amy's old room. I thought something in the style of Gauguin.'

'What? You want us to paint in the style of Gauguin, just like that? That would take years of training.'

'Aha, Jemima! Not at all! Look at what I managed to find this morning in that Art for All shop on the King's Road.'

Laura walked over to the dresser and fetched a cardboard poster tube, from which she coaxed a print of five Tahitian women sitting on a bench in dappled sunlight, with a sixth walking away from them. The women were straight-backed and elegant, their hair thick and dark, their long, plain dresses in sumptuous colours.

'It's beautiful, isn't it?' she said. 'The Tahitian name for it is *Ta Matete* which translates as "We shall not go to the market today". Gauguin naturally breaks up into blocks of colour anyway, and I'm good at mixing colours. Perhaps you, Hugo, could just copy the outlines on to the wall?'

'It'll be hard,' said Hugo, a trifle anxiously.

'No it won't! You could do it like we used to at school, break the painting into squares and then just copy the squares on to the wall.'

Hugo was keen to be loyal to his wife, so he said, 'I'll give it a go.'

'I knew you could do it!' enthused Laura.

'It'll be harder than it looks,' said Jed.

'That kind of negativity won't get you anywhere, Jed. If you are to make a success of your life, you have to give it a go, isn't that right, Hugo?'

Husband and wife shot each other a look of appreciation; Jemima and Jed, irritation.

'And I have a further idea, folks,' continued Laura, in a tone that would sit happily in any creative boardroom. 'If it all goes smoothly, and we get more confident as we go along, why don't we replace these six Tahitian women with ourselves? Wouldn't that be a good joke?'

'Oh Mum, please!' said Jemima. 'Do you know how hard it is to get a likeness? You just can't expect us to do that!'

'Do you know what that great artist Rothko said? Painting is as natural as singing. Relax, Jemima. So what if it does go a bit askew? We can give it a go, can't we?'

'Since when have you been quoting Rothko, Laura?' asked Hugo, impressed.

'Oh you know,' she said breezily, 'I've been going to a few lunch-time lectures recently in Chelsea. In fact a rather nice gentleman I met there told me he would put my name down for the Arts Club. I said, "Yes please," but I know there's a long waiting list. Do you know, the greatest regret of my life is that I never took up my university place to read …'

'We know, Mum,' interrupted Jemima, 'History of Art. But what I want to know, Mum, is this. There are only five figures sitting on the bench. Which of us is going to be the one walking away?'

'I haven't thought about that,' said Laura, chastened for the first time. After some moments, she said, 'Perhaps we should just have the family. After all, Jed and Amy won't be living with us forever.'

'Nor will we!' said Jemima. 'And I'm going to refuse to be in this painting unless we paint both of them!'

'No,' said Leo, 'me neither!'

'You win!' said Laura, at least half of her delighted, and the other half a smidgeon anxious. She paused just a moment to look at her children, but not long enough to ask herself the questions she might have done. 'Perhaps we should have six of us on the bench, with no one walking away. Are you okay with that, Hugo?'

'I wouldn't have wanted it any other way,' said Hugo. He smiled at Amy, who had been completely won round by the idea, and was grinning broadly. But when Laura tried to catch Jed's eye, he was already standing in the frame of the kitchen door.

'I'm late,' he said.

Jed smiled shyly at that happy group sitting round the kitchen table, and was gone.

Laura didn't sleep well. Despite barely catnapping for the previous thirty-six hours and feeling unutterably exhausted, she was worried about Jed. They had been so close for so long. She missed their afternoons together, and she thought of how Jed must miss them, too. How patient he was being, what admirable qualities he had. Before the school holidays began, Laura had insisted they think of them as a diet, the one time when you hoped time would pass quickly, but by the end of it, life would seem more delicious than ever. But now she realised, as she tossed and turned, that a diet wasn't quite the right analogy. In a diet you could control things. But when two people who loved each other were apart, anything could happen. It frightened her to think of it. She badly wanted some time alone with Jed to re-establish things. She yearned to embrace him, kiss him, be reassured that things were all right between them. It was only after she'd decided to get out of the house with Jed the following afternoon – take him to some gallery or other – that she could get any sleep at all.

She spent the morning researching exhibitions she could take Jed to. There was a show of a new young sculptor, Marc Quinn, at the White Cube gallery in Duke Street called 'Emotional Detox' – seven twisted torsos in lead representing the seven deadly sins. But Jed always became impatient with her when she suggested he become a sculptor himself, and of course she would. Then she saw there was an exhibition of dead poets at the National Gallery, but realised she didn't know much about poets and poetry and there was too little time to gen up. But at last she found one that was quite perfect for her needs: Andrew Wyeth's Helga pictures had finally come to London and were being exhibited at the Institute of Contemporary Arts in Nash House. Laura had adored Wyeth's paintings as a teenager: fresh, innocent American landscapes, where you could feel the breeze blowing off the stubble. But this was the reason Laura's mood suddenly changed for the better, why it even danced through her mind that they might briefly stop off at a day hotel (she'd only recently learnt about day hotels: dark, seedy places where there was black satin on the beds and businessmen took their mistresses over the lunch hour). Laura remembered the moment some years ago now when the great artist told the world for the first time – and the world included his wife – that he had secretly been painting a neighbour of his over fifteen years, a red-headed German woman called Helga. Everybody of course wanted to know whether the two had been lovers, and perhaps no one would ever know. But there was no doubt that the great artist was obsessed with her, and a number of the nudes were distinctly erotic.

Laura longed to run upstairs to the kids' floor after lunch and be with Jed for those precious moments when he woke up. She needed to tell him all about the plan she was hatching. But she knew that

Jemima was in her bedroom revising for her GCSEs – in fact Jemima had positively astonished the family by how much work she was getting done this holidays – and the last thing she wanted to do was explain herself to her. So with a good deal of impatience she waited for Jed to appear in her kitchen at three.

She was about to give him a friendly kiss on the cheek but noticed that Jemima was right behind him.

'Jed! Jemima!' she enthused. 'How are things going? How's *Macbeth*, Jemima?'

'Awesome,' she said. 'The best play ever.'

'I imagine you're here for some brain fuel.'

'What's that?' asked Jemima.

'You need a snack,' explained Laura. The truth was, she would have happily fobbed her daughter off with a packet of biscuits and told her to go back upstairs.

'Ah no,' she said. 'I'm not hungry. I just want a break, that's all.'

'And a break is what you deserve,' said Laura.

Jed was helping himself to cereal and had his back to them both.

'How was work?' asked Laura.

'Good,' said Jed, as enigmatically as ever.

Laura fetched a bottle of milk and put it on the kitchen table. Jed sat down and poured it on to his cornflakes.

'Thanks, Laura,' he said.

Laura sat down next to him and, elbows on the table, rested her chin on her hands.

'I've been thinking,' she began, the moment Jemima left the kitchen. 'We haven't been to an exhibition for ages. What about if we go this afternoon? There's a fantastic artist who I know you'd love and there's an exhibition of his paintings in Nash House, a terrific venue just off Trafalgar Square ...'

Then Jemima walked in again, with a few letters from the afternoon post in her hand. 'Did I hear you say the word "exhibition"?' she said. 'If you did, take me! It's about time I got out of this house. I'm getting cabin fever.'

Laura forced enthusiasm into her voice. 'That would be wonderful,' she said, 'if you feel you're sufficiently on top of your work ...'

'I am *so* on top!' she said, smiling at Jed. Laura missed their little secret, because she was still trying to think of an excuse for her not to come. Jemima stood in front of her, beaming. 'Jed tells me you've been educating him. I should love it if you educated me, too.'

'Gosh, you're in a good mood,' Laura said. Her mind went into overdrive now. What warning, bribe or promise would allow her and Jed to have the afternoon to themselves? The idea of Jemima tagging along was unbearable. But when she finally realised her dream was just not going to happen, she gave in. 'It would be terrific to have you on board,' she said.

Laura was someone who could make the most of any situation, and just looking at her radiant daughter in the bus gave her a surge of pride. Wherever had the bolshy teenager gone, who had watched wall to wall television over the Christmas holidays? When she'd complained to Rachel about it, Rachel had assured her it was just a phase all teenagers went through, and that Clara had been a zombie for at least two years. She now counted herself lucky that Jemima's grouchy moods had been so short-lived, and her heart warmed when she remembered how she had defended her over the mural. She was pleased Jemima was coming with them. It was a sign that she was at last growing up. Anyway, it would be good for her GCSE.

Laura looked at Jed, too: inscrutable and beautiful as ever. He was wearing the same biker's leather jacket that he always wore, and which she'd found so attractive the first time they met. How she yearned to slip her arms under it and feel his warm flesh! Well, there were only five more days left of the holidays. She would just have to wait for him.

As they walked up the Mall, Jemima asked her mother about the exhibition. 'Who's the artist?' she said.

'I doubt you will have heard of him. Andrew Wyeth.' She wanted Jed to be listening, too, before she carried on, but he was walking some steps ahead of them. Jed had never been to the Mall before, he'd told her in the bus. Laura watched him taking it all in, enjoying the breadth and the grandeur of it, the large white buildings against a blue sky. It was one of the reasons why she loved him. Jed took nothing for granted, and through his eyes she saw the world anew.

It was only when they were queuing up for tickets that she had the full attention of both of them. 'Andrew Wyeth is generally thought of as an American landscape painter,' she began. 'But unbeknownst to anyone, even his wife, over a period of fifteen years he was painting a series of paintings of his German neighbour, Helga.'

'Then they would be bound to be having an affair,' said Jemima immediately.

A man in his sixties who was queuing in front of them looked round to see who'd spoken so emphatically. He smiled when he saw Jemima. How Laura wished she'd been able to give Jed her little lecture back in the privacy of their kitchen – that's what normally happened when Laura took him to galleries, and he was a model pupil.

Laura kept her voice low: 'Whatever gives you that idea, Jemima? He was extremely happily married to a woman called Betsy.'

'Helga the mistress, Betsy the wife. You can tell just from their names who's who. You'd tell your wife if this Helga was just a model, don't you think so, Jed? If you're sleeping with someone, and you're not supposed to, that's when you have to keep it secret. What more can you say?'

'Shh, Jemima, this is a gallery, you know. Keep your voice down!'

'Well, Mum, I'm right, aren't I? You know I'm right!'

'Betsy was his most devoted fan. She became his trustee after his death. She wouldn't have spent her life looking after her husband's name and reputation if she'd thought they'd been lovers,' insisted Laura.

'What a waste of a life. God, I'm not going to hand my life over to my husband's reputation. No wonder he had to go and seek out an adventure with someone else …'

'Shh, Jemima, do you know what a loud voice you have?'

They were standing three places away from the ticket window, and suddenly Laura realised that everyone was looking at them. She was fairly inclined to take Jed and Jemima away from that place there and then. The sunlight beckoned to them beyond the large glass window. Why oh why hadn't she taken them to the exhibition of dead poets instead? Anywhere but here. Perhaps they could see a film together instead. Or just go to the park on a lovely day like this. They could go and feed the ducks in the Serpentine, just like the old days when Jemima was still in pigtails.

'Why did painters always insist on nude models?' thought Laura. 'I don't believe for a moment it's to do with the beauty of the human form, or the difficulty in drawing it. That's what they say so that they can get away with it. Of course they have to throw in a couple of ugly, fat people just so they can keep up the pretence. But really it's just an excuse to be titillated. It's about wanting to see nakedness for its own sake. God I pray there's not too much nakedness in the exhibition! What will Jemima think?'

And then Laura had a new worry: 'Will Jemima ever twig that I was all set to bring Jed here without her? Won't she suspect something? Please God! Jemima hasn't even seen the Rembrandts at the National Gallery. Why did her artistic education have to start here?'

But alas, on the nakedness front at least, all Laura's fears were realised. After the bright, sunlit foyer, the room in which the paintings hung was dark, subdued. The first few afforded Laura a temporary respite: Helga was actually wearing clothes, and looked handsome and wholesome – wrapped in sheepskin in a field in winter, or donning a German peasant dress. But her young charges swiftly walked by them, as though they were of no interest. Then when they were mesmerised by others, seriously profound, intensely erotic, and stood a while to study them, Laura wanted to push them on with a cattle prod. One called *Black Velvet* featured Helga, naked apart from a black choker round her neck, lying on what should have been a bed but which Wyeth had transformed into a black, velvety void. She seemed suspended in mid-air, her face turned away, her arm resting protectively on her midriff.

'Oh God!' thought Laura. 'Why aren't I at Jed's side now? Why am I standing behind them, playing the prude, when I'm not, I'm just so not!'

'What d'you think, J?' she overheard Jed say to her daughter. The tone was so easy and familiar that Laura suddenly loathed both of them simply for being friends. Jed and she were lovers: didn't that cap mere friendship? The better part of Laura said to herself: 'Let them be friends! Think how miserable things would be at home if they weren't!' And rather less generously: 'Less than a week till Jemima's safely back at school!'

Jemima read out Wyeth's caption underneath his painting.

'"My struggle is to preserve that abstract flash – like something you caught out of the corner of your eye, but in the picture you can look at it directly. It's a very elusive thing." Do you understand a word of that that, Jed?'

'Nope,' said Jed.

'Nor I,' said Jemima. 'Mum, what the hell's he going on about?'

Grateful for being consulted, Laura now came forward to look at the painting more carefully. She took her place between them, relishing the fact that they were all ears.

'The thing about painting,' she said, authoritatively, 'is that it catches a moment in time. Usually moments run so fast we don't notice them, we don't notice what they can say to us. It seems to me that Wyeth is saying he's found a moment and he's captured it.'

Then Laura couldn't think what else to say. The painting was so tender and true, the body language so intuitively recognisable – the arms that had so recently embraced her lover now protecting herself from him. Has she not known that mysterious moment herself?

'What moment has he captured, Mum?'

'The moment afterwards,' she said. This was for Jed, but Jed was far away and lost in the painting.

'The moment after what?' asked Jemima, disingenuously.

'The moment after making love,' declared her mother, in a voice rather too full of feeling.

'You are *so* embarrassing, Mum,' said Jemima. 'She's embarrassing, isn't she, Jed?'

'I don't think your mother's embarrassing,' said Jed, diplomatically.

Laura looked at Jed gratefully and Jed smiled back – but his smile was polite rather than conspiratorial. Laura suddenly felt inexplicably sad.

'Let's move on,' she said.

Alone with Jed, how slowly they would have enjoyed these extraordinary paintings, how long they would have lingered at the nudes, how close they would have felt! But Laura would have sooner had the three of them munching greasy burgers at McDonald's than endure the agony of holding in everything she wished to express. Now she was trying to keep her heart and soul in check as she sped on her little party as fast as she feasibly could. Drawing after drawing, how exquisite they were, Helga with her arms over her head, or asleep, or naked under trees; Helga naked on her knees, arms behind her back, looking out of a window. How Wyeth had loved this woman, thought Laura, how Wyeth had revered every inch of her soul and body!

They had been in the gallery for barely half an hour. Jed and Jemima were laughing somewhere, of that Laura was dimly aware. The painting she was looking at was called *Overflow* and depicted a sleeping Helga on a bed in front of a window, naked, her arms stretched over her head and a sheet draped over her thighs.

Below the title, Wyeth had written: 'I think one's art goes as far and deep as one's love goes.'

She looked across at Jed. Jed was telling Jemima she should plait her hair. They had rushed through the entire collection and were sitting near the exit waiting to go.

'I would lay down my life for that man,' she said to herself. 'I'm not sure he would lay down his for me.'

8

On the last Saturday of the spring holidays – the night before the children were due back at Bedales – Hugo and Laura were getting ready to go to the wedding feast of an old friend of Hugo's. Despite it being a second wedding, the friend had connections in high places, and the dinner was taking place at James's Palace. Hugo, anxious that he was losing his sexual allure – his forty-fifth birthday was looming, and a couple of pretty secretaries had recently given him the cold shoulder – had been on a fitness regime and had lost a couple of inches round the waist. Laura had celebrated this fact by buying him a new suit in deep blue velvet. And for herself (why not? – it had been ages since she had bought something truly spectacular) she had bought a really gorgeous dress in lilac satin from Harvey Nichols.

'You look like a Greek goddess,' said Hugo proudly, as they walked down the stairs into the hall.

'And you look like James Bond at a casino, winning!' was Laura's riposte.

Jed, Amy, Leo and Jemima were in the sitting room watching telly together.

While Hugo admired himself in the hall mirror, adjusting his bow tie and silk waistcoat, Laura walked into the sitting room, first and foremost for Jed to see her, but also to remind Amy that there was a Waitrose moussaka in the fridge, and she should think of putting it in the Aga soon.

Then Hugo followed her in.

'Amy,' he said, 'did you remember to pick up my suit on Wednesday? I can't find it.'

Amy had not remembered, but his tone irritated her. Even though she passed the dry cleaners on her way home, and Laura would have had to make a special journey, was this really *her* job?

'I forgot,' she said, coldly.

Hugo sighed. He wanted to say, 'Look at me when I'm talking to you,' but realised that would be out of order. Jemima said, 'Shh, everyone, can't you see we're watching *Blind Date*?'

'We know when we're not wanted!' laughed Laura. 'Come on, Hugo, let's go.'

But some moments later Laura was popping her head round the door again. 'Amy, I forgot to take two chickens out of the freezer and they really should thaw all night because …'

'Got it. I'll take the chickens out,' said Amy, without taking her eyes off the TV.

As they walked up towards the common to hail a taxi, Hugo said to Laura, 'Amy seems a bit out of sorts tonight.'

'Does she?' said Laura, who was replaying Jed's admiring gaze in her head, and taking pleasure in the feeling of the satin against her thighs as she walked. 'I didn't notice.'

'No,' said Hugo, 'she's definitely a bit off-colour.'

'Probably PMT,' suggested Laura, helpfully.

'Ah yes, I always forget about that,' said Hugo, reassured.

When they heard the front door slam shut, the young people visibly relaxed. Amy took off her shoes and tucked herself into a corner of the sofa.

'They so boss you!' said Jemima. 'I'd rebel. Tell Dad to pick up his own stupid suit. But listen, Jed and I are going out tonight. Don't worry about cooking for us. We'll just grab some sandwiches and go.'

'You didn't say,' said Leo.

'And guess why not, blabbermouth? I'm going to see where Jed works, aren't I, Jed? You can only tell Mum if I'm still not back when you wake up. If I'm not, you'll know I've been sold into slavery.'

Leo looked alarmed, but he said, 'It's your life.'

'Damn right it's my life, Leo.'

'There's no point in setting off before ten, J,' ventured Jed. 'Let's eat first. It'll be a long night.'

'Okay. But you don't budge, Amy. I'll put the moussaka in the oven. Anyone for peas?'

Everyone wanted peas, and Jed and Jemima went into the kitchen to sort out supper and discuss the night's adventure.

'What do you want me to wear?' asked Jemima, flirtatiously. 'Or should I ask you "How much do you want me to wear?"'

'It's a cold night. Dress warmly. A thick coat.'

'I don't have a thick coat.'

'Borrow one of your mum's. She's got a nice fur coat.'

'But she loves that coat. She'd be furious if something happened to it.'

'You'd look good in that coat.'

'We're not going anywhere … what I mean is, if someone spilt wine on it …'

'Trust me,' said Jed. 'No one is going to spill wine on that coat. You get it, J. It's a waste, all that warmth just sitting in your mum's cupboard warming no one.'

'Okay then, Jed, I trust you.'

Once the moussaka was in the oven, and the peas sitting in cold, salted water on the hob, ready to go – Jemima had never even boiled peas before, but she decided it was time she should – the two lovers sat down at the kitchen table to chat. Jemima poured Jed a glass of wine and fetched a vanilla-scented candle from the dresser, which she lit and placed between them.

'What's this?' asked Jed.

'When I was growing up, Mum always used to light this when she was having supper with my dad. I don't know why, but she doesn't any more. It seems a shame to waste it. I like the smell. It used to waft into my bedroom when I was going to sleep. It's kind of comforting, don't you think?'

'What, you mean the smell went up three flights of stairs?'

'Oh no! Things were very different then. We only had one house for a start. And Leo and I slept on the first floor. In fact, we shared the room where Mum wants to do her mural.'

'Sounds cosy.'

'Did you share a room, too?'

'Still do,' said Jed.

'Gosh! Is your house very small?'

'You'll be able to judge for yourself. We'll be dropping by tonight.'

'Do you mean I'm going to meet your parents?'

Jemima was alarmed. It had never occurred to her that Jed might have real living parents of his own.

'Just my mum. And my little brother Charlie, who's three, Lisa who's four, and Stacy, who's eight.'

'You never told me you had a family. It's weird they've all got names.'

'Why?'

'I don't know. It makes them seem so ... real.'

'Most people have got families.'

'I suppose I imagined ...'

'What did you imagine?'

'It's embarrassing, really. That you just somehow, that you just ... existed.'

'That's funny.'

'Why?'

'I think your mum thinks I just exist like that, too.'

'But it's true, when you meet someone, you don't think of them being in a family, do you?'

'I think of you as being in a family.'

'Well, that's not fair, you live with us. But if you just met me in the street, you wouldn't think "Ah, there's a girl with a family."'

'You're right. I'd just think, here's a class act. I wouldn't have thought I stood a chance.'

'Jed, you don't think I'm snobbish, do you?'

'Not one bit. Nor your mum. You're really good, kind people.'

'You know I'm really left-wing!' said Jemima, proudly.

'I'm sure you are, J.'

'I really believe in equality, you know.'

Jed laughed good-humouredly.

'No, I really do.'

'Once people believed in God. This was the message from the rich to the poor: "Be like us and you will be saved!" Now people believe in equality. "Be like us and you will be saved!" What's the difference? You, J, are middle class, and you think like a middle-class person. I don't blame you for it.'

'But can't you see how it's all so unfair? If I had my way, I'd split this house in two again and give you and your brother and your sisters and your mum the other half! It seems so obvious!'

'Oh yes? And when would you start accusing us of being lazy, of saying that we didn't deserve it? That capitalist crap, aspire! Do well at your fucking school, listen to the fucking teacher, or you'll end up at Tesco, the lowest of the low! Aspire! That's the trumpet call of the fucking capitalists. But I'm not listening, J. And I wouldn't want my family to listen, either. I'm not into money. When I start wanting it I won't be me.'

'But can't you see how poverty traps you, Jed? Can't you see how free we are? Dad says he's going to buy a new Range Rover soon. We might be going to Morocco this summer, and Mum says we're going to be kitting out our house in beautiful things. I think everyone should be allowed that freedom.'

'You call that freedom?' said Jed with some passion. 'You're just the servants of capitalism! Can't you see that? I'm the free one round here. I'm no one and nothing's servant!'

'You're so angry, Jed!' said Jemima, wounded to the quick.

The sweet smell of aubergine and garlic began to waft from the Aga. Jemima was grateful for an excuse to turn away from Jed, while she put the pan of peas on the hotplate. She had only wanted to tell

Jed she was on his side. She couldn't for the life of her understand where his rage was coming from.

When she sat back down at the kitchen table, she said, with an altogether lighter air: 'Anyway, what do you think of my family? What do you think of my parents?'

'Great,' said Jed, sounding more like himself.

'That wasn't very heartfelt,' observed Jemima. 'My dad first. What do you think of my dad?'

'I don't love him as much as I love your mum.'

'What, do you love my mum?'

'Yep. You've got to agree, J. She's a sweetheart, isn't she? She's stuck in the middle class, but we're all of us carrying shit.'

'You really think it's a problem being middle class, don't you?' said Jemima, longing to get off the subject and on to something rather more romantic.

'If you're an obedient kind of person, who likes a bit of structure in life, then not at all. But I think your mum's more interesting than that.'

'But am I more interesting than that?'

'Is being middle class a problem for you? I don't know, J, is it? Don't you ever find it a bit boring? All those rules you have to follow to keep your membership up to date? I mean, to be middle class you have to be a winner, don't you? You have to have a job that pays well. You have to work hard and be good at it, so everyone else in the middle classes can say, "Well done, mate!"'

'Please, Jed, don't sound so sarcastic. It's just not like you. Not all the middle classes are like that. You're painting a horrible picture, and it's not true, either. I know of a woman who lives in a car in Chiswick. We learnt about her at school. She used to be a pianist, teach in a music college, live in a fine house. Then she lost her job, got evicted, and started living in the car right outside her old house as a protest. But as far as I'm concerned, she's still middle class. She's polite and proud and spends her days in a music library reading through scores. She doesn't have a penny to her name, but she's cultured. Being cultured isn't crap, Jed. It's a good thing.'

'That's what they teach you at school, is it?'

'Well, they do, yes. I mean a school really has got to say it's better to be cultured than ignorant. Even your school must have thought that.'

'This was what my school was like,' said Jed. 'Sit down, stand up, get your backside out of my classroom, yes sir, no sir, sorry miss. We never got culture there, J. Culture's something you get from your parents. Or don't get.'

'I wouldn't call my parents cultured. They're just rich.'

'You mum likes her art.'

'That's probably just a pose to impress you. She never takes *us* round galleries. She wouldn't have taken *me* to that exhibition we went to on Tuesday if you hadn't come, too. She's trying to educate you, Jed. You're her project. Tell me the truth. Do you really enjoy all those afternoons you spend with my mum?'

Jed closed his eyes and thought of Laura. No doubt about it, her lovemaking had gone from good to fucking brilliant over the last few months. Her blow-jobs were second to none. 'I really do,' he said with feeling.

After supper, Jed and Jemima set off on their adventure. Jemima wrapped herself up in her mum's fur coat and Leo called after her, as they left arm in arm through the front door, 'You'll be sorry!'

Amy took the two chickens out of the freezer and spotted a couple of little cartons of Häagen-Dazs ice cream, chocolate brownie flavour.

'Here you are, Leo,' she said as she tossed him a carton. Leo was already back on the sofa, looking through the TV channels for a good movie to watch. It was ten o'clock, well past any kids' watershed. He was looking for a horror film to enjoy with Amy. He enjoyed horror films, and didn't get too scared. Sometimes, when he spent the night with a gang of school friends, girls said to him, 'I'm not watching this!' and hid their faces in his lap. Leo yearned for Amy to hide her face in his lap. Even the thought of it gave him a hard-on.

'I thought we could watch a horror film,' said Leo, pointing the remote control at the screen.

'I hate horror films,' said Amy. 'Where's the paper? There must be something on.'

When Amy suggested *Last Tango in Paris*, Leo said, 'That sounds incredibly boring. I hate dancing. I hate anything to do with dancing.'

'I'm sure you'll like dancing one day, Leo,' said Amy.

'God, that is so patronising!'

'No, just the truth. Anyway, it's not about dancing. It's about sex.'

Leo's body suddenly became taut.

Amy took off her shoes and jumped back into the corner of the sofa. But this time she didn't cross her legs, but stretched them out over Leo's thighs.

'Have you ever had sex?' asked Amy.

'No,' said Leo. There was no point in lying.

'Good,' said Amy.

'Why?'

'Because you're barely fifteen. You've got your whole life before you. Kids have sex far too early nowadays, in my opinion. Has a girl ever given you a blow-job?' Amy sucked on her spoon.

Leo shook his head. He concentrated on keeping Amy's legs away from his crotch. He could not bear the humiliation of her feeling quite how aroused he was.

'Have you ever felt inside a girl's knickers?' continued Amy, remorselessly.

Leo looked down at the bulge in his jeans. He knew that Amy could see it. He remained perfectly still.

'Inside her bra?'

Amy tossed the empty carton of ice cream into the bin across the room.

'Good shot,' said Leo.

Amy took off her jumper and then her shirt and picked up the remote control.

'Let's watch that film,' she said.

Jemima had never been so far out of central London. She had friends in Kew, Ealing, Islington and Wandsworth. She'd been travelling on the tube on her own for the last two years. She had always imagined herself streetwise. But even though Jed sat beside her, a protective hand on her knee, the people on the train frightened her.

They frightened her because they were looking at her. There were all sorts: a black man, old with white hair, weary and thin, who couldn't keep his eyes off her. What was he doing on the train at a quarter to eleven at night? Surely he hadn't been working till this hour? Why was he there? There was a Japanese woman of about thirty-five with bright red lipstick and chopsticks in her hair. It crossed Jemima's mind she was a prostitute, but she didn't know why. She also stared at Jemima. She wished she hadn't worn her mum's coat. She wished she didn't look so young, so rich. She'd have been better off borrowing her dad's anorak.

At Northfields a group of youths who got on the train were either stoned or drunk or both. There was only one girl among them, who was short and fat and wore a tiny mini skirt. She had a ring in her nose and countless studs in her ears. Jemima tried smiling at her, but the girl was far too cool to smile back. Jemima felt stupid and turned away. The stations went past: Boston Manor, Osterley, Hounslow East.

'Where are we going, Jed?'

'Nearly there,' said Jed, reassuringly.

'I didn't know London was so big.'

'Oh, it's a big place all right. We live right on the edge of it.'

'Are you taking me to your home first?'

'Yep.'

'Are you not going to tell me where we're going to after that?'

'I've been keeping that to myself for three months. Why spoil the surprise, J?'

'What would my mother think if she knew where I was going? Would she be pleased?'

'I once thought of taking her, not you. But she's the one who takes me places. I'm the one who takes you places.'

'So it's not dangerous?'

'Trust me,' said Jed, kissing her.

At Hounslow West Jed took Jemima's hand and said, 'Here we are.' Once they were out of the underground and on to the main road Jemima looked so anxious Jed had to hug and kiss her all over again. 'Cheer up, Jemima,' he said. 'Come and meet my family.'

At eleven o'clock on a Saturday night the only pockets of activity were near the pubs and the Indian takeaway. Jed was pleased Jemima had come, he felt protective of her, and they walked hand in hand to his home. Jemima was shocked to see how many people lived in this faraway place. She looked at the closed curtains and the lights peeping out behind them and wondered about all the people she had never met.

Jemima couldn't believe a house could be as small as Jed's. There were four windows: two downstairs, two upstairs. She was so nervous she felt sick. She wished she wasn't wearing her mum's coat. It embarrassed her.

Jed put his key in the lock and brought Jemima into a tiny hall: there was a door on the left, a door on the right and a small flight of stairs straight ahead of them. Not even a hook on which to hang her coat, thought Jemima.

Then Jed brought Jemima into the sitting room. The backs of two heads and a sofa greeted them. Jed's mum briefly turned to look to see who it was but then turned back to the TV. They were watching *Last Tango in Paris*. Then another figure sat up, a girl of about eight years old in a grubby pink nightdress and said, 'Hey, Jed! What are you doing here?'

'This is crap, Stace. Shall I take you up to bed?'

Stacy wondered briefly which of the two offers was the most tempting, a story with Jed or a film with Mum.

'Okay,' she said, and clambered over the back of the sofa.

Then the man turned round and looked at Jemima. He was dark, unshaven, fat.

'Nice coat,' he said.

'It's her mum's,' said Jed's mother.

'Well, actually it is!' laughed Jemima.

'Come with me, J,' said Jed.

The three went upstairs: Jed leading the way, his little sister Stacy right behind him, and Jemima trailing.

Stacy's bed was next to Jed's. The other two beds in that tiny room were already filled with sleeping children, pretty blond things of indistinguishable sex. Jed crept past them and lay down on his bed. Stacy followed and leapt into hers, which was squashed up against his.

Jemima stood awkwardly at the doorway, wondering where there might be room for her.

'Take off your coat,' whispered Jed. 'Slip in here.'

Jed pulled up his duvet and gestured to Jemima to come and join him. Jemima snuggled down inside the bed and put her arms around Jed's waist, whose attention was now wholly diverted to his sister.

'Well, Stacy,' he said. 'What story do you want me to tell you?'

'I want to hear the one about the boy who had a ladder so high it reached the moon,' said Stacy.

'You've already had that one twice this week,' he said.

'What about the girl who makes a rocket in her back garden?'

'Mm,' said Jed unenthusiastically. 'What about the one about the boy who gets lost in the middle of a beautiful lake?'

'Is it frightening?'

'Oh no, it's not frightening.'

'Okay then,' said Stacy.

'Once upon a time there was a boy called Luke,' began Jed.

'I know a boy called Luke,' said Stacy.

'Do you want me to tell you this story or not?'

'Yes, please,' mumbled Stacy, sleepily.

'Once upon a time there was a boy called Luke who was eight years old. Now Luke had never seen the sea before, and he could barely imagine it. Once he went on a camping holiday with his mum and dad, and when they were going for a walk one day they came to a large lake, and his parents teased him and said, "Luke, that's the sea, you know." Well, he didn't doubt them, because no one doubts their mum and dad when they're small, and when he saw a little boat moored to the shore he had an idea. Because, Stace, he thought he knew how to row, because the family went to Thorpe Park for their last holiday and his dad let him row on the boating lake, and kept saying, "Well done, you're an expert rower!" So one night, when his mum and dad were asleep, he took a torch and set off to the lake. It was so dark, Stacy, and he was just a bit frightened …'

'This is a scary story, Jed,' mumbled Stacy.

Jed was quiet. He leant on his elbow and watched her fall asleep. Then he turned around and saw that Jemima was sleeping, too. That would never do. There was a long walk ahead of them. The night was still young.

Leo hadn't much enjoyed *Last Tango in Paris*. To begin with, there'd been this ache in his balls for what seemed like an eternity. He hadn't understood the story. He didn't even know if there was a story, and was too shy to ask Amy what was going on. He had secretly hoped it might be a good chance for him to learn how to make love to a woman, but all the sex he saw was violent and strange and didn't help him to understand what a woman's body was actually like. And then there was the scene when Marlon Brando uses butter. He wanted to ask Amy, 'Why does he need butter?' but he didn't want to seem naïve. And he wanted to ask, 'Why does the butter seem to hurt the woman?' But he didn't dare. He knew Amy would laugh at him. Amy was kind. Her laugh would be kind. But that didn't make things any easier.

But he really enjoyed the bits when he saw the woman naked. She had a very beautiful body, he thought. He had once seen a girl's breasts before when he was twelve, but she was only twelve, too, so they barely counted, lovely as they were. He'd seen posters of naked women, photos in magazines. But he'd never seen a naked woman move before. He was transfixed. He yearned to touch her full breasts, and to know what lay beyond her thick, triangular bush.

'So what did you think of that?' said Amy, as she pointed the remote control to the TV screen and switched it off.

'Good,' said Leo.

'What did you think of the main actress?'

'I thought ...' began Leo.

'Yes?'

'I thought she looked like you.' Leo wanted to say, 'I bet that's what you look like with your clothes off.'

Amy said, 'Do you want to see if she does?'

All Leo could do was nod.

Amy looked at her watch.

'I don't suppose your parents will be back for a while, but I suggest we go upstairs. We don't want to be rushed, do we?'

'No,' said Leo.

'Your place or mine?'

Leo couldn't think, let alone speak. He followed Amy up to the third floor.

'I'll come to your room,' she said.

Leo was pleased she'd said that. After all, how many times had he imagined that she might just come into his bed in the dead of night? A couple of weeks back, he had gone into the bathroom to do his teeth when Amy was already there doing hers. Amy had taken the brush out of her mouth and said, 'Come in, Leo! Don't mind me!' She had been wearing a little slip of a nightie in pale blue.

Doing his teeth with Amy had counted as the most erotic experience of his life. Clumsy conversation wasn't allowed, therein lay the relief of it. He was able to look at her, admire her, cast his eyes upon the contours of her body without having to justify himself. And though at the beginning their eyes were laughing, there was also a moment when they looked at each other in perfect seriousness. And that was the moment Leo would play back in his imagination countless times, that was the moment which gave Leo hope that one night his bedroom door would open and a female form would slip into bed beside him.

And now it was happening.

Except, when Amy turned on the light in his bedroom he was suddenly ashamed. It wasn't just that he hadn't made his bed and there were clothes all over the floor, it was the silly photos on his desk of him and his school friends clambering over each other in games kit. It was the posters on his walls: Steve McQueen on a quad bike, Bart Simpson. It was the stupid curtains his mum had chosen for him when he was a boy, bright yellow, spattered with matchstick sportsmen playing different sports.

He was so ashamed he said, 'Perhaps we should go to your bedroom. You've got a bigger bed. And it won't be such a tip.'

'Hey, Leo,' said Amy, 'I like your room.'

Amy sat down on the bed and patted the space next to her.

'Sit down,' she said.

Leo did as he was told and tried to kiss her, but Amy stopped him. She undid his shirt buttons and slipped his shirt off him. Leo felt thin and puny and pale. He wished the light wasn't so bright. He wanted to get up to turn it off but felt powerless. Amy took her pants off and threw them on to his chair.

'This is your first time, isn't it, Leo?'

Leo nodded.

'You'll come quickly, don't worry. The first time is always fast. To be blunt, Leo, I suggest you just fuck me now, and then when we do it again we'll take it long and slow. The night is only just beginning. Do you know that Patti Smith song, "Because the Night"?'

Amy sang the refrain.

'I think so,' said Leo, lying.

'This is your night, my dear little Leo.'

Amy patted his knee affectionately.

'Can we turn the light off?' Leo asked.

'If you feel more comfortable. Let's put the bedside light on. You're right, Leo, it's gentler.'

Leo stood up to turn off the light. Meanwhile, Amy lay on the bed, hitching up her skirt.

Leo took off his trousers and Amy waited patiently for him to continue. Then he took down his boxer shorts and instinctively hid his penis from her. Amy just smiled at him, generously.

Leo sat down on the bed beside her and learnt what it was like to feel a woman for the first time. Even their skin felt different, it was so soft. Amy didn't instruct him, didn't tell him what gave her pleasure, but let him explore her with his fingers. That was arousal enough. After some minutes, Amy whispered, 'Come on, Leo, you know what to do!'

The sex lasted all of a few seconds. It was an outpouring of everything he had harboured in his heart and body for weeks. The kissing came afterwards. Leo was overwhelmed with feelings of gratitude and love. Amy, too, was touched that she could have had such a deep effect on the young lad. If ever her motive had been to take revenge on his father, the feelings she had for Leo now were new and uncorrupted.

'The night has just begun,' were the last words Amy whispered in Leo's ear before the two fell fast asleep, wrapped in each other's arms.

Jed let Jemima sleep for twenty minutes, and then woke her.

'Let's get out of here,' he said.

Jemima wanted to say, 'Please let me sleep some more, I'm so tired!' But she didn't want to seem weak in the eyes of her beloved, and managed to rouse herself.

'Are you okay?'

'Oh yes!' said Jemima enthusiastically.

They wriggled past the three beds with three sleeping children, and Jemima put on her coat. The sitting-room door was closed. Jemima suggested saying goodbye and thank you to his mum, but Jed said, 'What for?'

Once out in the fresh air, Jemima said, 'What's your mum's boyfriend like?'

Jed didn't bother to answer her. He just took her hand and they began to walk. It was now one in the morning. Jemima was too tired to chat, and anyway Jed had a look on his face she didn't recognise. It was set and hard and it frightened her. They seemed to be walking in the direction of the airport, and it crossed her mind that this was what Jed did at nights: he broke into the cargo sheds and dealt in drugs or stolen goods. She imagined herself in court justifying her presence at the scene of a crime. 'Your honour, I wasn't his accomplice! He was my lover! I trusted him!'

Onwards they went: street after street of nondescript houses, most as small as Jed's, some with tended front gardens, some with sheds, some with smart half-glazed front doors and paths leading up to them. Jemima was relieved by how normal they looked, as though normal people lived inside them, and overjoyed when Jed suddenly went up the path of one of them and knocked at the door. An inviting crack of light cast a glow from between the curtains, and she could hear the friendly sound of a western on TV. 'That's what Jed does,' she thought to herself. 'He babysits for the nightshift workers at Heathrow. How silly we all were to imagine anything different! And how happy I'll be to sit on a sofa with my head on Jed's lap, snug and safe!'

And sure enough, when a middle-aged woman in a tracksuit greeted Jed and asked them both to come in, a boy of about seven called down from the top step, 'Jed! Jed! Come upstairs!'

Jemima glimpsed inside her sanctuary of the night and was satisfied: a coal-effect fire, bookshelves with books and trinkets, and above all, a sofa to die for, covered with an orange mohair throw.

But Jed said, 'Not tonight, Tom.'

'Just one story, Jed, please!' said the boy, as he began to come downstairs.

'Hey, no you don't,' said his mum. 'You go right back to your bedroom!' and she followed him up.

Jemima whispered, 'What's going on here?' while they were waiting in the hall.

Jed shrugged. 'It's nothing,' he said.

But Jemima had guessed right. When the woman appeared again

she had cash with her. 'Three nights I owe you for, don't I?' she said, counting it out. 'See you Tuesday.'

'See you Tuesday,' called a voice from upstairs.

Jed took the cash and they were back on the street.

'Is that it?' asked Jemima. She tried hard to sound less disappointed than she felt. 'Are we going home now?'

Jed looked at her as though she were crazy. 'You've got to be fucking joking, J.'

Jed held her hand firmly, with no sentiment, and on they went. This wasn't the easygoing dish of a bloke that happened to be her mum's lodger. This wasn't the Jed who made her laugh, who flirted with her, who made her feel like a beautiful young woman. In fact, she had never felt more like a girl, and though for weeks she'd been pleading with Jed to take her with him, what she would have given to be back at home in her bedroom, flicking through fashion magazines, or watching some horror film with Amy and Leo.

Onwards they tramped in the yellow sodium light. The sky was clear and the air cold. Jed mentioned the stars and Jemima looked up, but there were no more stars in Hounslow than Clapham. She began to tell Jed about her grandparents' house in Dorset, 'where the stars are simply amazing', but she could see he wasn't listening.

'We have to cross over a few fields now, climb a few gates. You're not frightened of horses, are you?'

Jemima was frightened of horses. When she was thirteen she'd been thrown off a friend's pony. 'Oh no,' she said, breezily.

They climbed over the first gate, Jemima looking after her mum's coat as though her life depended on it. Jed had a small torch, which he shone at the horses one by one.

'Six,' he said. 'There were only five on Thursday.'

'Were you really here just on Thursday?'

'You know I was, J. And on Wednesday. And on Tuesday. And on Monday.'

'Why don't you come on a Saturday? Why is it different on a Saturday?'

Jemima fancied she saw the horses' shadows looming up behind her and broke into a run. She clambered over the next gate and then paused to catch her breath. She could just about make out Jed stroking the muzzle of one of the horses. Then, far away, she could hear music. Not only music, but one of her favourite songs of all time. Oasis was singing 'Wonderwall'. She even had a poster of Liam Gallagher up on the wall in her dorm at school. Feelings of relief flooded through her. Jed was taking her to an all-night party.

But when Jed jumped over the gate to join her, he said, 'Fucking music, what a pollution. You wanted to know why I don't come here at weekends. Listen to that fucking noise.'

'But how can you not like music, Jed? I didn't think there was anyone in the world who didn't like music.'

Jed didn't answer her. They crossed another field or two; then the land became scrub and the music became louder. Jemima could hear U2, Annie Lennox, Michael Jackson, all her favourites. But Jed was so far from her now, marching ahead in his solitary rage, that she kept quiet and concentrated on keeping up with him.

At last they came to the source of it.

About twenty young people were sitting on the bank of a stream, close to a bridge. The place was lit by oil lamps and flaming torches that had been stuck into the ground. Some were lying, some were sitting cross-legged looking out on to the water, some were smoking, some were snogging. The boom box took pride of place. Jemima thought, 'What a really good scene.'

When Jed walked up to them, no one greeted him. Some were visibly afraid. Then Jed remembered Jemima and took her hand. He was gentler this time, and seemed happy that she was with him. Jemima was grateful for his tenderness. 'This is my place,' he said to her, ignoring the others, who slowly began to relax again.

Jed took her under the bridge, where he'd installed a single table and a gas ring. A large canister of Butane gas stood underneath it. Over the table were strewn slices of white bread, half-eaten packets of ham and sliced cheese; and on the ring was a large pan half filled with lukewarm potatoes.

'Hungry?' he said to Jemima.

Jemima shook her head. She wondered if this was some kind of test, whether he'd fly off the handle if she said she was. But instead he found a fork and began to eat himself.

'It's good,' he said to Jemima. 'Here, have some.'

She did as she was told. But still the expression on Jed's face worried her. She wanted to be part of the gang, she wanted Jed to introduce her to a couple of friends. But when they emerged back into the party on the bank there was a tension Jemima couldn't understand. He stared at them; they stared back. They stared at Jemima, too. A part of her wanted to desert Jed and go to the other side. The boom box blared 'Thriller' and Jemima got the feeling that if Jed wasn't there there'd be dancing by now, and Jemima loved to dance.

Instead Jed took her deep into a copse nearby to show her a wigwam he'd made out of hazel branches. More cleverly still, he had woven dried reeds into the structure, like darning.

'Come,' said Jed.

But when they approached they heard a soft moaning coming from inside. Jed walked up to the entrance and put his head through it. 'Fuck you,' he said to the lovers on the hay floor. Then he took Jemima's hand and said, 'We're fucking getting out of here.'

The young people looked up in alarm when they saw Jed coming back.

'You're a load of fucking idiots,' he said to them.

One of them dared to say, apologetically: 'How did we know you'd turn up tonight?'

Jed didn't even bother to look at him. The boom box was now playing 'Beat It'. But Jed didn't beat it. Instead, he picked up the hideous object and threw it into the stream.

'Come on, Jemima,' he said. And the pair walked on. Not even a murmur of protest emanated from those they left behind.

And on they went. The land they crossed didn't have so much as a footpath running through it. If it had been daylight, they would have seen willow, alder, oak. Underfoot they crunched over broken twigs and branches. Jed moved quickly, occasionally forgetting that he wasn't alone. Sometimes he'd look back and point his torch at Jemima. 'You okay?' he'd ask. Jemima always said, 'I'm doing fine.'

After some twenty minutes they arrived at the perimeter fence of Heathrow Airport.

'This is a good spot,' said Jed.

Jemima looked through the fence trying to think of something positive to say about the few British Airways aircraft she could see parked outside a hangar, or the pretty stripes she could just about make out on a United Arab Emirates plane that was parked relatively near them. Or perhaps she could say how clever it was that they could light up such a vast space. Or perhaps she could say that the light was ugly and meant you couldn't see too many stars. Or she could mention the high fence with the rolls of barbed wire skirting the top of it. Or she could ask Jed why he didn't like music. Eventually she said, 'Yes, it is.'

Jed stood holding on to the fence, seemingly mesmerised by what he saw. His face became like a boy's, relaxed and eager.

'You should see this place in the day,' he said. 'It's my first memory, watching a plane taking off.'

'How old were you?'

'Two, perhaps three.'

'Who took you here?'

'My dad, of course. He loved the planes, too.'

'I can't remember my first memory,' said Jemima.

'Perhaps it didn't mean much to you, then.'

'What's so special about watching a plane take off?'

Jed looked back at Jemima in disbelief and Jemima regretted saying anything.

'Planes fly!' he said.

Jemima wanted to say, 'But of course planes fly, that's what they do,' but she didn't dare.

'They take you away, they lift you up and over, they take you over the curvature of the planet, Jemima. You know the world is round, don't you?'

'Of course I do,' said Jemima.

'That's just because someone told you it was.'

'How else do you know anything?'

'That's how we're different, you and me.'

Jemima felt hurt but emboldened. 'I've flown loads of times,' she said. 'Corfu, Turkey, LA, Tunisia. And I can tell you, you can't tell the earth is round at all. You just fly from A to B over the clouds and you can't tell where you're going.'

'Then you weren't concentrating,' said Jed patiently.

'Have you ever flown?'

'Once.'

'And did you feel the earth was round?'

'We didn't go far enough.'

'Excuses, excuses!' said Jemima lightly.

But Jed gave her a thunderous face. 'I trust my dad ahead of you,' he said. 'Come on, let's go.'

They walked on beside the perimeter fence and Jemima said, 'Jed, please don't walk so quickly. Aren't we going home yet? It's three in the morning. I'm so tired I can't go on. Can't we just sit here and rest a while?'

'I warned you you'd be tired, didn't I? I told you it was a bad idea.'

Jed began, if anything, to walk more quickly. Then Jemima just gave up, slumping down with her back against the fence.

Jed came back for her. Here was the old Jed again, kind and encouraging. He took Jemima by the hand and pulled her to her feet.

'I'm really sorry, J,' he said to her. 'But you can't give up now. We're so close, just a few minutes more. It'll be worth it, you'll see. We're heading that way.'

Jed pointed to some tall trees and a huge patch of dark.

'Did you build a wigwam there?' Jemima had visions of being tucked up inside it.

'This is on another plane, J. You'll see. You won't be disappointed. There's a fence we have to climb, but it's not too high and there's no barbed wire on the top.'

'But my mum's coat …'

'You'll have to throw that over first. You're tall, you'll manage fine. There's a bit of a jump from the top but I'll catch you.'

'I trust you, Jed,' said Jemima. She was so tired she would have handed herself over to anyone.

When they got there Jemima looked through the metal bars of the fence and tried to work out what she was looking at. Jed was watching her, she could feel it. She so wanted to say the right thing.

'Is there water there?' she asked him.

'Dead right there's water. Billions of gallons of the stuff. I've been watching them build it. It's a reservoir, but it's fucking amazing. It's huge. And look at this.'

Jed shone his torch through the fence. Jemima couldn't see what she was supposed to be looking at.

'They planted reeds. And not only reeds, but sedge and willowherb.'

Jemima had never heard of sedge or willowherb.

'Why did they build a reservoir here?' asked Jemima.

'Good question, and there's an awesome answer. It's pure ecology, totally natural. These plants, this water, which is as clear and clean as could be, absorbs the pollution from the airport. I've even drunk it.'

'You've drunk the water?'

'Of course. I keep a cup in the boat.'

'The boat?' asked poor Jemima, aghast. The idea of yet another adventure appalled her. 'You've made a boat?'

'One day I'll make a boat. This one's just a little rubber dinghy. I suppose they use it for maintenance or something. But it's comfortable.'

'We're going in a boat?'

'Hey, don't look like that, J. You can sleep in the boat. Don't you want to sleep?'

'How long is the boat trip? Are we going anywhere?'

'In a way, yes, in a way, no.'

'How long is the journey?'

Jed looked at his watch. 'About two hours. Is that all right with you?'

Jemima's stomach sank.

'But you say I can sleep,' she said.

'It's cold,' said Jed, 'but I've got a haul of old blankets. You can sleep.'

'Where are we going?'

'Just you wait. You won't regret it, J. You've come this far. Here, let's get over this fence. Give me your coat. I'll toss it over.'

Jemima did as she was told. Almost immediately she began to shiver.

Jed wrapped up her mum's fine faux fur coat, value one and a half grand, into as small a bundle as it would go and threw it over the top. Jemima couldn't even see where it landed. But she was so tired that she barely cared.

'Now, put one foot here and get yourself over the top, J. It's only a six-foot drop on the other side.'

Jed interlocked his fingers and offered her the palms of his hands.

'I'm heavy,' she said.

'No you're not,' said Jed.

Jemima was by now too tired to be afraid of anything. She put her foot on to the proffered step and heaved herself up. If Jed should drown her, she scarcely cared any more. If it had been day, she would have hovered on the top too anxious to go one way or the other. Now she almost threw herself into the unknown and landed well.

'Good girl,' said Jed.

Jemima picked up her coat and was thankful that it still had the warmth of her body locked inside it. She put it back on and felt better about things. Jed landed right beside her with a thud.

'I'm proud of you,' he said.

It was all okay now. Odd how a few comforting words from the man you love makes things all right again. Jed retrieved a black bin bag stuffed with blankets from under some scrub, and together they walked down to a small jetty.

The blow-up yellow dinghy they found there was modern and clean. Jed threw the bag into it and told Jemima to jump in. Then he got in himself and pushed the boat away into the middle of the water with an oar. It was romantic, even Jemima saw that. But the slither of moon that had been there earlier was nowhere to be found, and even the few faint stars had disappeared behind the clouds. What eerie glow there was came from the yellow lights on the inside of the perimeter fence. But when, after some minutes, Jed put down the oars and came and sat next to Jemima, suggesting they could lie down together to watch the dawn, Jemima felt that this was the moment she'd been waiting for.

Jed lay down blankets on the bottom of the boat, and more to serve as pillows. 'Come here, J,' he said tenderly, and Jemima got down to lie with him and put the skirt of her coat over Jed's legs.

'I love you,' she said to him.

Jed paused and said, 'You're a great girl, J. You'll make a fine woman.'

That satisfied Jemima, and she snuggled up to her man.

'Is this really where you've been coming, night after night, even in the middle of winter?'

'Yep,' said Jed, in a matter-of-fact sort of way.

'But what happens?'

'Often, nothing at all. But tonight it's going to happen, just you wait.'

'I don't see how anything could happen, out here in the middle of nowhere.'

'I'll give you a clue, J. It's spring. It's the twenty-second of April. It's a new year.'

'Daffodils,' guessed Jemima.

'So what's your idea? That the heavens are going to open and pour millions of daffodils on to the lake? Nope, have another guess.'

'I don't really know about these kinds of things.'

Jemima half-waited for Jed to be angry with her. But he wasn't. Instead he put an arm around Jemima and hugged her.

'Just you wait,' he said.

Jemima drifted into sleep for an hour, and when she awoke she could see that Jed was on full alert, and hadn't slept for a moment. He seemed happy to see her back with him, and kissed the top of her head.

'Have I missed anything?' she said.

A light breeze blew over them. Jemima gave herself to the gentle rocking motion of the boat.

'An hour to wait,' said Jed.

An hour suddenly seemed no time at all.

'It was a wonderful thing when you came to live with us,' said Jemima.

'You're a great family,' said Jed. 'It's been good for me, too. I love you all.'

'All of us?'

'Perhaps just you and your mum. She's great, your mum, isn't she?'

'Yeah, I s'pose.' Jemima didn't like it when Jed went on about how great her mum was, even though she thought so, too. 'How do you know Amy, anyway?' she asked him, changing the subject. 'That's why you came to stay with us, isn't it? You're Amy's friend.'

'I am,' said Jed.

'Didn't you ever go out with her? Amy's so nice. And she's so pretty. Don't you think she's pretty?'

'Yep,' said Jed.

'But didn't you ever fall in love with her? I mean, I would fall in love with her if I were a bloke. She's so sweet.'

'Yep,' said Jed.

'Yep what? Did you go out with her or not?'

'I never did.'

'I can't think why not.'

'Sometimes things happen, and sometimes they don't.'

That didn't quite reassure Jemima, who sighed.

'Here, have some water,' said Jed.

Jed produced a small, slim metal cup from under the air-filled rim of the boat. 'Let's make a toast,' he said.

He leaned over the side and filled it with water. 'To Jemima!' he said, and drank it down in one.

A couple of hours earlier Jemima had sworn to herself that she wouldn't even taste it. She didn't like the idea of all the pollution of Heathrow Airport being dissolved into it. But she so loved Jed that she took the cup from him and sank it deep into the water.

'The water's freezing,' she said. She saw that the sleeve of her mother's coat had got wet but she was beyond caring. She raised the cup on high and cried out, 'To Jed!' Even if she was poisoned to death, what did that matter? The water was, thankfully, so cold that she couldn't taste it.

Then Jed took the cup from her and dipped it down into the water a second time. 'To water,' he said, 'to all the water everywhere in the whole world and in the whole universe.'

Jemima thought what a beautiful toast that was and took the cup from Jed and did the same. 'To all water everywhere in the whole world and in the whole universe,' she said. She gulped it down.

'Good,' said Jed.

Jemima didn't want to disturb that 'good' and therefore said nothing. It was now half past four, and slowly, gingerly, the light of the new dawn was beginning to come. Jemima suddenly understood that that was what Jed was waiting for, that was why he went there night after night. Looking above her, she could make out a deep purple.

'Oh God, Jed, it's so beautiful.'

'Just wait,' Jed whispered in her ear.

For Jed, practised in the art of listening to birdsong, the first silvery trills silenced him. He held Jemima tight, and when she tried to say something he said, 'Shh, J.'

At first the sound was sporadic, one bird calling to another. The notes were clear, distinguishable, like a conversation was going on.

'That's a whitethroat,' whispered Jed.

Then the warbling began, fuller-voiced, lower in pitch, rhythmical. It was answered by clear, musical notes.

'The sedge warblers and the kingfishers. You hear that sharp-whistled call? That's a kingfisher, I know it. The kingfishers are back, J.'

And then other birds joined them. The black caps, the wood-pigeons, the reed warblers, the thrushes, the blackbirds, the wrens. They were a choir where every verse was new, where every song demanded a reply.

Jemima looked down on her lover, who was lying down again on the floor of the boat resting his head on her lap. There was no point in saying anything. She had never heard birdsong so loud or so joyful. There were whistles, trills, real tunes that you could hum along to, an impenetrable wall of sound. The tears streamed down Jed's cheeks. Jemima felt that she was witnessing something she had no right to witness and looked away.

The journey back to the tube station at Hounslow West seemed to take no time at all. The sky was now a deep, majestic blue, not a cloud in sight, and tinged with the red of the dawn. The party-goers had all gone home, and the streets were empty, bar a few weary faces coming home from the night shift, and a few less weary setting out for a day's work.

The first plane of the morning took off and they paused a while to watch it. Jed was silent and took hold of Jemima's hand, as though in the presence of something holy. The plane flew right above their heads, rumbling, roaring, then higher and higher, further and further, leaving a great arc of white across the sky. Everything was still again.

'The birds have come back from Africa, you know, J,' was all Jed said to the young Jemima.

'Your dad left you, didn't he?' said Jemima, quietly. 'He just flew off, didn't he?'

'Yes, he just flew off,' said Jed.

SATURDAY 8 JULY 1995

At seven in the morning Laura is polishing her new kitchen table. It's a glorious thing: vast and circular and made of hand-cut glass. Her kitchen cupboards are made of glass, too. Ann teases her and tells her she never realised the chaos that lies behind the façade. She teases her because Laura remains immaculate inside and out: nowadays, she even orders her cereal packets according to size, and persuades her children to do the same.

Things have moved apace in the Glass household. Hugo has contacts in *Interiors*: there's a big photo shoot next week. They simply *love* the glass idea. Transparency, simplicity, honesty: these, they say, are the new values of the new society, and there's a lot of money to be made.

Laura's new best friend is Sarah, whose husband Mark has left her for Arabella. She thinks Arabella has behaved disgracefully, and they're not even on speaking terms. Laura has been all compassion towards her new friend, who goes running with her every morning. She's barely spoken to Rachel since the dinner party. Rachel makes her feel anxious while Sarah makes her feel good about herself. Isn't that what friends are for?

The mural hasn't worked out too well, but it's still there. The colours are good, the paint's top quality. There is even something vaguely reminiscent of Gauguin lurking there. But however hard Hugo and Laura try to capture something of their lovers, some essence, some hidden spark, they fail miserably. Laura secretly thinks that one day she'll take them out completely, and stick with the family sitting on the bench together as a happy foursome. But she's in no hurry.

The greatest fan of the mural is Amy. She persuaded Laura to let her sleep in her old room again, even while the mural was in progress, though her real motive was to escape from Leo. Leo has been behaving like an over-sexed puppy, always trying to put his hands inside Amy's bra, telling her she 'owes it to him'. Leo is angry with her for letting him fall asleep after having sex with him, and then disappearing off to her bedroom.

Laura and Jed are still getting on well. But the intense eroticism of those early weeks has given way to something more nurturing. Laura is determined to persuade Jed to go back to school, take his A levels, go on to university. 'You're so clever, Jed, so talented! You have your whole life before you! Do something special, the world is out there waiting for you!' Jed is touched by Laura's concern but in May he ran away for a week when she suggested Hugo was going to help him 'succeed' by making him manager of one of his new branches of Second Helpings.

Jed has also moved back into his old room on the first floor. Laura explained it felt unwholesome to be making love to him on a floor packed full of her kids' paraphernalia, and she didn't know where to shower after they'd had sex. Two in the afternoon remains a special time for them both, though Laura's given up taking Jed to galleries. He once said to her, 'I don't get why people have to look at things through someone else's eyes, why we can't just look ourselves.' Anyway, Laura needs the time to concentrate on her new business.

Hugo comes down to breakfast at 7.30. He's in his jogging gear and shows off his new trainers to his wife. 'Expensive,' he says, 'but so light.' He helps himself to a bowl of Shreddies and Laura casts an anxious eye to make sure Hugo puts the cereal packet back in the right place. He does.

'What time's everyone coming? I'm pleased the good weather's holding out,' says Hugo.

'Normal time.'

'Have you told Amy and Jed to move upstairs again?'

'Of course I have, Hugo. Their bedrooms are immaculate.'

'I like your parents.'

'And I like yours, Hugo.'

'And it's so lucky they like each other so much. That can't happen often.'

'We're from good stock, you and I. We had a good start in life.'

'I'll start the barbecue at midday, then,' says Hugo, as he gets up from the magnificent glass table. As he does so, he catches a glimpse of himself, and approves. Not bad for forty-five, he thinks.

When he's gone, Laura checks that everything's in order in the fridge. There's a plate of lamb cutlets marinated in mint, a couple of packs of chilli sausages, a bowl of chicken drumsticks dipped in Moroccan spices. Is that enough, she wonders, for the eight of them? She takes out a packet of hamburgers from the freezer and leaves them on the side to defrost. She'll make the couscous later.

Laura has become passionate about everything Moroccan. In fact, the family are heading down there in their new Range Rover at the end of the month. They'll be taking the overnight ferry to Santander, driving gently down south – five nights of glorious paradors – and then picking up the ferry in Gibraltar.

Laura's particularly excited to go to Morocco because she'll be visiting an ink factory there. Hugo has so usurped the glass furniture arm of her new company Glass Ink that she's determined to keep him away from the dyed linen. Hugo seems more interested in making their holiday tax-deductible. Well, that's Hugo for you, she smiles to herself.

Laura begins to worry that Amy's not come down to breakfast yet. She works at the salon on Saturdays. At half past eight Laura goes upstairs to the kids' floor and knocks at her door. When there's no answer she creeps in.

'Amy,' she whispers, 'are you okay? It's late.'

'I've got the day off,' mumbles Amy.

'Well, you deserve it!' says Laura, but secretly she's thinking, 'I don't want Amy at our family lunch. Perhaps I should tell her to keep herself scarce.'

But she thinks the better of it, and tiptoes away.

Laura has begun to prepare salads at ten when Amy comes down to breakfast. She helps herself to muesli but leaves the packet on Laura's new table. Amy reads her mind and says, 'Jemima eats muesli. She'll be down in a minute. She's in the bathroom.'

Laura makes a gesture that says, 'Honestly, I'm not concerned about something as trivial as that!'

Amy asks who the salads are for.

'The kids' grandparents,' Laura says. 'Thanks for moving upstairs, by the way. They're arriving at lunchtime.' She still can't bring herself to say, 'We're having a barbecue and you are absolutely not invited.'

'Is there anything I can do to help?' Amy asks. 'Can I grate the carrots?'

'No really, don't worry,' says Laura.

Jemima comes in wearing a pretty blue check halter-neck dress and espadrilles. She is looking the picture of health and happiness.

After her night out with Jed, she doesn't know what to think of him. She's a bit scared of him, if truth be told. Some weeks ago, she found a knife in his room with a wooden handle, and remembered the party and the music and the fear. She'd forgotten about the wigwam, and how nicely made it was.

Recently she's started going out with a boy from her school who's the drummer in the school band. His name is Korel and he's half-Turkish. He has straight shoulder-length black hair and a long fringe, which he's forever putting behind his ear. Jemima has told her mum that she's no longer a virgin. Laura was pleased that her daughter confided in her. She took that as a good sign.

Laura's faux fur coat survived its journey to Hounslow West and is living out the summer safe and sound in Laura's wardrobe. Jemima brushed the sleeve that got wet in the reservoir with a hairbrush, and it came out just fine. But she forgot to take out her tube ticket from the pocket, dated Saturday the twenty-third of April, issued at Hounslow West. In late November, when she slips her coat on again at the first sign of frost, Laura will find it there and she'll question her daughter. But things will have moved on, and come a day or two, they'll even have a laugh about it. Jemima will tell her mother all about the crush she used to have on Jed, and about her adventure on the reservoir. Laura will tell her daughter nothing.

Jed strolls into the kitchen at about eleven. Laura is happy to see him, she always is. He's a good listener. Laura makes two cups of coffee and sits with him while he eats toast. She hears the front door open: Hugo's back carrying a couple of bags from the off-licence. He takes them to the pantry and tries to find room in the fridge for two bottles of champagne and half a dozen beers. Then he disappears upstairs to take a shower.

Laura is telling Jed all about sepia ink.

'There's a species of cuttlefish called *Sepia officinalis*,' she says. 'They've got these little ink sacs in their bodies. In the eighteenth century that's where most people got their ink from. It's a lovely red-brown colour. Do you know the word "sepia", Jed?'

'Yep,' said Jed, though he doesn't, and he doesn't much care what 'sepia' means.

'Well I've found this factory just outside Marrakech that makes ink in the old way, and I'm bringing over some natural linen curtains which they're going to dye for me. They're going to be such a beauti-ful, earthy colour, I'm sure of it!'

'I'm sure you're right, Laura.'

Then Jed takes Laura's hands in his and says, 'I've always thought your hands are really beautiful, really fine.'

'Oh Jed!' she says, and she thinks what a lovely young man he is and how guilty she's feeling that she hasn't yet invited him to their family lunch.

'Have you got any plans for the day?' she asks him.

'Yeah, I have,' says Jed.

'I'm so pleased,' says Laura with feeling. 'It's a sort of family event we're having, you know. Grandparents and all that.'

'That's okay,' said Jed.

'I hope you're doing something fun,' says Laura, glancing at her watch. 'Gosh, it's getting on. I ought to wake up that son of mine.'

'Hey, before you do,' says Jed. He stands up and gives her a look abounding in affection. He tries to put into words something he wants to tell her, but fails. She kisses him lightly on the cheek and laughs, but her mind is somewhere else. Leo's been wearing these filthy jeans ever since he got back from school, and worse, there are holes in the knees. She put new jeans on his chair the previous evening, and she has to make sure he's seen them.

'I'll be right back,' she says. But she's not right back. Leo says he doesn't like the new jeans, they don't fit him properly, they're too long.

Laura says, 'No problem, we'll just roll them up.'

'I'm not seven years old,' says Leo.

'Well, what other trousers have you got? What about the corduroys?' And so on. And so on.

At midday Hugo lights the barbecue, the first of the season. The barbecue is only two years old: state-of-the-art, stainless steel, double-sized. He wipes it down with pride, and then fetches his butcher's apron from the kitchen drawer.

'It's lovely out there,' he tells Laura, 'so warm.'

'Here, you couldn't lay the table out there, could you?'

Laura hands Hugo a red-checked tablecloth and some cutlery, and he takes them outside.

Laura begins to lay out the food on the kitchen table. What a fine spread, she thinks to herself. Leo comes in wearing last year's knee-length khaki shorts.

'Thank you, Leo,' she enthuses.

She suddenly realises Jed has gone, but that's fine, that's good. Amy, too, seems to have got the message.

It's going to be a really lovely family day, she thinks.

And she's right.

It's two in the afternoon. Amy and Jed are in the attic. They're standing at the window together, watching.

'They're a good family,' says Jed. 'I like them.'

'Me, too,' says Amy. 'They're lucky kids, Jemima and Leo. A mum and dad who love each other. Four grandparents, all of their own.'

Hugo has his arm around Laura, while pouring her another glass of champagne. Leo is in earnest conversation with one of his grandfathers, Jemima is laughing with her grandmother, who is trying to put a bloom in her hair.

'I'd say, they're the perfect family,' says Jed.

'Will they miss us, do you think?'

'Not really,' said Jed sadly. They watch a while longer. Now Laura is standing with her dad. They can't see her expression, because her back is towards them. But they can see his. And what they see is a man so proud of his pretty daughter, so full of love.

'I liked being part of a family,' says Jed.

'Me, too,' says Amy.

They watch a while longer. They can't hear what they're talking about, but Hugo is making them all laugh. Then he's back at the barbecue wielding his giant-sized spatula, persuading them one by one that they could manage an extra drumstick, an extra lamb chop.

Suddenly Jed smiles. 'I never showed you this,' he says proudly.

Out of his pocket he produces a brand new British passport, his first.

'Oh Jed!' Amy says, happily. 'It finally came! Where shall we go?'

Amy and Jed have been saving for some months now. Amy has about six thousand pounds, and Jed about six hundred. Over the double bed are scattered clippings from the travel sections of Sunday newspapers. But they've never slept together, Amy and Jed. They know they have all the time in the world for that.

The family don't hear the taxi arrive at the front door. Jed helps Amy with her case. Jed doesn't have much, just a rucksack.

When they tell the taxi driver they want to go to Heathrow Airport, he asks them, 'Are you going somewhere nice?'

'Oh yes!' they say in unison. The whole world stretches out before them. They are holding hands on the back seat, like children.